Titia Sutherla[...] [...]ry and has spent much of her a[...] [...]tchy education at various day s[...] [...]subject in which she received a good grounding. As a child she started many novels which were never completed, and she and her brother wrote and acted in their own plays. In her late teens she spent two years at the Webber-Douglas School of Drama and a short period in repertory before marrying a journalist. The birth of a baby put an end to acting. Following a divorce, she had a series of jobs which included working as a part-time reader for a publishing firm, and designing for an advertising agency.

She started to write when her children were more or less adult and following the death of her second husband. Her first novel, *The Fifth Summer*, was published in 1991. She has four children, enjoys gardening and paints for pleasure when there is time.

Also by Titia Sutherland

THE FIFTH SUMMER

and published by Black Swan

Out of the Shadows

Titia Sutherland

BLACK SWAN

OUT OF THE SHADOWS
A BLACK SWAN BOOK 0 552 99529 0

First publication in Great Britain

PRINTING HISTORY
Black Swan edition published 1992
Black Swan edition reprinted 1993

Copyright © Titia Sutherland 1992

The right of Titia Sutherland to be identified as author of this
work has been asserted in accordance with sections 77 and 78
of the Copyright Designs and Patents Act 1988.

Conditions of sale
1. This book is sold subject to the condition that it shall not,
by way of trade or otherwise, be lent, re-sold, hired out or
otherwise circulated in any form of binding or cover other
than that in which it is published and without a similar
condition including this condition being imposed on the
subsequent purchaser.
2. This book is sold subject to the Standard Conditions of Sale
of Net Books and may not be re-sold in the UK below the net
price fixed by the publishers for the book.

This book is set in 11/14pt Melior by
County Typesetters, Margate, Kent

Black Swan Books are published by Transworld Publishers Ltd,
61–63 Uxbridge Road, Ealing, London W5 5SA, in Australia by
Transworld Publishers (Australia) Pty Ltd, 15–25 Helles
Avenue, Moorebank, NSW 2170, and in New Zealand by
Transworld Publishers (NZ) Ltd, 3 William Pickering Drive,
Albany, Auckland.

Printed and bound in Great Britain by
Cox & Wyman Ltd, Reading, Berks.

For Bill, Diana, Justin
and Matthew
with great love

Chapter One

Alone with his mother, Simon Playfair showed signs of distraction, repeating himself, stirring his tea and then leaving it to get cold. Eventually he crossed to the windows and stared out thoughtfully at the garden. Rachel knew it boded ill; he was about to make a comment or raise an issue that would annoy her. She could tell by the way he rocked gently backwards and forwards on his heels; an irritating habit inherited from Henry and about the only similarity between them.

Her eldest son was satisfactory to look at, she admitted silently from her seat in front of the fire, and not in the least like either parent. Where had the blond hair sprung from, and the even features? Henry had been not unlike an attractive gargoyle, and her own face appeared to her in the mirror as uncoordinated.

There were times when she did not like Simon very much, which she had come to accept recently as normal. It was, she realized, quite possible to love one's child at the same time as disliking it. Certain characteristics of his, such as pomposity and an eye to the main chance, seemed to be on the increase. He had been a cuddly little boy, more so than Christian who was thin as a rake and all angles. Watching Simon's back view, hair exactly the right length above the maroon-striped collar, she mourned the transition of small child to glossy, self-indulgent man. She dreamt always of her children as small, and Henry had frequently accused her of indulging in nostalgia. But then, it was the job of historians to look backwards.

There was a patch of thinning hair high up on Simon's head, she noticed sadly.

'The garden looks good,' he remarked out of the blue.

Pleasantly surprised by such unusual praise, she went to stand beside him.

'I *am* rather proud of it this year.'

'That choisya is growing into the lace-cap,' he added, spoiling it all. 'Have you noticed? Something ought to be done about it.'

'I suppose so, but it will have to wait until autumn.' She knew her voice to be acerbic. She could not help it. Why not mention the amazing spread of lilies of the valley, out a month early, instead of picking on defects? Before he had married Camilla he had taken no interest in the garden, could not tell a tulip from a rose. He was merely throwing his weight about as he used to do as a boy, bossing the other two. Turning away abruptly, she said, 'It's stopped raining. Shall we have a walk round?'

He glanced at his watch. 'Right. I mustn't be long, though. We ought to be on the road by sixish.'

Their feet squelched on the puddled stone paths. They skirted the lawn in need of cutting, and the sagging boughs of cherry heavy with dripping blossom; stood while she pointed out the glories and hurried on past the neglected bits. Behind them the dog pressed his nose against the french windows reproachfully.

The air was raw with rain and more to come. Simon paused by the door, replacing a flattened daffodil against its supporting cane.

'Of course,' he remarked, not looking at her, 'it's a large garden for London. An awful lot of work.'

'I'm cold,' she said, shivering, her arms about her, refusing to acknowledge his statement.

In the drawing-room, while she bent to light the gas fire, he came out with what he had been meaning to say all along.

'You're over-housed, Mother. Don't you think you ought to consider selling?'

He had not pursued this theme for quite some time. Nevertheless, she was ready for him. She picked up an armful of wriggling dog to use as a hot-water bottle and smoothed her cheek on the rough coat.

'No, I don't,' she said. 'I'm not quite ready for a granny flat, thank you, darling.' She let go of the dog and reached for a cigarette. 'Besides, have you considered how inconvenient it would be for you and Camilla? There would be no room for Emily when you wanted to dump her.'

On this occasion, Simon had brought his daughter Emily to stay with her grandmother for three nights while he and Camilla took a break at a country hotel. Father and child had arrived at the hour that Rachel thought of as tea-time although Simon invariably told her not to bother. ('She never has it at home. Doesn't eat much, as you know.')

Rachel, who knew this to be a fallacy, was cutting a plateful of smoked salmon sandwiches and another of gentleman's relish, in order to snub him. Through the semi-basement window she watched Emily's spindly legs climbing the steps, her own miniature umbrella held aloft and the small suitcase clasped tight. Rachel knew what it contained; a change of everything, the contents listed by meticulous Camilla so that nothing got left behind when repacking. There would be a pair of jeans for messing about in, which generally remained pristine since Emily showed a distaste for the great outdoors, being completely happy alone with a book. She would have been approved of in a Victorian household but for her acute powers of observation and the voicing of them. She could spot a cobweb or a crooked picture at a hundred yards.

In the hall they kissed each other with the reserved warmth of adults, while Simon hovered on the doorstep. 'I've brought the bike. Shall I leave it by the back door?'

'Yes, please.'

'You've moved the snuff-boxes.' Emily gazed round the drawing-room, scenting out change like a bloodhound.

'They're behind the sofa.'

'And the photographs are different. Mine used to be this side, and Christian's, then Mummy and Daddy getting married.'

'I like a good switch-round occasionally.'

'Why?'

'It relieves boredom. Have a sandwich,' said Rachel, waving a plate.

'Sit down if you're going to eat,' Simon ordered, being unnecessarily parental. He peered at the plate, took two triangles and subsided into an armchair. 'Mmm. I shouldn't think you'll like these, Em, a bit sophisticated for you. Delicious. Terribly bad for the figure.'

'I don't suppose it matters if you are still pumping iron,' said Rachel mildly.

'I like gentleman's relish. We never have it at home.' Emily sat on the tapestry stool by the fireplace, ankles primly crossed, nibbling thoughtfully. Her eyes, enlarged by glasses, wandered over furniture and grown-ups alike without expression. Rachel poured tea, dressing her granddaughter mentally in pantaloons and pinafore, wishing she could have a drawing of her that way, a pastel. Watching Emily caused her thoughts to leap-frog unaccountably, to a plan of action that she had in mind; research of a different kind to any that she had undertaken before, and for her enjoyment only. She felt in need of a change, an interest that would absorb and relax her but make no demands. Simon would not approve. There was nothing lucrative in what she proposed, merely a means to satisfy a certain curiosity.

Recently she had finished researching a book on morale and mental health among the Forces during the two World Wars edited by a media journalist. It had been a lengthy business and she had found it depressing, the perusal of endless medical reports and sad letters laying bare the secrets of shattered lives. Before the end, she was beginning to experience personally the mud and cold of the trenches, to hallucinate with pilots deprived of sleep. No other research had affected her this way. Her morale sank to a low ebb. This was not a break-down, she wasn't the type. But she could understand how such a situation evolved, how it might creep up on one unawares. She

11

came away from a visit to the doctor with some well-intentioned advice which she rejected and a prescription for mild sleeping pills which she reluctantly handed in at the chemist. Then she had lunch with her friend Phyllida.

'Well, what did he say?'

'He told me to take a holiday.'

'Sounds sensible. Why not? When did you last have one?'

'I stayed with Carrie and George last September in the Isle of Wight,' Rachel mumbled into her salad Nicoise. 'Oh, and I took Louisa away for a long weekend when she first got pregnant.'

Phyllida said scornfully, 'Ten days with a couple of alcoholics and a weekend with a weepy daughter? I mean a real, proper, get-away-from-it-all holiday, being totally selfish.'

For some reason the idea made Rachel feel tearful. Going away by oneself was no fun and fraught with difficulties, not the least of which was the supplement levied by hotels on single people. But Phyllida, being intrepid, could not be expected to understand.

'Have a brandy,' she suggested, drink being an infallible source of comfort in her view. 'All this,' she said, making a sweeping gesture with her arm to cover Rachel's problems, 'is a build-up of post-Henry misery. You bottled it up and now it's coming out at last. Better to have let go at the beginning.' Phyllida was strong on psychology. 'You know, what you need now,' she added, uncorking the bottle with a symbolic jerk, 'is a bloody good affair.'

She is wrong on both counts, Rachel decided. I cried for the entire night when Henry died. But after that it was over. The numbness commonly accepted as nature's anaesthetic following a bereavement seemed to have lasted her quite happily for nearly five years. Being forced to think about it, she realized a shaming fact: that if she missed Henry at all, it was either in bed or as a travelling companion. He shone at both, but she could hardly admit that to Phyllida.

'I'm no good at affairs,' she said sadly. 'They're so transitory. You need courage.'

'Can I get down?' Emily was asking.

'*May* I,' said Simon. 'We all know you can.'

'Don't be so pedantic, Sim,' Rachel said crossly. 'Yes, of course you can, Em.'

The child had eaten nothing to speak of, but Rachel was not worried. The rest of the sandwiches would disappear at supper, plus large chunks of chocolate cake. Emily's tiny appetite was an act put on solely for Simon's benefit, to gain his attention. She seemed to have been born with a sixth sense for such things. Simon had this effect on people of making them feel placatory for no reason. He wore his parenthood uneasily, like a new pair of shoes.

'Am I sleeping in the room next to you, or the nursery?' asked Emily from the doorway.

'Next to me.'

'I think I'll go and unpack then.'

Rachel nodded, Emily smiled, their expressions bland. Simon thought he could detect a flash of complicity pass between them, and felt excluded.

And now, chilly from the garden, Rachel was regretting bringing Emily into an argument about the house.

It was unfair to use her as a missile.

'Honestly, Mother, I thought you liked having Emily here. If I'd known you had thought of her as being dumped—' He turned red. His fair skin always flushed easily when thwarted.

'I do. I don't.' She held out her hands to the flames of the fire. 'I love having her. I merely meant to point out that the house is still serving a purpose.'

He grunted, fumbled in a briefcase for papers. 'Yes – well, I've brought some up-to-date bumf, a simple layout of incomings and outgoings so you know exactly where you stand—'

'Simon, Morgan's do all that. I've had their statement and I know where I stand.' And where she sat and slept, and where she intended to stay. 'You shouldn't go to all that bother.'

'You told me once you couldn't make head nor tail of their figures.'

'I can if I concentrate, enough to realize what I've got to live on, anyway. It bores me, that's all.'

'I thought you liked us to have the odd discussion,' he said, looking wounded.

She ignored it. She was making a stand against intimidation, for so she had come to regard his repeated attempts to organize her life.

'I'm happy to discuss anything except the house,' she told him, rising to wipe dust from the mantelpiece with a forefinger. 'And that's really what you want to talk about, isn't it?'

He opened his mouth, shut it, opened it again. 'I do worry—'

She knew what worried him: being hit by inheritance tax when she finally keeled over.

14

'There's no need,' she replied cheerfully. 'I've got the immediate future mapped out, if you're interested.'

He nodded apprehensively.

'I've decided to give up work for a while.'

She saw the apprehension deepen and wanted to laugh. The money she earned as a researcher was a mere pittance, but she regarded it as hers to squander as she wished without eating into the children's rights.

'I've finished Rex Hoskin's book and I feel I need a break.' He would not understand that reading about misery could affect one's health and she did not bother to explain.

Simon said, 'Oh. Well, I do see if you're tired – I suppose you'll miss the cash, though.'

'I'm going to take a lodger.' She smiled at him. 'I don't know why I haven't thought of it before.'

'You mean, a career woman wanting a London pad?'

'No. I mean a man, they're easier. They go out more often and don't impose on your life.'

'A man?' repeated Simon, stunned.

'Why not, for Heaven's sake?'

'How do you know they're not rapists? Or unreliable, at any rate?'

'They come with references, I gather, from the Ministry of Defence.'

'That doesn't stop them from making passes,' he said disapprovingly.

'A nice thought, but hardly likely in my case.'

He grunted.

'You're surely not denying me the small pleasures left in life, are you?' She eyed him curiously, wondering how he would take it if she were to remarry. 'Do stop being nannyish, darling.' Briskly she crossed to

15

her bureau, pulled out the bottom drawer, found what she wanted and tossed it into his lap; a roll of thick paper tied by tapes. 'And that is my hobby and my therapy.'

'Therapy?' He frowned. 'You're not ill, are you?'

'No, just tired.'

He looked at the roll, holding it in his hand. 'What on earth is this?'

'Deeds. I'm going to research the history of the house.'

'I've never seen this.' He unrolled it with a flicker of interest. 'It's written in longhand. Copperplate?'

She nodded. 'It's the original. I can't think of a better way to relax for a month.'

She had always known there was a resident spirit on the top floor. Its domain was the nursery; Louisa, when eight or nine years old, talked of someone tucking the bedclothes round her late at night. Rachel herself had been aware of it from the moment she viewed the house with Henry. Since he was a strong disbeliever in the supernatural, she mentioned the subject only once, bringing down a deluge of reasons on her head as to why ghosts did not exist; all of them extremely logical. The spirit was quite amiable, it disturbed neither Rachel nor Louisa, and kept itself to itself, never moving from the nursery floor, possibly because of Henry's scepticism. The rest of the house remained free of any occupants but the Playfairs, until the afternoon when Rachel walked into the drawing-room and realized she was not alone.

It was the same day on which she had been to the doctor and lunched with Phyllida. Exhausted by hours of being told what was good for her, she arrived home rather more depressed than on setting out. Closing the front door behind her in relief, she felt the house fold itself round her with familiar warmth. The dog, Morecombe, scrabbled round her feet in ecstasy at her return and escorted her to the drawing-room where the hair rose on his back, he gave a low growl and bolted downstairs to the kitchen. She looked into the room cautiously. It was empty as she had left it. But the air stank as if there had been a party, thick with the smell of Turkish cigarettes and a particularly heavy scent.

She moved slowly towards the fireplace, puzzled rather than frightened. Lighting the fire, she became aware of someone close by, sensing it only, because there was nothing to be seen. Whoever it was stood beside the pie-crust table with the lamp, leaning one arm on the mantelpiece. She could find no explanation for this ridiculous conviction when she thought about it later; no outline, no hazy spiral of smoke from a cigarette. Nevertheless, she could have drawn the figure she had in mind. She left the room feeling eyes in the small of her back, and when she peered in after an hour or so, the air was clear. They had departed.

Since then their visitations had been spasmodic and always with the attendant smell of sophistication. Rachel thought of them in the plural because of the social atmosphere they induced. They did not worry her, but she was intrigued by their obvious modernity and why they should manifest themselves after twenty years of dormancy. She found these questions occupying her thoughts more and more; they made a welcome alternative to wondering what positive use she was to anyone. Her curiosity grew and, at the same time, the

17

idea of doing something about it. But this was not for Simon's ears. He would think her alarmingly eccentric.

Scrutinizing the Deeds, Simon remarked, 'There are surprisingly few changes in occupancy. People seem to have stayed put for years.'

'Exactly,' replied Rachel pointedly. 'It is very much a family house.'

'If that's a dig, Mother, it's uncalled for. All I've ever suggested is that one day it will all get too much for you; the stairs, for one thing.'

She began weeding out dead flowers from a bowl of daffodils with swift expertise and an inclination to empty the contents over her child's handsome head.

'A moment ago you were worried to hear I was stopping work for a while. Now you are worried that my legs are about to collapse under me.' She laughed without humour. 'Not very consistent, are you?' Brittle daffodils hit the waste-paper basket in a screwed-up ball. She threw herself down in an armchair. Then she began to laugh.

'I'm hopeless at rows. Look, I'm shaking.' She held out her hands. 'I hope you realize you've made me long for a cigarette and I'm trying to give up.'

Simon gave a weak smile.

'I think we'd better make a pact,' she said, 'not to discuss this again. Because I've no intention of leaving for the time being.'

'Fine. OK. It's your decision, naturally,' he said, backing down in relief. Her anger could still scare him, take him unawares in its rarity.

'Do I *look* decrepit?' she asked, voicing the worst of her hurts.

'Of course not.' In fact she looked almost indecently young, he thought; fine brown hair caught back in combs from a face shiny as a schoolgirl's, and wearing jeans. There was nothing wrong with her figure.

'Of course not,' he repeated. 'I'm sorry. Let's forget it.'

She got up and moved to give him a quick kiss on the cheek. 'You probably think I'm a selfish old cow. The point is, I'm happy here,' she said, without elaborating on the pain of dragging up roots. He would not have understood. 'Meanwhile, if I go entirely senile you can stick me in a home,' she told him.

He grinned at her levity. But the argument had left them uncomfortable with each other.

The moment he had left, Rachel thought how much, after all, she loved him. She wished she had told him so; perhaps, in his case she had never said it enough. But then it was difficult to get it right with children.

Emily lay flat on her stomach, sucking a strand of hair, a book propped against the pillow. Somewhere a baby cried. The noise, gentle but persistent, as if the child was tired, gradually penetrated her concentration, forcing her to stop reading and listen unwillingly.

The red suitcase sat where she had left it, still packed, her mind having been distracted immediately by the whole of one bookshelf devoted to herself. Rachel wouldn't mind if she never unpacked so long as she cleaned her teeth. The swift disintegration of her mother's ideals instilled in Emily had begun, seeping away to leave a sense of drowsy content. Rachel called it 'settling in'. Whatever, it was comfortable.

19

After another two-and-a-half pages the wailing started again, but she was too involved with *The Wind in the Willows* to bother. At the end of the chapter she yawned deeply, rolled on to her back and stared at the ceiling where weak sunlight made watery mobile patterns. She wished she was allowed to call Rachel by her name instead of Granny. Emily herself was called Rachel; Emily Rachel Playfair. They called her Emily because to have two Rachels in the family would have been muddling, so they said. Emily loathed 'Emily'.

The crying sounded like a cat. Perhaps it was a cat. She sat up, unhooked her glasses, spat on them and rubbed the lenses with the cuff of her jersey. Laying the book flat on the bed, she padded to the door and opened it. The only sounds now were the ticking of the grandfather clock in the dining-room and a clunk as the central heating turned itself on. The staircase on the top floor was a semi-spiral like the lower one, only steeper and narrower. There were thirteen stairs. She counted as she climbed, stepping one back and up again because thirteen was unlucky. The landing carpet had a threadbare patch by the nursery which had been there as long as she could remember. The door was open; Rachel left a lot of doors open to let in the light. Emily peered in. It was orderly and unoccupied, a large room facing north over the square and redolent of baby powder. The bed was an unsullied sea of white under its cover, the curtains with yellow and blue posies hooked back from the unopened windows. A small wooden horse on rockers, its scarlet paint worn to a few scattered patches, was the only sign of childish inhabitance.

Emily was disappointed. Because of the crying she

was half-expecting to see her cousin Robin. She did not normally approve of babies, they were messy and boring, but she found it possible to overlook such drawbacks in Bins. For one thing he was a strange and lovely colour, exactly the colour of Rachel's breakfast coffee when she stirred in the milk. Neither did he smell, like other babies, of nappies and sick. His smell was the same as something that Rachel grew in the garden, which was surprising since Louisa was a careless sort of mother, not one to worry much about washing Bins or his clothes.

Emily had mixed feelings about her aunt. She pictured her now sprawled on the bed, the cover all rucked up, her dark hair falling over her face, cuddling the baby and reading *Elle* at the same time. Louisa was beautiful. She represented everything that Emily instinctively knew she would never be able to emulate. But you never knew where you were with Louisa; she could be enormous fun or really snappy, and she hated the baby to be nick-named Bins. Emily decided that perhaps it was more comfortable without them after all.

The crying had stopped; had stopped ever since she came up here, she realized. The next-door room was Christian's whenever he was at home, and still smelt of school socks, although he was grown up now and in the Army. By the window she stood on tip-toe and saw, way down below her, her father and Rachel in the garden, their figures distorted from above. From this height the double row of gardens seemed like one big orchard, the pinks and whites and yellows of spring billowing into each other. Emily breathed heavily on a pane and drew a face in the mist. She wondered how long it would be before her father left and she could 'settle in' properly.

Simon, as he headed west along the M4 with Camilla by his side, had a lingering sense of injustice. If he lusted after a portion of the family finances, it was on behalf of Camilla and Emily and the second child. The Consort Terrace houses must be worth a bomb. Mother was stubborn, always had been. All the same, he had made a mistake in banging away at the issue; coaxing rather than coercion worked better with Rachel, every time.

He wished sadly that he had not always, even as a child, found her somehow out of reach. In those days there had been a feeling of not quite belonging; a pairing off: Louisa with Father and Christian with Rachel and himself as odd-man-out. The feeling had never completely left him. He still felt ostracized occasionally, even from the carefully erected structure of his own nest.

'You're terribly silent,' said Camilla accusingly. Pregnancy made her inclined to petulance.

'Sorry. I'm having to concentrate on the traffic.'

He had started the journey with the idea of discussing Rachel's attitude, but the desire had left him. While she got on perfectly amiably with her mother-in-law, Camilla was secretly scared of Rachel's intellectualism. It made no difference that Rachel in no way made it obvious; Camilla felt inferior and an excellent way to combat this was the occasional grumble about Rachel's scattiness. But Simon was thinking of a certain look in Rachel's eyes which reminded him of a small cornered animal whose young are endangered.

He supposed the house had taken the place of her children to some extent, become her security. Brought up for most of his life in Consort Terrace, he remembered loving it once, yet he would hardly feel a pang of regret if it were sold. Could anyone mind that much about bricks and mortar?

He put a hand on Camilla's knee. 'All right? Not uncomfortable, darling?'

She was only six months pregnant and already having trouble doing up the seat belt. He could not recall her being as large with Emily. They had better make the most of this weekend; another month and making love would be awkward. He put his foot on the accelerator and switched to the fast lane.

'I thought Bins might be staying as well,' said Emily, popping a sandwich into her mouth absently. They were in the kitchen and Rachel was stacking tea things into the dishwasher, glad of an excuse to use it for once.

'Oh. Why?'

'I heard a baby crying, quite near, like upstairs. I thought it might be Bins. But he never does, does he? Cry, I mean.'

'Not often.'

'It sounded really close.'

'One of the neighbours' children, I expect.'

'Do any of them have babies?'

Rachel paused. 'Not that I know of,' she said thoughtfully. 'Are you still hungry after all those sandwiches?'

'Starving.'

'Then we'll have omelettes for supper. Cheese or ham?'

Later she sat in bed with the Deeds spread across her lap, a mug of hot milk and whisky on the table beside her.

This aspect of being single was one she enjoyed enormously, the freedom to read, drop biscuit crumbs in the sheets, spread things all over the bed and listen to the radio before dropping off to sleep. No grunts of disapproval, no huge sighs or demands to have the light out. She had come to the conclusion that, for sheer bliss, it beat sex by a short head, although it was some time since she had had a chance to confirm her theory. A sudden clear vision, the memory of standing in the hall while Henry climbed the stairs, flashed into her mind. Her hand lay on the banister rail, she could feel the slippery polished surface under her palm. She was thinking, this is where we're going to live, this is it and I've found it, he must like it, he *must*. Because if Henry did not approve, then the whole idea must be ruled out. Her happiness was completely dependent on his happiness.

Or so it was in those days, she reminded herself; until I discovered what a lying, two-timing bastard he could be. She took a sip of her drink, shifted her feet under the duvet, allowing herself to finish her memory since it was so vivid.

He had tried to make love to her upstairs in the main bedroom, this room. They had stood by the window, he rocking on his heels, she twittering like a bird – 'You do like it, don't you, darling?' – and then he had caught her by the wrist and pulled her on to the bed, giggling, horrified because the house was occupied and someone might appear at any moment. They had rolled and wriggled, half-joking, half-overcome by passion, leaving the oyster-coloured satin cover creased and unresponsive to her attempts to iron it out with her hands. Her face was aflame, her wrists marked from his grip. He had left her to cool off by the open window while he went downstairs to have a discussion with the unsuspecting owner.

The agony, the terrible agony of loving as acutely as she had loved Henry. It should be passed on as a warning from mother to daughter not to marry in a state of emotional slavery. She had never told Louisa; but then it was difficult to imagine Louisa so inflicted, and in any case the young today went about things in an altogether more realistic way, having long trial runs before deciding on anything permanent. For all Rachel knew, falling in love might have gone completely out of fashion. Of her own children's relationships she knew little, could only guess. She sighed and picked up her mug. The milk had gone cold. She turned her attention back to the names and dates so meticulously inscribed under her gaze.

Her ghosts were certainly not products of the last century; no lavender water and smelling salts for them. They were emancipated women, smoking and sloshing on the scent; probably sloshing back the gin as well. Mrs Pankhurst had been and gone. She fumbled for pad and pen and started to write down names that fell in the right period. From 1910 to 1930 the house was owned jointly by a Colonel Bruce-Hardy and a Mrs Frances Tavistock. A love-nest or merely a brother and a widowed sister sharing a home? Rachel wondered.

In 1930, Mrs Lilian Fane Rumbold became sole

owner; a widow or a divorcee, or possibly a dominant woman insisting the house should be in her name. She appeared to have stayed until 1943, after which there was a gap of four years before the next resident, probably due to the war damage sustained by the Terrace. Rachel stared at the ceiling, tapping the pen against her teeth, her eyes held by a long black thread of cobweb which surely had not been there yesterday. She shifted a pillow and felt her eyes grow heavy. Rumbold was a singularly uninspiring name. She put a question mark by Colonel Bruce-Hardy and fell asleep with the light on, the pen making a thin streak of blue on the sheet as it rolled away.

A crack of thunder directly overhead jerked her awake and brought a white-faced Emily to share her bed, burrowing under the duvet until only a few wisps of hair showed. Rachel, abandoning all thought of sleep, settled back philosophically. Lightning flickered through a gap in the curtains.

'If you come out, I'll read to you,' she said eventually. Emily emerged slowly. 'My book's next door,' she pointed out.

'So?'

'I'm too scared to get it.'

'Thunder doesn't hurt. Noise may be unpleasant but it can't actually hurt you.' Rachel swung her legs out of bed, giving in to this one Achilles' heel of the composed Emily. 'I'll come with you.'

'I think I'd rather talk.'

'In that case, we may as well both have something to drink.'

'Mummy lets me do this when there's a storm,'

confided Emily when they were back in bed. 'But I'm not allowed to talk. It keeps Daddy awake.'

'Men can be boring,' agreed Rachel.

'What's this, Granny?'

'It's the Deeds, a list of all the people who lived in the house before us.'

'How long ago does it begin?'

'From when it was built in 1837; a hundred and fifty-five years ago.' Rachel spread them out. 'There you are.'

'Goodness.' Emily blinked, trying to envisage such an immeasureable length of time. 'I'd better get my glasses.'

Thunder ignored, she was back in seconds to sprawl with her nose two inches from the paper.

'If you have to read that close, the lenses can't be strong enough,' said Rachel.

'It's funny writing, I can't read it anyway.'

'Actually, it's clear and perfect. You aren't used to it, that's all.'

There was a distant growl of thunder. Emily yawned, losing interest.

'The storm's over,' said Rachel hopefully. 'It's rolled miles away.'

'Can I sleep in your bed?'

'Neither of us would *get* any sleep.'

'Just five minutes, then. Please.'

Emily lolled against Rachel's shoulder and stuck a thumb in her mouth, removing it after a minute or so to say, 'There's a cobweb up there,' and adding as a complete *non sequitur*, 'Mummy's pregnant, did you know?'

'Yes, I did.'

Emily was silent.

'Are you pleased?'

She shook her head. The thumb had gone back in again.

'Why not? You like Robin. Now you'll have a baby to yourself, so to speak.'

It was no use trying to explain even to Rachel that no baby could be like Bins; that she, Emily, knew for certain that this one would be pink and slobbery, quite, quite different.

'It moves,' she remarked in disgust. 'Mummy got me to put my hand on her tummy, and it wriggled. It feels creepy.'

'At least it's alive and well,' said Rachel.

'I know,' said Emily gloomily.

'Come on, I'm taking you back to your bed now.'

She hovered, fingering the Deeds, using delaying tactics. 'What are you going to do with this, Granny?'

'I'm going to research one of the families; find out about their lives and what happened to them.'

'Can I help?'

'I don't see why not.'

'How will you choose which one?'

'I've boiled it down to two: Colonel Bruce-Hardy and Mrs Rumbold. Which do you think?'

'Not Rumble,' said Emily immediately. 'It's what insides do when you're hungry.'

As Rachel tucked her into bed she asked, half-asleep, 'Are there ghosts here?'

'Absolutely not,' said Rachel firmly. She was not going to risk a discussion that might incur Camilla's disapproval. 'Good night, darling.'

* * *

Camilla was lying in a four-poster bed wearing nothing but a look of satisfaction. She was rather off sex at the moment but she was quite good at pretending, and Simon was satisfied which brought its own slightly pious reward.

'I adore you when you're all pink and rumpled,' he said, smiling down on her.

She hated to be either. 'Thunder,' she murmured.

'Miles away. London, I should think.'

'Oh dear, I hope Rachel can cope. You know Emily and thunder. God! I'm hungry.'

He patted her stomach. 'Then we must feed little Basil.'

'Don't, it's a ghastly name. Anyway, it's a girl.'

'Hope not, because then we'll have to try again and we can't afford it. Sandwiches and champagne?' He reached for the telephone.

'Cocoa, please, darling. I'm hooked on it.' She opened large blue eyes and smiled at him affectionately.

Privately, she had no intention of 'trying again'.

Shortly before morning, Rachel dreamt of Guy Fawkes' night; a bonfire in the garden, shadowy children's figures darting here and there holding sparklers, and Henry about to set light to a huge rocket aimed at the house. He was smiling and the smile terrified her. She woke as she was about to pull Louisa from the rocket's path.

The dream with its unacceptable connotations might have lingered like a hangover if it had not been for the company of Emily. The smell of wood-smoke lingered in any case, pungent enough to make her gaze at the grate in the drawing-room, half-expecting to see the ashes of a real fire instead of a gas replica. The power of imagination was an extraordinary thing, she told herself, and forgot the matter until Emily, eating her toast, asked what was burning.

Chapter Two

Letter from Florence Codie, cook, to her sister.

7 Consort Terrace. April 1942.

Lisa went back today, up Norfolk way. Maybe the air'll do her good, put some colour in her cheeks, poor mite. Makes your heart bleed seeing her like that, white and thin as a peeled stick. Didn't do her no good coming home, that's for sure. Compassionate leave's a daft name for it, her ma don't know the meaning of the word. You'd think she'd know how to handle a grieving daughter, she's seen enough death driving that ambulance of hers. But it's my belief she looks on it as more of a nuisance than anything, Robbie's having gone missing, maybe killed and all. Interferes with life, a death does.

Spent most of her time down with me in the kitchen, Lisa did, just like she done when she were a kid hiding away from that old bitch of a nanny of hers. Course there was staff in them days and me just the kitchen maid doing the veg and the rough and Lisa'd be all round Cook looking for biscuits and cakes, it's my belief the child was half-starved, who can blame her? Come for the

31

company too, most like, bit of human kindness and it were warm down there, still is more'n the rest of the house. Madam thinks coal and logs come easy like always, never mind the flippin' war.

Don't call her 'madam' no more, don't call her nothing, not even Mrs Rumbold. She ain't said nothing about it, feared of losing yours truly, the flamin' dogsbody. Yells down the back stairs yesterday like always, 'Codie, bring some logs, fire's going out,' and up I goes with what's left and there's Lisa all huddled up in a chair and wearing one of Robbie's old jerseys, s'pose it give her a spot of comfort. Her ma's all tarted up in a black frock ready to go out and trying to pour gin down the girl, that's the only comfort madam's got to offer. Lisa come down to me later and smoked me fags and we had a talk, even made her laugh telling her how me old man buggered off. Could see she never think I were married what with me wonky leg and thick specs but it take her mind off things for a while. She's happy being a land-girl, likes the country and the cows and all but her ma reckons it's beneath her, ought to be in the women's Navy or a FANY whatever that is, sounds downright rude to me.

Then what happens but they whisks Lisa off to some hotel or other, nothing's going to interfere with madam's precious evening out with her fancy man, Yank he is, something high up. Makes her feel better to take Lisa too, I reckon, but the girl don't want to go, never could stand up to her ma. Oh Gert, you should've seen her, her frock hanging on her like Orphan Annie and her face like whey. Worse'n that, they give her too much to drink, she come home at two o'clock in the morning, sick as a cat she were and her ma not with her neither. The Yank bring her home, leastways he's a gent, helps her up the stairs to me, seems madam stayed on dancing with friends. I ask you, she didn't ought to have a child.

It all come out next day, that's today like, house like a morgue and madam not up by noon nursing a bloody great hangover for sure. Child ain't just grieving over Robbie, she's feared stiff of him coming home scarred, skin burnt off of him so's she won't recognize him, don't think she'd cope with that somehow and nor do she. Plane went down in flames, see, and they tell her not to hope, but you never know, do you? Wondered why she turn his photo face down, see that when I done the room. You'll manage, I tells her, if it happens. Didn't help much but no use pretending. Anyway she seem a bit happier when she leave, glad to be going if you ask me. Don't know how she'll manage without Robbie, needs a man that one does to look after her. Used to be a lovely girl, well she ain't so lovely now, poor little beggar. Can't seem to stop thinking about her, Gert, alone and all of a muddle, feared of him dying and feared of him living.

Chapter Three

Consort Terrace bordered the south side of Edgehill Square, its identical Victorian houses in solid contrast to their more graceful neighbours. The north, west and east sides were built in the eighteenth century; earlier in some isolated cases, their windows long and lean and their porticoes curved and elegant. Beside them the Terrace appeared as plain and plebeian as a cart-horse amongst racehorses. Rachel mentioned something of the sort to Emily without imagining she would be in the slightest degree interested, and was surprised when she sprang to the defence of Rachel's property.

'I like our house much the best.'

'The ones in the square are far more beautiful.'

Emily stared disparagingly at a perfect example of Georgian architecture. 'The windows are dirty. And they haven't painted the front doors real colours, only black or white,' she announced, and that was that.

Rachel disentangled the dog from Emily's legs before continuing on their way to the butcher. It was true the Terrace had its own charm, particularly on a spring morning with the sun softening the uncompromising façades and setting alight the cherry blossom in the front gardens.

It was on a morning such as this that Henry had died swiftly and untypically without fuss at the breakfast table. The image in Rachel's mind at this moment was not of him, however, but of Christian struggling down the front steps with his tricycle, in tears from a scraped ankle. Simon and Louisa might have been there as well but it was Christian whom she saw vividly in a striped T-shirt, bony knees protruding from below dark blue cotton shorts. She was seized with a sudden and overwhelming desire to be able to talk to him, touch him, convince herself that the fear which stalked her daily had not become fact and he was not lying in a ditch, the latest victim of an IRA bullet.

'On we go, then,' she said cheerfully.

'When will we go to the Town Hall?'

'After we've bought the chicken.'

Emily was a surprising child. The weather had swung to summer overnight and Rachel had suggested several outdoor activities. But Emily was bitten with the idea of research and could not be deflected. Her enthusiasm would probably turn to boredom by the end of the morning, when she realized it was not grand detection but a tedious plodding through a history of Kensington. Rachel could think of nothing more imaginative than a visit to the Public Library with no clear purpose in mind apart from making Emily feel she was helping.

Lambe's was a family butcher, uniquely long-lasting amongst the Indian grocery, Chinese estate agent, Italian bistro and the Mexican arts and crafts. Emily lolled in the doorway with Morecombe panting beside her in the sun, while Rachel waited her turn. The smell of meat, clean yet repugnant, drifted outwards. Emily's nose wrinkled in distaste. On the red-brick building

opposite there was a blue-and-white plaque com-
memorating a poet/playwright. She had never heard of
him but she knew you had to be famous to have one of
those stuck on your wall. That happened after you
were dead so you would know nothing about it. It
seemed a pity; a bit pointless, really. She drew a
plaque in the sawdust with the toe of her trainer and
tried to write Emily Rachel Playfair, but there was not
enough room.

The thought of death made her remember, for no
particular reason, the baby crying upstairs in Rachel's
house. Despite Rachel's comments, Emily was convinced that it did not belong to neighbours; the sound
had come from directly above her, in fact. Rachel had
seemed not to want to talk about it, which was unlike
her. In Emily's experience grown-ups behaved like this
when they believed what you said was probably right,
but they were not willing to admit it. Her mind skipped
to what Rachel called the 'Deeds'. One thought led to
another. Emily would have liked to tidy them into a
neat pattern but the connection eluded her. She
scratched the back of one leg with the other foot, half-
listening to the conversation going on between Rachel
and the butcher. A chicken was in the process of being
degutted by his trembling hands. Mr Lambe was as old
as God in Emily's eyes.

'Doesn't seem like nearly fifty years, does it, madam?'

They were talking about the war. One could rely on
much the same conversation with Mr Lambe each time
one entered the shop: the war was his favourite
subject. Rachel had no difficulty in guiding him along
the right lines. It had occurred to her that his memory

might well stretch back to residents he had served in the past. Such snippets of casual gossip were quite often valuable.

'But of course, you wouldn't remember the war, madam. You wasn't born.'

'Thank you, but I was. I remember bits of it quite well. Gas masks, dried egg, that sort of thing. The shop was here before that, I believe you told me?'

'Since 1930.'

The year the house was sold by Colonel Bruce-Hardy. There would be no information about him from this source.

'I worked here from the day it opened; sixteen, I was. Started as Dad's errand boy, delivered to all the houses round here; Edgehill, Consort, Frederic Gardens, all of 'em. They had staff then, of course.' (Rachel could have recited this bit word for word.) 'Funny to think of it now.'

He wrapped the chicken slowly in two layers of paper and put it reverently in a plastic carrier. 'All through the war I ran the shop. Dad died 1938 and I was on my own, except for Nellie. We was married by that time.'

He shot a nervous glance at Mrs Lambe sitting in a glass cubby hole, hair fiercely permed, sharp eyes on her husband to make sure he was behaving himself. Rachel took the carrier from him.

'I wonder,' she said, 'whether you remember the people living at my address during the war?'

'Now that would be Consort, wouldn't it? Number eight?'

'Seven.'

'Of course it is. Never could remember numbers.

Now people, that's a different matter. I used to put the houses to the names when I did my deliveries. If the families changed, it threw me out. Number seven. Let me think.'

He put a hand to his forehead, looking like an elder statesman in deep contemplation. Rachel drew out her wallet in readiness, waiting for his thoughts to assemble.

'It was one of the houses got damaged by an incendiary, that I do know. Two of them, there was. One was the Brownlow's and the other people – it's on the tip of my tongue.'

'Rumbold?'

'That's it. Mrs Rumbold.' He looked at Rachel, perplexed. 'Fancy you knowing and me not able to recall.'

Rachel decided on the direct approach. 'I'm doing some research; West Kensington during the war years. I happened to notice the name in the Deeds of my house.'

'Ah.' Mr Lambe seemed impressed. 'So you're still writing, then?'

'I don't write,' Rachel explained patiently. 'I just do the spadework for other people's books.'

Mr Lambe ignored the modesty. 'I was saying to Mrs Lambe only the other day, wonder if Mrs Playfair's still in the publishing world.'

Rachel gave up. 'Did you know Mrs Rumbold? You see, Mr Lambe, I'm like a detective, gleaning information any way I can and sticking the bits together to make a whole. Every little helps.'

She smiled encouragingly at him.

'Well, madam, I didn't rightly know the lady.

Beginning of the war people had staff, like I say, then later they was called up. But Mrs Rumbold had a cook right through, so she was the one I saw when I took round the rations.' He paused, watery blue eyes on some distant picture. 'Had a limp, the cook did, that's why she was let off war-work. Though I seem to recollect war-work might have been preferable, from what she said.'

'Oh, why was that?'

'Bit of a tartar, that Mrs Rumbold, so I heard.' He lowered his voice. 'Quite a looker, though, she was. I seen her once or twice in uniform, Red Cross I think it was. Very smart, it suited her.' Becoming serious, he added, 'She had her troubles, poor lady, what with the bomb and all.'

'Yes, I gather the top floor was destroyed.' Rachel, aware of Emily fidgeting, picked up her parcel. 'A fire must be terrifying. But they certainly rebuilt expertly.'

'They had to put things back just the way they was, after the war. Didn't cost a penny, neither; Government compensation.'

'How wonderful,' Rachel sighed. 'I could do with some of that right now.'

Mr Lambe's expression was sombre. 'Yes, madam. But it wasn't so for Mrs Rumbold. Wouldn't have made up for the loss of a daughter, would it?'

'A daughter?'

'Yes, madam. The only casualty with them incendiaries; that's how I remember it. She was married, I believe. Now *her* name doesn't spring to mind. Tragedy, that was.' He shook his head.

Mrs Lambe pushed her torso out of the cubby hole. 'You shouldn't tell about such things, Cyril,' she admonished. 'Mrs Playfair won't be wanting to know who died in her house and when.'

'I really don't mind.' Rachel, sensing a whole new aspect to her project about to take shape, paid her bill and smiled comfortingly at the butcher. 'Thank you, you've been such a help. What happened to Mrs Rumbold, do you know?'

He straightened up from giving Emily a sweet. 'She left the area. The cook went with her and that's all I can tell you. Never had sight nor sound of her since. She'd be a very old lady by now. Doubt if she's still with us.'

'If you do think of anything else, would you please let me know, Mr Lambe?' Rachel scribbled her number on the back of an old envelope. 'However unimportant it may seem.'

Emily, her cheek bulging with a humbug, struggled for speech. 'Was there a baby there? When the house caught fire, I mean?'

Mr Lambe looked down at her and across at Rachel in bewilderment. 'A baby? No baby what I know of.'

'Funny the things kids come out with,' he said to his wife when his customers were out of earshot.

While Rachel disposed of the shopping, Emily answered the telephone.

'It's a man.'

'Christian?' asked Rachel quickly.

'No, just a man.'

She took the receiver in resignation, sudden hope squashed. Emily heard her say, 'Sorry, Renton, I can't. I have Emily staying.' There was a pause, then Rachel's huffy voice, 'Of course, my granddaughter, who else? Yes, fine, some other time.'

The receiver clicked down sharply.

'Who was it?' asked Emily.

'Just a friend, Renton Thirsby, wanting me to have dinner with him.'

'You weren't very nice to him,' observed Emily.

Rachel smiled at her. 'Men can be boring, as we agreed last night.'

'He can't be a real friend.'

In fact, that was exactly Renton's role. He was the only one left over from a small coterie of men who used to pay her attention after Henry's death. There was a period when she had welcomed such invitations, savouring the feel of new-found freedom, enjoying the preparation and the dressing-up more than the actual event. It was short-lived. Gradually they had drifted away because she had not the slightest inclination to sleep with any of them, and it dawned on her slowly that this was the common lot of women who suddenly found themselves single once more. They were expected to provide a kind of unpaid escort service. She was left with no regrets except the foolishness of her naïvety, and with Renton, solid, unimaginative Renton. He was a source of mild irritation but he had undoubted loyalty.

'He always rings at the wrong time,' she said, 'and we have important things to do.'

There was no longer a lack of purpose in visiting the Town Hall. Her mind was made up, caught by a thread in the reminiscences of the butcher. And as they walked, passing in and out of the shade from the plane trees, she explained to Emily the purpose. Emily thought privately that Rachel was making a mistake, but she was far too content in the company of her grandmother to complain.

Louisa Playfair telephoned her mother to no avail. She wished, not for the first time, that Rachel would overcome her aversion to technical devices and buy herself an answerphone. One should be able to reach her, especially in a state of emergency like now. Louisa was in need of a haven since her own seemed to be collapsing around her ears.

The breathtakingly beautiful morning had not begun auspiciously for her. There had been two rows, no less, followed by a joint exodus by her lover, Vijay, and her daily nanny. Nanny, like several before her, had finally rebelled against what she called 'chaotic conditions' and what Louisa regarded as 'lived in'. The battle with Vijay ran along familiar lines but with more verve than usual. He disapproved of working mothers; no high-caste Indian approved of them, according to Vijay, not quite in those words. Louisa accused him of chauvinism, told him to get stuffed and battle commenced. The impasse remained.

To lose a child-minder and a lover in one morning was worse than bad luck, more like a full-frontal attack from the gods. Vijay might return, Nanny never. Seething with frustration, Louisa picked Robin out of his cot where he was sleeping peacefully and brought him back to the sofa. He made no objection, merely yawned and grinned and reached for her glasses while she telephoned to cancel an interview with the photographic agency who needed a model combining innocence and sensuality. At this moment Louisa felt she possessed neither quality but it was a potential thousand pounds down the drain. She kissed the top of Robin's downy head, breathing in the baby smell, and wondered whether she could spare the time for a good cry.

She thought about Vijay as she cleared the breakfast things, unable to work out how much she would miss him if he walked out on her. He wanted to marry her. 'He has to be joking,' she told the marmalade spoon, tossing it into the sink. The whole problem lay in the difference in cultures; quite simply it did not work. Perhaps over breakfast had not been the most tactful time to tell him about the possible assignment modelling beach clothes in the West Indies; but then it was difficult to find a right time. The evenings were no better; he was often late and irritable after directing all day. What he really wants, she decided, is a subservient doormat in a sari to do his bidding. She paused in the middle of her anger to consider this, and regretted it. For whatever else Vijay was, he was quite the most beautiful man she had ever seen.

She began to pick up a trail of objects that led from the kitchen far across the living-room. Holding in her arms a pink rabbit, two plastic bath toys, baby-grows and her handbag, she sank on to the sofa. Her eyes wandered over the huge room which once, in the first euphoric fervour of coming to live with Vijay, she had helped to decorate. The pale walls and covers were unsuited to having children, but then Robin had not been planned. It was impossible to recall her misery at becoming pregnant, impossible to imagine being without him. He had never been allowed to suffer as a result of her work and it was cruel of Vijay to suggest it. 'You are all I've got' she told him dramatically as she lifted him from the rug and added him to her armful. 'We'll go to Gan-Gan, shall we, and leave nasty Daddy to stew.'

There was still no answer from Rachel's telephone. Louisa gave a sigh. There were friends she could run to, but it would be much better to go to Rachel. She loved Robin and there would be built-in baby-sitting. Louisa had not been home for some time. She had no difficulty in persuading herself that this was a duty visit and nice for Rachel, choosing to forget the things that annoyed her about her mother, like her extreme reticence in prying into other people's lives. Louisa longed to be asked questions and took such tact for lack of interest. Henry had been the opposite, openly inquisitive. She suffered one of her pangs for her father despite the damage he had done her, which Rachel never appeared to notice. But it was typical of her mother's ostrich attitude. Henry had made her miserable. It was her own fault; she should have shown more spirit, taken a leaf out of my book, Louisa told herself smugly.

She had one last attempt at dialling Rachel's number, trying to ignore a desire to bury her head in her mother's lap and cry her eyes out. But Rachel was at this moment browsing in the Public Library.

Rachel found what she was looking for in a volume of *A History of Kensington*. Chapter twelve covered the war years, 1939–45, and it included the exact dates of local bomb damage, going so far as to list the streets and squares, and the type of bomb involved. Three isolated incendiaries had dropped on Consort Terrace and Edgehill Square, causing considerable fire damage and one fatality. The year was 1943 and the date the seventeenth of July. It was enough for one morning. She drove Emily to Richmond Park for a picnic lunch underneath an oak and amongst new green sprigs of bracken.

Emily was still convinced that the Rumbold family were a poor substitute, as subjects of research, for the mysterious Colonel Bruce-Hardy and his lady. Rachel, who felt obliged to keep the supernatural aspect from her, could not say what she felt. Death as a result of a fire was a violent death and possibly the only one of its kind in the entire history of the house. The restlessness of spirits often sprang from violence, and the war years suited her particular spirits admirably.

'I wish you hadn't changed your mind, Granny. That Colonel and Mrs Thingummy are much more fun, the ones who were living together,' Emily was saying as she threw crumbs to the sparrows.

'What do you mean, living together?' asked Rachel cautiously.

'Well, they weren't married, were they? They've got different names. It's called "living together" if you aren't married, like Louisa and Vijay.' Emily's tone was kindly explanatory. 'That's what Mummy and Daddy said.'

'Surely they didn't say it to you?'

'No. I overheard,' said Emily calmly, watching a sparrow trying to launch itself into the air with a crust.

'Have a ham sandwich.' Rachel sought to guide the conversation into less perilous waters. 'Anyway,' she said, 'I would like to know more about the people called Rumbold. They lived in the house during the last war and that's an interesting period. A lot of sad but exciting things may have happened to them.'

A lame explanation, but it was not easy to find a better one. Any further discussion was diverted by an alien creature crawling inside the leg of Emily's jeans and her insistence on undressing behind a tree. 'Do we *have* to eat out of doors, Granny?' It seemed that Emily and nature would never be reconciled.

She was quite won over by the second visit to the Town Hall, however. In the Reference Room copies of newspapers were kept on micro-film, the tapes stored and labelled in months and years. They were to search for the daughter who had died in the fire.

'It's not going to be easy,' Rachel told Emily, 'because she was married and we don't know her name.' She took a pen and notebook from her bag. 'We'll just have to hope her maiden name is included.' She worked her way patiently through the death columns from July the seventeenth, nineteen forty-three onwards, and found what she was looking for in *The Times* of the twenty-fourth. While she copied down the announcement, Emily sat riveted to her chair, eyes on the screen, lips moving as she read.

'Kincade. On July the seventeenth as the result of an air raid, Elizabeth Jane Kincade (Lisa) aged twenty-two, wife of Robert Kincade presumed killed in action, and beloved daughter of Lilian Fane Rumbold and the late George Rumbold. Private funeral service at St Jude's Church, Millhurst, Sussex on July the twenty-eighth at three p.m. Family flowers only. Donations if desired to the Red Cross. No letters please.'

A tragedy in six lines, Rachel reflected; widowed and killed before life had begun. It struck her as a strictly factual account that amounted to coldness. No résumé of young lives, no softening apart from the obligatory 'beloved'. Was Lisa loved?

'That's as far as we can go for the time being,' she said, questioning the wisdom of dwelling on the morbid. She need not have worried. Emily was interested in facts, not sentiment.

'Twenty-two is very young to die, isn't it?' she said on the walk home. 'That's younger than Louisa. I wonder why Mrs Rumble didn't die too? I suppose the girl was stuck at the top of the house. I think it's rotten her mother didn't rescue her.' She stopped to fix the elastic band more firmly round her pony-tail of straight brown hair. 'Think of being frizzled up,' she said cheerfully.

'Don't be such a ghoul,' Rachel told her. 'Lisa would have known nothing about it. Smoke fumes make one unconscious. Do hurry up, darling. Morecombe will be bursting to go out.'

'You know something,' said Emily, undaunted. 'Lisa and her husband could have had a baby, couldn't they?'

Rachel felt suddenly tired. 'It's possible but unlikely; I don't suppose they were married for long. And by the way,' she added firmly, 'Mummy and Daddy will not approve of today's activities. The less said the better, otherwise my name will be mud.'

'I wasn't going to tell them,' Emily said with dignity. She knew when not to pursue a subject. Some while later she asked, 'We found out a lot, didn't we? I suppose that's the end of the research?'

'We've done well,' replied Rachel, 'but it's only the beginning actually.'

*　　*　　*

Emily went home on Sunday evening. Alone, Rachel toured the house, standing for a moment in the nursery, her mind on Lisa Kincade. For some reason, possibly the similarity in names, her thoughts switched to Louisa. It was warm and airless and she opened a window to let in a gust of north wind. The weather had changed again and the gale had blown a pink carpet from the cherry trees and flattened the last of the daffodils.

In Emily's room she closed a book lying open on the bed, marking it with the dust cover and putting it back on the shelf. 'Will you let me know what happens?' Emily had whispered before leaving, twining her arms round Rachel's neck and pulling her down to child-level. Her reserve had vanished only temporarily; when they met again it would be with the usual formal greeting. 'What will you do next?'

The Rumbolds had become a saga to be divulged in instalments.

'I'll let you know,' Rachel promised.

Her parents had driven Emily away, Simon genial and Camilla pink and complacent with pregnancy.

Missing her, Rachel sighed, opened a top drawer and discovered a pair of pop socks and a sweater. She had forgotten to check.

It was not the only matter that had slipped her mind. The Ministry of Defence found her a prospective lodger and she was thrown into confusion by the unexpected swiftness of events. Any further research had to be shelved. The spare room on the top floor destined to be a bed-sitting-room needed attention.

Several hooks were missing from the curtains, the bedside lamp did not work properly, a small rug must be bought to cover a worn patch on the carpet and a portable television hired. Anyone with a modicum of method would have organized such things before putting in an order for a paying guest, thought Rachel wearily as she trudged her way round Peter Jones. She could imagine Simon's smug expression if he were to know. She herself began to regret the whole idea as she stood on the step-ladder cleaning out shelves while the telephone rang insistently. Louisa, plaintive but autocratic, was on the other end.

'Not until the end of the week,' Rachel said more firmly than ever before. She searched for a place to put the wet jay-cloth she was clutching.

'Why?' asked Louisa, openly amazed at this lack of enthusiasm; Rachel, of all people, who adored Robin and loved her daughter and was always, but always, available.

Rachel did not know why exactly; an overdose of housework, perhaps, a pervasive tiredness, but mostly because she felt a strong and selfish urge to get on with her own life without interruption.

'Various reasons,' she told Louisa. 'I was going to ask you the same question.'

'I've told you, I've left him.'

'Yes, darling, I know. What's the trouble this time?'

'Oh, the usual. He's a shit, that's all.' The voice wavered on the brink of tears. 'No, I don't mean that, I take that back.' An enormous, dramatic sigh. 'It's the culture gap, I suppose.'

There was a pause which Rachel felt too irritated to break.

'Anyway, I'm not going back. I've made up my mind, I'm never going back.'

Like last time, and the time before that, and the one before that, thought Rachel. 'Good,' she said. 'Quite right.'

'You mean it?' Louisa asked, taken aback.

'Definitely.'

'You've never had an opinion about it before.'

'Well, I have now.'

'Oh.' Louisa began to cry. 'He wants me to give up my work.'

Was that so terrible? Rachel wondered. To lie back and be kept in luxury by one's gorgeous film-director lover did not seem too painful a prospect.

'Where are you staying at the moment?' she asked.

'With Gilly and Paul. But they can't have me for long, they've got friends coming from abroad,' Louisa sniffed.

I bet, thought Rachel. 'How's Robin?' she asked, refusing to discuss these problems further.

'Lovely. I thought you'd be dying to see him.'

'So I am, but not until Saturday.'

When the receiver had finally gone down on her daughter's reproachful voice, Rachel broke her rule of never having a drink before six-thirty. She had not been very nice to Louisa. Tolerance in later life was a fallacy; the older the crabbier. Slumped in a chair, sipping her whisky, she foresaw a host of minor difficulties, not the least of which was Louisa, Robin and an unknown male sharing the top-floor bathroom. There would be tights and bras hanging to dry and very definite evidence of a baby littered around. All this must be explained to the Colonel who was viewing the bed-sitting-room the following evening. He was bound to be fanatical about tidiness, despite his surprisingly young and pleasing voice. How like Louisa, she reflected with a sigh, to upset the best-laid plans.

Half an hour later, soaking in a hot bath, she viewed the situation in a better light. The step-ladder and the bucket of dirty water sat where she had left them and there they could stay until morning. She had planned her evening; an old Hitchcock thriller on television and an early night to recharge the batteries. Lying back with her head resting on the bath cushion, her face well creamed and her hair floating around her shoulders like seaweed, she very nearly fell asleep where she was. The sudden fierce peal of the doorbell she was inclined to ignore, if it had not been repeated so insistently.

'I'm only asking,' Louisa said on the telephone to Simon, 'because Mum has barred the door to me; just until Saturday, so I wouldn't be staying long. I wondered whether you and Camilla would be absolute angels—'

'I'm sorry,' lied Simon firmly, 'but Camilla isn't up to it just now. She's been very tired recently and the doctor has ordered her to rest. Well, you know what it's like.'

The door to the drawing-room was open. He could see Camilla glowing with health, writing out a recipe.

'Oh well,' Louisa said crossly, 'I can't think what to do. I feel like some sort of refugee.'

It was on the tip of his tongue to suggest she should return to her own comfortable pad and make it up with Vijay. He thought better of it and changed the subject.

'I'm slightly worried about Mother, actually. She's given up her normal work and proposes to delve into the history of the house. Nothing wrong in that, I suppose, but it won't make her any money. And she's getting a *male* lodger.'

'So? I don't see anything wrong in that, either.' Louisa, having been refused a favour, was prepared to be quarrelsome.

'As long as she doesn't get involved with someone unsuitable.'

'Honestly, she's hardly the age.'

'I don't know. Her figure's pretty good still.'

'Maybe that's what she wants. Who knows? After all, it's five years since Fa—'

'Besides all that,' interrupted Simon, 'Emily seems to have got it into her head the house has ghosts. She wouldn't have thought that one up on her own. Mother must have been filling her up with a whole lot of nonsense.'

'It *is* haunted,' Louisa said.

'You must be joking.'

'The nursery is, always was. I don't mind when I sleep there with Robin. It's quite harmless.'

'Lou, really!' Simon was angry. 'I've never seen anything.'

'No. You wouldn't.'

'And Father was extremely sarcastic about things supernatural, if you remember.'

'I didn't agree with Fa about everything, personally,' replied Louisa sweetly. 'Anyway, Emily has her own ideas, she's that sort of child. I doubt if it has anything to do with Mum.' There was a pause. 'You're quite sure about not giving me a bed?'

'It's not on. Sorry, Lou.'

She rang off morosely. The childhood war between herself and Simon had become a cold one in maturity. At times like this, however, she recalled a day when he ran across the lawn shouting, 'Lou-Lou! Lou-Lou! Clean the loo, do, do!' And she, taunted beyond endurance had fired a home-made bow and arrow and hit the wrong man. Christian had lain as dead, three years old and pathetic as a scrawny baby bird, a hazel stick embedded in his temple. 'He got in the way!' she sobbed furiously, panicking in the face of parental wrath. Christian had got up meanwhile and asked if it was time for tea, and Simon got off scot-free and smirking. There was no justice in life.

Phyllida came to lunch, bringing a bunch of tulips and a collection of travel brochures.

'I've solved your holiday problem,' she said, dropping them beside Rachel who was frying fish-cakes.

'What problem?' Six weeks had passed since lunch in Phyllida's kitchen; six weeks in which Rachel's mind had been occupied with other matters. Life had become unusually full and holidays had not entered into it.

'I'll find a vase, shall I?' asked Phyllida, diving into a cupboard and coming up with an object as straight and uncompromising as the flowers. 'Don't you remember? We decided you needed a holiday and you were being feeble about it, putting up every kind of objection. The chief one being you don't like going away on your own.'

'Was I?' Rachel turned off the gas. 'Oh well, it

doesn't matter now. I can't possibly go, I'm far too busy. Would you like some wine?'

It was better to let Phyllida elaborate on her latest scheme, however, otherwise she would not pay attention and Rachel had a lot to talk about.

'I knew you'd be defeatist about it.' Phyllida crammed the flowers into water in one go. 'It's no use messing around with tulips, they're naturally ungraceful. Thanks, cheers.'

She picked up the pamphlets and waved them in Rachel's direction. 'The answer for you is a tour. Everything done for you, luggage taken care of, no worry over bookings and tickets. And company; plenty of people to chum up with.'

'I don't like plenty of people.'

'Like-*minded* people. These are cultural tours, not your ordinary run-of-the-mill stuff. They are designed for people with similar interests.'

'I don't think I'm very cultured.'

'They have painting holidays, photographic holidays, archaeological holidays; just about everything you can think of. Mind you, they're not cheap, but they're comfortable. And everyone is one of us.'

Rachel slid a plate in front of Phyllida. 'How do you know all this?'

'Cissie Matthews. She goes each year, always somewhere different and always the most wonderful places.'

'What happens to Dennis?'

'Oh, she leaves him behind. Can you *see* Dennis on a cultural tour?'

'No.' Sensible old Dennis. Rachel speared a piece of fishcake and pulled a brochure towards her. There was

54

a picture of a lavender field in Provence on the cover. She turned to the prices page. 'It says here you have to share a room. No singles.'

'Well, obviously they have to fill the tour, don't they?' Phyllida pointed out, looking evasive. She sipped her wine. 'You could go with a friend. Or share with a kindred spirit already booked. *I* wouldn't mind, personally.'

Rachel tidied the pamphlets. 'You must be mad,' she said. And then, seeing the colour flush up Phyllida's neck, she added, 'I'm sorry. That was very rude of me.'

This was not at all how she had meant lunch-time to be spent. The trouble was, fond as she was of Phyllida – the length of their friendship stretched back to school-days – they viewed life from totally different angles. Henry could not stand her, had always been atrociously cruel to her. The thought of it caused Rachel to reach out and squeeze Phyllida's hand.

'I'm sorry, darling,' she repeated. 'I'll keep the brochures in case I change my mind. But I don't think it's quite my form.' She filled their glasses. 'The fact is, I really haven't thought about going away, what with one thing and another.'

Mollified, Phyllida said, 'Well, you're looking better. What have you done to your hair?' She did not wait for an answer. 'So what's new?'

Rachel hesitated. It was no use expecting Phyllida to be remotely interested in any kind of research. But an account of Rachel showing a stranger round the house in her dressing-gown might amuse her, particularly since a male was involved.

'This is the room.' Rachel had switched on the light

and stepped aside to let her prospective lodger see for himself.

It was an unfortunate start. She had not envisaged herself leaning out of the bathroom window, dripping wet and demanding to know who he was. He had been very apologetic, standing diffidently in the hall and insisting that it was his fault, he must have mistaken the day; offering to go away and return tomorrow. Rachel ushered him upstairs quickly. She had a distinct impression that despite his apologies, he was trying not to laugh.

Standing on the threshold while he wandered around, she was past caring about the step-ladder and the bucket sitting where she had left them. It did not matter. She was convinced that he would not want the room, would bow himself out with a polite excuse and disappear to find a less chaotic lodging place. The fates were against this meeting. It might be a blessing in disguise. Perhaps he was the psychopath Simon had predicted.

'It's much bigger than I imagined.' He turned a smiling and unmurderous face towards her. 'And you've made it so attractive. I love the curtains; they're Laura Ashley, aren't they?'

'That's right.' She was taken aback by the unexpected interest in interior decoration. Could he possibly be gay? 'They aren't meant to sag at the end. Two hooks are missing. I didn't get round to fixing them.'

'Have you got them here? I could do it for you, if you like.'

She fetched them from the chest of drawers, conscious as she did so of her short towelling robe and her legs the colour of boiled lobsters from the hot bath-

56

water. It was a relief when he turned his back.

'This is always happening at home,' he said.

Home means married, she thought; highly satisfactory. She watched while he busied himself, reaching easily without the help of steps.

Henry had not been a do-it-yourself man; he had left such things as the changing of plugs to Rachel, to whom they did not come naturally either. She had learnt of necessity. This man's backview with its broad shoulders seemed suddenly the personification of security; the everyday sort of security where doors would be locked properly and household crises dealt with calmly. Having him in the house would be a bonus, she reflected, allowing herself a small ray of hope as he stepped back saying, 'There we are.'

He stared critically at the curtains, his head bumping the ceiling light and setting it swinging.

'Thank you,' she said. 'That light is going to be a nuisance for you. You'll always be knocking against it.' And then, embarrassed, 'But how stupid of me. You obviously want to think about it before deciding—'

'Oh, no.' He smiled at her. 'I've quite decided, if it's all right by you.' Glancing at the bookshelves, he asked, 'Did this room belong to one of your children?'

'No. It's always been a spare one, or where the home help slept when we had one. The books are an overflow from the nursery.'

'That's nice,' he said, reading the titles. '*The Wind in the Willows* and *Biggles*. I shall enjoy myself.'

'You're joking.'

'Absolutely not,' he told her seriously.

'All the children slept up here on this floor at one time,' she said. 'Christian, the youngest, still does when he's home on leave. He's the only unattached one.'

'Where is he at the moment?'

'Ireland.'

'Ah.' He looked at her as if taking her in for the first time. 'I expect you find that pretty nerve-racking.'

'Yes, I do,' she said gratefully. 'Anyway, I have a feeling he will leave the Army at the end of his three-year commission, thank God.'

As they made their way downstairs she asked, 'When would you like to move in?'

'The end of the week, if that suits you?'

For a tall man he walked lightly, the stairboards hardly creaking under his weight as he preceded her. He was younger than she had imagined, his blond hair a shade darker than Simon's curling over his collar. Obviously her idea of the military image was completely out of date.

She felt elated after he had left and caught herself grinning foolishly in the hall mirror. Her triumph deflated a little at the sight of her gleaming face and hair hanging in damp strands. First impressions stuck. However good she looked in the future, this was how he would remember her. Annoyed by such unaccustomed vanity, she marched down to the kitchen and slammed a shepherd's pie in the oven.

The Hitchcock film was already halfway through and she had difficulty picking up the plot.

'Is that all?' asked Phyllida.

Rachel had fallen silent, gazing at a piece of brie on her plate.

'All what?'

58

'All you're going to tell me, for Heaven's sake. I don't know his name, or his age or what he does.'

Rachel ate the brie. 'Tom Crozier, fortyish I should imagine, and I don't know exactly what he does. He's a Colonel.' She started stacking plates. 'Nobody knows what people do at the Ministry of Defence. I couldn't appear too nosy, could I?'

'*I* could. And what is he like to look at?'

Rachel considered. 'I can't remember,' she said, hedging.

'But it was only last night that you met him.'

'What I mean is,' said Rachel, unashamed of her mendacity, 'he is one of those people you pass in the street without noticing. Ordinary, anonymous.'

'How disappointing.'

'He has nice hair; an unusual colour and very thick,' she said to keep Phyllida happy.

'Well, I suppose he sounds suitable,' said Phyllida dubiously. 'I hadn't thought of someone younger for you but it might be an excellent thing. Is he sexy, do you imagine?'

'Honestly, Phyllida, you've got a one-track mind,' Rachel told her as she marched to the sink. 'How should I know? I've only seen him for fifteen minutes.' Opening the dishwasher she added, 'And anyway it's irrelevant. I'm looking for a source of income, not a toy-boy.'

'But wouldn't it be nice if he turned out to be both?' Phyllida was irrepressible.

'Shut up!' said Rachel mildly. 'You can come and give me your advice on some cushion material I'm thinking of buying. That would be considerably more useful.'

The room was now ready for Tom Crozier, and Consuelo had been bribed by fifty pence an hour to include the extra work in her cleaning schedule. Since she was Spanish and male-orientated, she even went so far as to offer to iron his shirts. Any ironing for Rachel was undertaken with reluctance.

With time on her hands once more, Rachel started to enter notes on the Rumbolds in an exercise book, which was her usual system. The information so far was minimal, covering one page only. She sat in the garden and debated the next move: the Public Record Office for Wills, she decided, followed by St Catherine House. If Lilian Rumbold's death was established, those who had benefited from the Will might well be traced, given that they were still alive. She was convinced of the Rumbold mother's death for the illogical reason that it had to be she who dominated the drawing-room, smoked her Balkan Sobranies, brought to life the smell of scent and real log fires. The daughter, as pictured by Rachel, was a wan little thing; an ill-fated, over-shadowed innocent.

Research was made up of facts, not intuitions, she reminded herself sharply. Ghosts were insidious; it would be easy to allow them to cloud the issue. She did not entirely approve of her purpose when it came to St Catherine House. But fact or figment of Emily's imagination, she felt compelled to discover whether or not Lisa Kincade had had a child. One could never afford to leave stones unturned, however insubstantial. Besides, the question nagged her.

The sun held its first heat of summer, burning her bare forearms. She left it unwillingly to return her notes to the desk and to look at the diary. There were three days before the weekend when Tom Crozier was due, and Louisa would arrive with Robin, bringing chaos. Any research should be done beforehand while there was a lull. She was reminded with distaste that she had been invited to a dinner party the following evening, one that, had she been quick-thinking enough, she would have refused. Renton Thirsby was to give her a lift. Being paired off with Renton was a common occurrence.

Christian's letter stared up at her. She had been so relieved to see his handwriting, ripping open the envelope there and then in the hall, eager for news. There were three pages, a record for him. Looking at the letter now brought a resurgence of the uneasiness felt on reading it. She supposed she should be duly grateful for any confirmation of his safety. But it presented her with a totally unforeseen anxiety and for the life of her, she could not think how to word an enthusiastic reply.

Chapter Four

Letter from Florence Codie to her sister.

7 Consort Terrace. September 1942.

Didn't get much sleep last night, 'Jerry' give us a pasting, and a bomb drop on that block of flats down Gloucester Road. Direct hit, couldn't have been no-one left alive. To make things worse, I knew as how Lisa must be in the thick of it, she were due in Liverpool Street around an hour before the sirens went. Coming back on one of her forty-eight hours, she were, and come midnight she still weren't home. Stayed up for her, 'course, and smoked me way through a packet of Wood-bines, I were that worried. Hearing her put the key in the door were like music, I can tell you. She come home two o'clock in the morning, her face a sight, all smears and grime, but the odd thing were, it had an expression on it I never see before. All lit up. I never see her look that way, not even for Robbie. And she smelt of drink, and that weren't like our Lisa, neither.

'Course, I knew there were a man behind it and I were right. I made a cup of cocoa and we sit chatting for an another hour. She tell me all about it, how she run for the shelter down Cornwall Gardens when the raid start. Dead scared, poor girl, hasn't been caught in one before, seeing as how she's stationed Norfolk way, hasn't so much as heard a gun down there. Anyways, there's this American sitting beside her in the shelter, in the Air Force he were, and he give her a slug out of his flask, Yank whisky, she says it's called Burbon or summat, don't know how you spell it. I tells her, she weren't half taking a chance, it might of been drugged so's he could have his wicked way with her later on. She just laughs at me, 'Silly old Codie,' she says and goes on to tell me as how they have a cup of tea somewhere, and she's all upset 'cos that bomb drop too close for comfort, shelter's only a couple hundred yards away. So he's kind to her and they talk a long time, and she tell him about Robbie and everything, and then he walks her home, a proper gent like.

Well, that's all very nice and above-board far as it goes, but it's my belief it's going to go a lot further, I feel it in me bones. Wish I could of seen him, been able to do a bit of summing-up. He's stationed near to where she work on the farm, see, there's fate for you. I'm not saying he ain't a good bloke even if he is a Yank, but you never know, and Lisa's green as grass for all she's been married. Lonely too, and missing a man in her life, well, it's only natural, ain't it? 'He's nice, Codie,' she say to me. 'Different from the others I've met.' 'That's as maybe,' I tells her, 'but you don't know nothing about him, so you go careful, see?' She smile then and I know she ain't taken a

63

blind bit of notice, and she drifts off to bed with that silly smile still on her face. All I can say, Gert, if ever I see a girl in love it were her, for all she's only met him the once. And he may be the best man on God's earth, but if he do anything to harm my Lisa, I'll have his guts for garters, or summat worse what I won't mention.

Must end now and get some kip, me eyes is going. Hope all's well with you . . .

Chapter Five

Rachel could not understand why she had been invited to dinner by the Ferriers; to make up numbers, she supposed. In the dark days when it seemed that Henry and she would part, their friends had already started to take sides, anticipating the final rift which never came about. After the marriage had made a surface recovery, a certain amount of partisanship remained. Alistair and Susie Ferriers were decidedly in Henry's camp, accepting Rachel as a necessary but slightly boring addition; or so it had seemed to Rachel, who felt over-vulnerable at the time, as if recovering from a major operation. But was that not how they had always viewed her? They belonged to Henry's world, an exclusive and academic club for which she did not qualify. A Ph.D. was necessary for membership, and her lowly history degree did not count; from the beginning she felt like the eternal student basking in Henry's glory.

All contact with the Ferriers died with Henry; which suited us all, reflected Rachel, mulling over her wardrobe. Could they really be as awful as she remembered? None of her dresses hanging limply in the cupboard inspired her with enthusiasm. Henry had taken a positive interest in what she wore; one of his strictly limited bonus points. She had grown lazy about clothes now there was no incentive, and learnt not to bother about people she disliked, which ruled out the necessity for a new dress.

Nevertheless she bought one, catching sight of its peacock blue folds in a shop window on the way back from the dentist and jumping off the bus at the next stop to retrace her steps. Later, turning this way and that in front of her looking-glass one hundred and fifty pounds the poorer, she had no regrets but wondered what on earth had possessed her. The neckline plunged, the skirt floated above her presentable knees. Henry would have approved of the cleavage only on someone else's wife, she decided, grinning at her reflection.

Christian had decided to leave the Army, so he began his letter. It wasn't just Ireland, although that was a large part of it; it had to be the most useless, shittiest little war ever. But there was a lot more to his decision than that, and the answer was, he just was not cut out for it.

Rachel was ready early, knowing Renton's excessive punctuality, and she reread the letter while she waited. She was delighted about this part of it, delighted and relieved she would no longer have to live in dread. It was the last paragraph that disturbed her to the point of unhappiness, and she was unusually pleased to open the door to Renton on the dot of seven-thirty. He was quite good about listening to other people's problems as long as the circumstances were right, and she made them so, pouring the statutory gin and tonic mixed half-and-half with two lumps of ice and a slice of lemon, and seeing him settled in his favourite chair, a bowl of nuts beside him.

'We mustn't be long,' he warned her. 'Can't be late for a dinner party.'

'Ten minutes late. Any hostess is in her bra and pants if one arrives on time.'

'How's the family? How's Simon?' Simon was the one he approved of, married, one child and another on the way, worked in the City; straightforward, uncomplicated.

'He's fine, thank you. It's Christian I'm slightly worried about. He wants to leave the Army.'

Renton made one of his typical faces, pursed lips and a small frown. 'I wouldn't think that was a good idea. Has he given it serious thought?' There was another very definite reason, Christian had continued, for why he wanted out.

'Yes,' Rachel replied.

'It's not going to be easy for him to get a job. What is he going to do? He hasn't any qualifications.'

'Just because he didn't go to university doesn't mean he's a moron,' said Rachel, bristling. 'You had no more qualifications than Christian when you started out, if I remember rightly, and you've done all right, Renton; chairman of this, that and the other.'

He took a careful sip at his drink, eying her over the rim of the glass. 'I didn't need them. Things were easier when I was his age.'

Funnily enough, Christian wrote, it wasn't the fear of being killed that got him down so much as the fact they were hated by both factions. He found it difficult to take being spat at, abused in the streets. Complete hatred demoralized completely.

'I shall be glad when he leaves,' she said. 'It's what he's decided to do that I find perturbing.'

67

'Well, at least he's decided; that's something. What does he have in mind? I might be able to help him with contacts if it's anything to do with industry.'

'I doubt it.' Rachel smiled wanly. 'He wants to join the Church.' That silenced Renton. He was out of his depth; the Church stood beyond criticism or the old-boy network.

'Well, well,' he remarked at last. 'I never knew he was religious.'

'He wasn't. This is sudden. He was an atheist like Henry. He became everything that Henry wanted him to be. That's why he went into the Army.'

'You don't look very happy about the transform-ation. Why not? It's nothing if not an honourable profession. And vicars aren't so poor as they used to be. They can afford a wife and three children these days; and a centrally heated vicarage.'

'It's a bit of a shock, I suppose.' The idea of Christian as a clergyman was not in itself unsettling. The disturbing factor was the Catholic priest who appeared to be the influence behind his new-found faith; Father Someone about whom Christian wrote with such enthusiasm she could almost see the fervour shining out of his eyes. Conversion, Roman Catholicism, the priesthood: celibacy. Rachel's thoughts read rapidly between the lines and her heart sank. He would be lost to her, to all intents and purposes, parted by beliefs and rules that were alien. And there would be no children, no replicas of Christian with their bony little bodies and huge dark eyes.

She could not explain to Renton. If she spoke of it, she would start to cry, her mascara would run and he would be overcome with embarrassment.

'I expect I'll get used to the idea.' She jumped up. 'You're right, we should be there more or less on time.'

The following day the telephone rang while she was in the garden planting aubretia. She rose from her knees, spearing the trowel in a flower-bed, reluctant to leave the smell of damp earth. It was Emily.

'Em, what a surprise! No school today?'

'I've god a code.'

'Yes, I can hear. Poor you.'

'Have you found out more about you-know-who?'

'Who?'

'About the research thing. *You* know,' Emily said rapidly. 'I can't speak too loud. Mummy's in the kitchen making something but she might come in at any moment.'

'Right,' said Rachel. 'Well, some time this week I'm going to St Catherine House where they have useful documents, so I hope to learn a little more.'

'I wish I could come with you.'

'I wish you could, too,' said Rachel truthfully.

'Will you ring me up if you find out anything exciting?'

'I can hardly do that if it's a secret, can I?'

'Pretend you're asking me what I want for my birthday. You can do all the talking and I can just say "yes" and "no". Please, Granny.'

'If there's something really important, then I'll telephone.'

'Promise?'

'Promise.'

'Perhaps you'll find out about the baby,' said Emily, uncannily near the mark.

Rachel, who was already in possession of more information than she was prepared to divulge, turned the conversation. 'How is Mummy?' she asked.

'All right, but she gets cross quite often. Daddy says she's tired so we're getting an au pair girl. She'll have to look after me when the baby's being born,' Emily said in disgust.

'You will probably find you like her.'

'I don't need looking after, I'm nearly eight. And she won't speak English, so how can I talk to her? I'd much rather come and stay with you, Granny. Can I? Shall I ask Mummy?'

A picture of Louisa, Robin, a lodger and Emily all occupying the house at once flickered in Rachel's mind, making her feel weak at the knees.

'Let's see, shall we? It depends . . .'

On what did it depend? Rachel was immediately ashamed of her prevarication; as a child she had been infuriated by those same meaningless phrases. Emily of all people had never been denied her escape route to Rachel. But the desire to have her life uncluttered at this moment in time was still strong in her; perhaps something to do with the onslaught of early summer. 'We'll certainly arrange it when the baby is born, before if possible,' she added as a sop.

She returned to the garden, her thoughts reverting to last night's party. As a social event it had been predictably tedious. But there had been an odd stroke of fortune in the shape of a guest as incongruous as herself. Drawn together in a conspiracy of misfits, she had given Rachel a piece of information more valuable than days spent amongst archives might have produced. Such flukes occurred rarely, in Rachel's experience.

When they did so, she felt as if an unseen hand had slipped a piece into the jig-saw puzzle and the seal of approval had been set on the project.

Alistair Ferriers had designed a house of unique simplicity which amounted to bleakness. There were no doors to the ground-floor rooms, very little furniture apart from enormous scatter cushions and fleshy rubber plants, and Rachel's heels clacked loudly as she walked on bare boards towards the hum of voices. The place was as she remembered it: a depressing leftover from the Sixties.

The change in her hosts was immediately apparent, however. At least in the old days there had been an impressive array of drinks, and ashtrays in abundance. Now she could see neither. Susie Ferriers, once terrifyingly glossy in her silk designer trousers and cleverly cut hair, advanced on Rachel and Renton wearing a dress of rusty Indian cotton and bearing two wine glasses. 'Lovely to see you both,' she said. 'White wine?' And without waiting for an answer she swept them into introductions to which neither side listened properly, before dividing them neatly as a sheep-dog and propelling Renton away to a remote corner. Rachel was left standing like an unclaimed parcel, wishing she could transform her wine into something stronger. Alistair and Susie appeared to have moved on to a higher and fashionably ecological plane while their personalities remained unaltered.

She no longer cared. Instead of the paralysing self-consciousness which once reduced her mind and limbs to jelly, she was able to make an assessment of her fellow guests and wonder why good looks and intellectualism seldom went together. She watched them conversing in uneasy groups, visibly missing the necessary alcoholic boost to get their egos working. It was difficult to imagine them participating in the *louche* romps that had always signalled the end of a Ferriers' party: nude bathing in the pool outside the dining-room window. Renton would be horrified; the Ferriers were only recent acquaintances of his and this was his first attendance. She could not help a snort of laughter at the idea as Alistair materialized at her elbow.

'Little Rachel,' he said, smiling with his mouth only.

He used 'little' as a disparagement. 'Henry's little virgin', he had wittily dubbed her during her engagement.

'It's good to see you are able to laugh. Tell me, are you *over* Henry?'

Poor Henry, made to sound like a bad attack of measles. She took a deep breath, astonished afresh at Alistair's gaucherie. 'I've got used to being on my own, if that's what you mean,' she replied coldly.

'Good, good!' he said, thrown off-balance by her new, self-contained image. 'Come and meet somebody. Let me top up your glass.'

She covered it with her hand. 'I'd rather have a whisky, please.'

'Ah, well.' His eyes, prominent and the colour of prunes, slid away from her. 'I'm afraid Susie and I don't stock spirits any longer. We've kicked the cigarettes as well. Unintelligent to hasten the ageing process, we feel. I dare say I might find you something,' he added unhopefully, his eyes making another swivel sideways as if a bottle might be hidden behind the curtains.

'Don't bother.' She opened her bag. 'I'll have a cigarette instead, since I don't pretend to be intelligent.'

Dinner was so long in appearing that Rachel began to wonder if they had given up eating as being another potential health hazard. She found herself seated between a monosyllabic architect and an American professor of philosophy and social psychology who claimed to have met her before; giving her this information as he stared dubiously at the first course. The food was vegetarian in deference to two of the guests, Susie dictating the fact from her end of the table. He looked far from philosophical as he forked over his spinach and avocado salad as if searching for slugs; giving up after a couple of mouthfuls to direct his attention and his horn-rimmed glasses towards Rachel. He had the smooth boyishness she had noticed in many Americans, making it impossible to guess their ages.

'You are Henry's widow?' It was a rhetorical question; he went on without a pause to remind her of how they had met on one of Henry's lecture tours in the United States. There had been a gathering at someone's hotel suite in New York. He could have sworn she was there, although it was some time ago; he remembered the hair and the eyes. Afterwards they had all gone on to dinner some place, and he recalled sitting next to her. They had, he was certain, an interesting discussion about sexual deviation. She shook her head; he faltered. It had seemed, he murmured, that she was attached to Henry at the time; obviously he was mistaken.

'It wasn't me,' she told him calmly. 'But then, Henry liked that type. He was quite consistent.'

The professor, aware of a social blunder, lapsed into silence.

The placidity of her reply belied a sudden dryness of mouth and a stab in the pit of the stomach; distant cousins of the despair she had once felt. She lowered her fork carefully to her plate, surprised that she could still feel anything about the Alison affair. For it was Alison whom her companion described, beyond doubt; Henry's second 'nut-brown girl'. Rachel had been the original; he had christened her so on one of their holidays when passion was still at its height between them. She remembered the exact hour and place, the room overlooking the harbour, the brownness of her skin against the white sheet, skin that turned the colour of toast without burning; and the sweetness of Henry's loving.

One of the hardest facts to take about this particular affair, she decided, was Alison's looks. It would have been easier to bear, less of an insult to be stabbed in the back by a voluptuous blonde rather than a younger replica of herself. None of Henry's other women had posed a serious threat. Rachel had almost, but not quite, come to accept those brief and unimportant adventures as being a necessary hazard of the lecture circuit. They reached her ears sometimes through gossip, more often by Henry's own admission. He found it impossible to keep a conquest secret; as incapable of reticence as a fisherman with a prize catch. They meant nothing, he claimed repeatedly, often enough for Rachel to believe him and to grow a second skin to protect herself from recurring hurt.

Alison was another matter; a thin, quiet, unobtrusive stumbling-block to happiness, she would follow Henry's every move with spaniel eyes, reminding Rachel sickeningly of herself at the outset of her marriage. The twice they met, she recognized danger with the terrible helplessness of someone trapped in the path of an avalanche. She recalled handing the girl a cup of coffee; their hands touching for a second, the prickling of her own flesh and the cold calculation behind the other's soft brown gaze. There had, of course, been one more meeting when the world turned upside down and nobody spoke a word. I could have killed in that brief moment, Rachel thought; I was capable of doing so.

Her eyes focused through the candle flames and she caught sight of Renton's balding pate gleaming in their light. He was watching her, his expression one of concern. She smiled at him, wondering what pain was reflected in her own face to cause it. On his right sat the woman whom she had met before dinner while searching for a bathroom along the reaches of the upstairs corridor. Large and friendly and shaped like a bolster, she had been sharing a drink with her godson, Oliver Ferriers. This single offspring of Susie and Alistair had been born late on in their marriage; a mistake, Rachel seemed to remember, in more ways than one. At least he was sharp enough to have usurped the whisky bottle. They were an ill-assorted couple, the boy with his pigtail and his spots lounging on the bed, and the godmother weighing down the end of it, as wholesome and rosy as a Victorian cook. Her floral dress was hitched comfortably above her knees to show fawn Directoire knickers. Rachel was welcomed – the woman introduced herself as Muriel Drummond – and the toothglass refilled and passed around between the three of them, while downstairs their absence went unobserved.

'A cup of coffee and then I'm off,' announced Muriel Drummond after dinner. 'Don't know what's happened to Susie's cooking. She used to produce some of the best food in London.'

They had retreated to a quiet corner occupied by two floor cushions and a rubber plant.

'Can't think why I was asked,' she continued cheerfully. 'They seldom bother. I suppose they're hoping I'll leave Ollie a fortune; "butter the old girl up, she's getting on a bit."' She laughed. 'God knows how I am going to get up from the floor.'

'I'll pull you up,' Rachel reassured her.

'A slip of a girl like you? Well, we can but hope. Do you want a lift home, by the way?'

'Thank you, but I'll have to go home with Renton since he gave me a lift here. We live in the same direction.'

'Is he the one I sat next to at dinner?' Muriel's expression registered what she thought of Renton, which was not much. 'And which direction is that?'

'Kensington; in my case Consort Terrace, but you won't know it. No-one ever does.'

'Bottom of Edgehill Square? Indeed I know it,' said Muriel. 'Used to know people who lived there, years ago during the war. Not well; they were friends of my mother's, actually. There was a daughter who was my

76

contemporary; I imagine the idea was we should become bosom chums but it didn't work, of course.' She paused to drain her coffee cup. Rachel watched a drip of pale brown liquid quiver and descend amongst the multicoloured ruffles of her dress. She waited, saying nothing, her mind alert with possibilities.

'Nice houses, though. I remember that.' The coffee cup was placed under the rubber plant, resting precariously on the rim of its holder.

'So you knew this particular house quite well?' asked Rachel.

'Good Lord, no. I believe I only went there once, for tea; a delicious one. Funny how these things stick in your mind. It was just after the war had started and there was no shortage, I suppose.' A dreamy look came into Muriel's blue eyes. 'Cucumber sandwiches and three sorts of cake.'

'And the family, the people who lived there?' queried Rachel, determined to drag the woman's memory away from food and back to the point.

'What? Oh, they were pretty ghastly. No, I really shouldn't say that. Speak not ill of the dead and so on. The mother terrified me and the daughter bored me, and so I never saw them again.' Muriel looked about her questioningly. 'Aren't we going to get a brandy? I must say, Alistair's becoming bloody mean.'

She sighed. 'Mind you,' she added, 'they were a tragic family. The girl was killed in an air raid; the house caught fire. And before that I believe she lost a husband.' She frowned. 'I wish I could remember their name. Worries me not being able to remember names. Sign of senility.'

'Would it be Rumbold?' Rachel held her breath.

77

'Good gracious.' Muriel stared at her. 'Don't tell me you knew them too? No, impossible; you're far too young.'

'I've heard of them through friends.' Rachel decided the butcher fell into this category. 'And I live in what was once the Rumbolds' house.'

'What a coincidence!' Muriel seemed delighted, shifting her bulk to a more comfortable position. 'Tell me, don't you mind the idea of a tragic death having taken place there? It would give me an odd feeling, I think.'

'I only learnt about it a short while ago.' Rachel considered. 'But I don't mind. In fact it's given me quite an interest in the Rumbolds.' More of an obsession, she thought. 'I find myself trying to picture what they were like,' she added.

'The daughter,' said Muriel, 'was quite lovely in a washed-out sort of way; do you know what I mean? Personally, I found her thoroughly wet and ineffectual, but I dare say that was jealousy on my part. I was no oil painting and much the same size as I am today. They couldn't find a uniform to fit me when I first joined the WRNS.' She snorted with laughter. 'The Rumbold girl should have been christened "Ophelia" or "Willow",' she said. 'She wasn't, of course. Elizabeth, she was called – Lisa for short; it's coming back to me.'

'Lisa Kincade,' murmured Rachel.

'What? Oh, I see, was that her married name? You seem to know more about her than I do.' Muriel eyed her with curiosity. 'There was some sort of scandal,' she said. 'You've probably heard of that as well. The story being that Lisa had a baby out of wedlock, as the saying was then. Everybody does it these days but at

78

the time it was a disgrace. It was well hushed-up, according to my mother; the husband had been absent far too long to have been the father. Mind you, it was only rumour; nothing was proved and my mother was a terrible old gossip.'

Rachel said nothing, thinking for a moment of Emily.

'I must say,' admitted Muriel, 'it's difficult to imagine Lisa Rumbold in those circumstances. Frigid as an iceberg, I would have thought; not enough energy for a roll in the hay. Life is full of surprises, isn't it?'

'That,' said Renton, breaking the silence on the way home, 'was the most boring evening I've had to sit through for a long time.'

'Oh I don't know,' Rachel smiled. 'I found it quite instructive.' She relegated Lisa Kincade to the back of her mind, to be brought out later at leisure. 'At least you didn't have to go for a skinny dip.'

'What *are* you talking about?'

She explained about the nude bathing. 'I suppose it wouldn't match their new puritanical image.'

He said through pursed lips, 'Remind me never to risk it again. Who was the old bat I sat next to at dinner? You seemed to have a lot to say to each other.'

'Oh, we did. She was splendid.'

'Well, she never drew breath with me. I couldn't get a word in edgeways.'

'I didn't imagine her to be your type, Renton.'

Renton's type got younger each year until it had finally reached the twenty-one-year-old daughters of his friends. His flirting was quite avuncular and nobody minded, but it made him something of a laughing stock.

He saw Rachel to her door, ever courteous, and bent stiffly to peck her cheek. It was all that remained of what had been a rather half-hearted courtship on his part. Rachel, who was fond of him, waved to him from the open doorway. She had gone to bed with him once, on a night of overwhelming and slightly drunken loneliness. It had been a mistake, since he had apparently enjoyed it and she had not. He had proposed to her afterwards, showing no signs of real anguish when she turned him down. Climbing the stairs to bed, she thought how simple life would be married to him, secure and predictable – and achingly tedious. Poor Renton, forever seeking and never finding; he had hated his evening, while she felt it to be well worth while.

The story of Lisa's baby both excited and disturbed her; she was not sure why. This research, which had started as an amusing pastime, had suddenly become more intricate than that. She had a wild feeling of being pulled backwards into the lives of these people almost against her will; that the characters involved wanted their lives investigated and were relying on her to act on their behalf. Simon would regard her as suffering from delusions, confirming his suspicions that she was fast becoming an ageing eccentric. Simon would never understand the delights of eccentricity.

'He has grown enormously.' Rachel pushed a rubber ball towards her grandson and watched with pleasure his wriggling efforts to reach it. 'It won't be long before he's crawling, will it, you fat little tadpole?'

Louisa bent down and picked him up, holding him, crowing with delight high above her head. 'He's not a tadpole. He's quite beautiful.'

The nursery, already strewn with the paraphernalia of mother and baby, had lost its impersonal bleakness and felt fulfilled.

Louisa removed a pile of her dresses and sat down on the end of the bed, Robin on her knees. She said, 'I love this room.' Without looking at Rachel she added, 'Thank you for letting us come.'

This was so unlike Louisa that Rachel was alarmed. She glanced sharply at her daughter, whose face was half hidden by the usual curtain of hair.

'Don't be silly, darling. You know you can stay any time; it's your home as much as mine.'

Louisa raised her head and glared, her eyes glassy with tears. 'I didn't think you wanted us much. You sounded pretty off-putting, and sort of harassed; not like you at all.'

'When you rang I was up a step-ladder; you caught me at a bad moment, that's all. I love to see you and Robin.' She sat down and put an arm round Louisa, who started to cry in earnest.

Rachel sighed. 'It's Vijay, isn't it? What *are* you going to do about him?'

'I don't know,' Louisa sobbed, her tears falling on a surprised Robin. 'I only know I bloody miss him.'

They sat there for a while, the two women and the baby huddled together. 'Perhaps,' said Rachel gently, 'it would be best to forget all this "different culture" thing and marry him.'

Louisa said nothing but the crying had stopped.

'Either that or separate completely,' Rachel added. 'It

can't be doing you or Robin any good, this nomadic life you're leading.'

Later in the kitchen Louisa said, 'I'll give myself the weekend to sort it out. I'll make up my mind by Monday.'

Watching her rinse the coffee mugs, her face pale and childish without make-up, Rachel felt a wrenching of the heart that she could no longer solve her children's problems. This was not the moment to ask Louisa to keep the bathroom tidy.

'I thought we might take Robin to the park this afternoon. It's such a lovely day and the chestnut trees are not quite over.'

'Good idea. Where's what's-his-name – Tom?' Louisa asked over her shoulder.

'He is away for tonight; taken himself off tactfully, I suspect.' Rachel felt herself growing hot for no reason. 'Actually, he's gone to see his children.'

'So he is married?'

'Getting divorced.'

'Is he fitting in all right?'

'As far as I can tell,' said Rachel primly, 'he's very pleasant. I've hardly had time to find out.'

She opened a cupboard and buried her face in its depths. 'Pleasant' was not, as a rule, part of her vocabulary. Louisa, diverted temporarily from her troubles, stared at her mother's back thoughtfully, her eyes bright with curiosity.

Rachel had arranged a bowl of stocks in the drawing-room to welcome Tom Crozier. She did not quite know what had moved her to do so; but their scent drifted into the hall where he stood amongst his two cases, a record player and a potted plant.

'You don't mind me bringing "Fred", do you?' he asked. 'He doesn't do too well in the office.'

'I don't mind.' Rachel looked at the plant. 'What is it?'

'Ceratostigma. Plumbago. He's rather nondescript at the moment but you should see him in late summer. Lovely blue flowers.'

'I didn't know you could grow plumbago as a house plant,' she said.

'I'm not sure you can. If he begins to droop, I'll give him to you for the garden.'

She took him downstairs for tea.

'What a lovely kitchen,' he said.

She switched on the kettle and looked round, trying to see the room through unaccustomed eyes. It needed redecorating like half the house and there was not the money for it.

'Thank you. It's large,' she conceded, 'which was a good thing when there were a lot of us here.'

'It's a really nice house,' he said. She waited for him to say wasn't it too big for her on her own but he did not. He wandered around peering at things while the kettle grunted and groaned as it gained momentum. 'So you have no children living at home now?' he asked, looking at the six-year-old Greek calendar which Rachel kept for the beautiful photographs.

'No.' She crossed to the cupboard beside him, searching inside for a teapot, seldom used. 'Simon is married; he's the eldest. Louisa is the one coming to stay with her baby. Christian you know about.' (She must find time to answer that letter.) 'Could you reach the teapot, please? Someone's put it on the top shelf.'

His arm shot out, lightly touching her hair. Now he was actually here, a solid and irrefutable presence in her home, she did not know what to do with him.

'You aren't going to make a pot for me?' When he smiled his eyes creased into blue slits. 'Why don't we just have mugs?'

'Do you mind? Right. Biscuits. Sugar for you?'

'Just one; I'm trying to cut down.'

Arranging the mugs on a tray she said, 'Let's have it in the garden.' Thank God for the garden and the weather. Out of doors would be less formal, prevent his arrival from becoming too much of an initiation ceremony.

'This is perfect,' he said with sincerity, leaning back in a chair and stretching out his legs.

She began to feel calmer. He was very appreciative; no reason to foresee difficulties. After all, she would hardly see him. Hadn't he mentioned going to the country most weekends?

'Do you have a garden at home?' she asked, pushing the packet of biscuits towards him.

He helped himself, breaking a chocolate digestive in half.

'Yes, we have rather a large one. Or rather, my wife does. We're not officially together any more.'

'You mean,' Rachel hesitated, 'you're divorced?'

He shook his head. 'We're in the middle of things. Possibly by the end of the summer the law will have severed us,' he said cheerfully. 'It seems the more amicable you are, the longer it takes.'

What did one say about divorce? Neither congratulations nor commiseration were in order. A bubble of something amazingly like happiness rose in her, lifting the corners of her mouth. She drank hastily. Whatever else, it was not the moment to smile idiotically.

'It's important to keep things friendly when you have children, don't you think?' he was saying. It was more of a statement than a question.

'Of course.'

'I go down most weekends to see them.'

'How many are there?'

'Two, both girls, Cassie and Kate. They're eight and six.' Emily was about to be eight; his daughters were her granddaughter's contemporaries. Rachel felt that piece of information could wait.

'I wonder if I could make myself another cup?' he asked.

'Yes, of course. I'll make it.'

'Please don't move. I'm competent with a tea-bag. Can I get you one?'

'Thank you. Very weak.'

Left alone, she watched the sun dropping behind the houses, the acacia tree casting a long blue shadow across the lawn. He did not seem shattered over the break-up of his marriage. She wondered whether there was someone waiting to become the second Mrs Crozier. For goodness sake, it was none of her business.

He stepped into the garden carefully with the dog doing his best to trip him up.

'Morecombe! Come here, don't be a bore.' Morecombe wriggled to Rachel, turning himself inside out with ingratiation. 'I hope you don't mind dogs. He's quite good really, just rather old and smelly.'

'We've got a Labrador. He is supposed to belong to the girls, but all his devotion goes on Hana. She's the one who feeds him.' He scratched Morecombe behind the ears. 'The Germans are apt to over-feed everybody, including the pets.'

'So Hana is German?'

'Yes.'

A dying shaft of sun pin-pointed his head. She imagined his children, seeing them quite clearly in cotton frocks, playing with the dog; fair hair and eyelashes like their father.

'I hope the tea's all right?' he asked.

'Lovely, thank you.' She sipped in silence, unable to think of a thing to say. Soon she must try to be efficient, explain the workings of the kitchen and the temperamental flushing of the upstairs lavatory.

'How long have you—?'

'What do you do—?'

They laughed. 'Go on,' he said. 'You first.'

'I was going to ask what you did at the Ministry of Defence. Now I realize it's a stupid question. You probably can't say.'

'I can; it's nothing very hush-hush. But I'm afraid it would bore you. I'm on a course; a six-month course learning about really exciting things like the deployment of missiles.'

'Ah.'

'See what I mean?' He smiled. 'I returned from Germany too soon. I really would like to have been there to see the Wall made redundant.'

'That *is* bad luck. Why weren't you?'

He hesitated. 'I was made redundant as well. How long have you lived here?'

'Twenty-six, nearly twenty-seven years; a large chunk of life.' On an impulse she added, 'People think it's ridiculous of me to stay on without Henry.'

'Are you divorced?' he asked.

She had expected a comment, not a direct query. Her face must have showed surprise.

'I'm sorry. I shouldn't have asked, of course.'

'It's all right. I'm widowed.'

How depressing it sounded, conjuring up pictures of eternal mourning. He did not attempt to sympathize. Getting up from his chair abruptly, he said, 'May I look around?' and wandered away. She watched him circle the garden, stooping now and then for a closer look at some plant or other. It would be polite to join him, she supposed, but from a distance she could observe and wonder. He had rolled up his shirt sleeves and she could see a dusting of blond hairs on his arms in the remains of the sun. He acted as if he was completely at home.

'What rose is that?' he asked as he rejoined her.' The climber over there? Surely it's early for roses?'

'Casino. Everything's a month early this year.'

'I'd find it difficult to leave here if it were me,' he remarked. She did not reply. 'Do you have to?'

'No, not just yet.' She put the mugs and the biscuit packet on the tray. 'But occasionally I get the feeling it is immoral for one person to wallow in so much space, quite apart from the upkeep.'

'It sounds as if someone is trying to make you feel guilty.' He took the tray from her and carried it to the kitchen, unloaded the mugs by the sink and ran the hot tap. 'Well, now you have the consolation of no longer being "one person". As long as you're prepared to give me a roof over my head, you can forget the moral issue,' he told her over his shoulder.

'I was going to explain a few domestic details,' she

said, 'but it hardly seems necessary.' The corners of her mouth curled upwards involuntarily and this time she let them. 'It's as if you had lived here for months.'

'Yes,' he agreed. 'Isn't it strange?'

She got the impression he was teasing her. 'Bottom half of the fridge for you; top half for me,' she said briskly.

'Will it matter very much,' he asked gravely, 'if my packet of fishfingers creeps up to join yours by mistake?'

'None of it matters a damn,' she said, laughing.

'Don't worry. I can promise you, I aim to be a model lodger. You'll hardly know I'm here.' He glanced at the kitchen clock. 'And to prove it, I am about to leave you in peace.'

'Oh.' She tried to make her voice neutral, keep the disappointment out of it. 'There's plenty to eat. I thought you might like supper here tonight; what with unpacking and so on.'

'It's a kind thought and thank you, but I'm having dinner with a friend. Is it all right if I have a shower?'

He smiled at her from the doorway. 'I enjoyed the tea. And the talk. But I don't want you going to a lot of extra trouble, Mrs Playfair.'

'Rachel, please.'

'Rachel.'

She heard his footsteps going lightly upstairs. Opening the fridge she removed a casserole dish to the kitchen table and lifted the lid. There was more than enough for two. Wishful thinking, she realized now, a picture of wine and conversation evaporating into thin air. Stupid woman, what had she expected?

Fetching Morecombe's dish, she spooned meat and gravy into it and returned the remainder to the fridge. She was no longer hungry; an egg would do. That night she found herself unexpectedly missing Henry.

On Sunday it rained, and Louisa's mood had changed from tearful to morose. She spent her time reading magazines between long spells of gazing at the water-shed pouring down the windows. Even the equable Robin was grizzly.

'He's teething,' said Rachel, and dosed him with gripe water.

'It's got alcohol in it,' protested Louisa.

'Not enough to harm.' The baby slept.

But Louisa was determined to find an alternative cause for complaint and made a ridiculous fuss over a small toy cat she had discovered on the floor of the nursery.

'It's got glass eyes,' she said accusingly, dumping the offending object on the kitchen table. 'Robin could easily have swallowed one.' Rachel sat the animal on the palm of her hand. The black fur felt real, like the pelt of a rabbit; its whiskers, exaggeratedly long, prickly as horse-hair. The eyes were a brilliant blue.

'I haven't seen glass ones on a stuffed toy for years,' she said with interest. 'Anyway, it's still got two of them so Robin is all right.'

'He might not be if he'd got hold of it,' Louisa said indignantly. 'What on earth were you thinking of, Ma, buying something like that for him? It's a danger to children.'

'I didn't buy it. I doubt if you could find a toy of this kind in the shops. In fact,' said Rachel thoughtfully, 'I would say it's an antique.' She had an odd presentiment about its origins.

Louisa put Robin in his chair and slumped herself down.

'Well, who did, then? It's extremely careless to leave things lying around,' she grumbled. 'I suppose it belongs to Emily.'

'No, it doesn't. Besides, she wasn't sleeping in the nursery, and the room was cleaned by Consuelo before you came.'

'I bet it's something to do with Consuelo, silly cow. She never had much upstairs.'

Suddenly Rachel had had enough. Consuelo drove her mad at times, but she was not to be castigated by a spoilt child. She gave up the struggle to be understanding and lost her temper abruptly, telling Louisa to snap out of it and adding, for good measure, the admonition about the bathroom. Words flew between them like short spats of gunfire, and died out as swiftly, leaving her with a thumping headache. She knew quite well that she and Louisa should have grown out of the necessity for these clashes. Never, particularly during the dreadful mid-teen years, had Rachel felt herself adequate to deal with Louisa's moods. Henry was the one who could calm her, restore her balance, get her to laugh at herself. Rachel knew he took a delight in his ability to succeed where she had failed. So it was until one evening when Louisa was fifteen or sixteen; Henry had gone to say good night to her and found her door locked to him. She refused to answer and his murmured pleas had switched to angry parental demands through the unyielding wooden barricade between them. Rachel could recall with cold clarity his face as he came slowly down the stairs, defeated. The expression of deep hurt had seemed out of all proportion to the situation; not unlike that of a rejected lover. She had never said anything to Louisa; that was her mistake. The barrier between them widened, and added to Rachel's inadequacy was the shame of moral cowardice; the sweeping under the carpet of unmentionable secrets. Only the arrival of Robin had drawn them tenuously together.

'I'm sorry,' said Louisa in a muffled voice.

Rachel shivered, the greyness of the day getting to her. She put an arm round her daughter and hugged her.

'He hasn't even bothered to ring me,' moaned Louisa, admitting the true cause of her distemper. 'Doesn't care if I'm alive or dead.'

'There's nothing to stop you ringing him,' Rachel pointed out firmly. 'One of you has got to do some pride-swallowing. What you need is a distraction.'

She fetched her research notes after they had finished lunch and left Louisa to read them with the pithy comment, 'There's a story in there that makes your life and mine look like a bed of roses. I think it might interest you.'

The notes were up-to-date; her visit to St Catherine House had been rewarding. Lisa Kincade had given birth to a son six weeks before she died. Rachel was not far out in guessing the child's age at around two months at the time of the fire. There was no death certificate for the baby that she could find, which made her curious to know how he survived the accident that killed his mother. Muriel Drummond's rumour had been proved correct and Rachel decided that she might be intrigued to know, making a mental note to telephone.

Confirmation of Lisa's baby was not the only revelation thrown up by the archives. Checking everything while she was about it, Rachel could find no record of Robert Kincade's death. Possibly this was because he was never proved killed in action. She was hazy on this point, but believed that after a certain number of years all missing persons were counted as deceased; she must check her facts. There was now the possibility that not one, but two Robert Kincades were alive, for Lisa had named the baby Robert Nathaniel, presumably as a strange acknowledgement of the two men in her short life. Had the lover Nathaniel meant anything to her, or was he merely a disastrous one-night stand? Either way, the picture of Lisa now emerging was one of awful sorrow.

And what part had the mother played in all this? Rachel wondered. She would hardly have been thrilled by an illegitimate grandchild in the days when such things mattered socially. Lilian: the very name intimidated. She would probably have insisted on adoption, and that of course, Rachel realized, answered the question of the baby's survival. It would be the perfect explanation also for Emily, who would go on badgering for one for ever. It did not quite explain her insistence on the sound of a child crying: but Rachel was happy for that to remain an enigma.

Louisa lay sprawled on the sofa, engrossed, while Robin on a blanket flexed his muscles by her feet. Eventually she closed the exercise book and stretched.

'Fascinating.' She looked at Rachel. 'I can see why

you're hooked on these people. Where will you go from here?'

'Florence Codie; the cook, or housekeeper. Lilian Rumbold left her a legacy,' Rachel said, putting the notes on her desk. 'If I can trace her, if she is alive, she is the only person with first-hand knowledge of what really happened.'

'She'd be ancient now; probably lost her marbles,' said Louisa callously.

'Not all old people are senile,' said Rachel with a touch of frost, 'and what I need now is an eyewitness. What a pity no letters have turned up. They're such a help.'

'It's Lisa you are interested in really, isn't it? I suppose because she and I have a certain amount in common.' Louisa swung her legs off the sofa. 'I wonder if I have a bearing on their appearance,' she added, wandering to the piano. 'Perhaps they're in search of an identity.'

She lifted the lid and riffled the keys. 'On the other hand, I haven't noticed them since I've been here. Lisa, in particular, you'd think would be curious. You don't think you've imagined them, do you, Ma?'

'The most puzzling aspect,' said Rachel, ignoring the suggestion, 'is why they should come back at all after twenty-six years of quiescence.' She lifted her head at the sound of a key in the lock. The rain had stopped; it was going to be a beautiful evening.

'That must be Tom,' she said with studied nonchalance, realizing that she had been subconsciously waiting for this sign of his return for the last hour; the key grating and then his footsteps in the hall.

He stood in the doorway, hesitating, as if uncertain

whether he should intrude. She decided he looked tired, noticing for the first time the way his face had creases which deepened when he smiled or frowned.

'Hallo, come in,' she said.

When she introduced him to Louisa, he looked as most men looked in the same situation; and Rachel, who had never minded before, minded now most acutely and turned away.

'And this is Robin.'

'Hi, Robin.' He squatted down and tickled the baby in the ribs. 'Nice to meet another man. I wish I had one like him,' he said to Louisa.

She got up from the piano stool and gave him an enchanting smile. 'I'm going to make his bottle. Anyone like a drink?'

She drifted away gracefully without waiting for an answer.

'You look as if it has been a tough day,' Rachel said when she and Tom were alone.

'Bit of a strain,' he admitted. 'Well, bloody awful to be honest.' He smiled at her. 'It rained all day and the girls fought non-stop. It's a difficult time; a lot of tension, and Hana's isn't the most placid of temperaments. Oh, well . . .'

He got to his feet slowly.

'I'm sorry.' She added, 'Your sweater's wet. You ought to change.'

'I think I'll get myself a drink. I've brought you a bottle, by the way. Shall I give it to Louisa?'

'Yes, please,' said Rachel, since that was what he was obviously longing to do, and he left, promising to return with a whisky for her.

For twenty minutes she waited, sitting on the floor

beside Robin while their voices murmured up from the kitchen, interspersed with sudden laughter. Any normal mother, she realized painfully, would be delighted at their immediate rapport. Her resentment built up steadily with each passing moment and the sound of their enjoyment mocked and excluded her. Totally forgotten, she faced the fact of her abnormality while Robin chewed a corner of blanket and her precarious burst of happiness drained away.

Later that evening and unable to sleep, Rachel switched on the garden lights and walked barefoot on the lawn. Illuminated, trees and shrubs took on a pale glamour. The sky was clear and star-pricked after the rain, and the grass, damp between her toes, smelled sweet like the country when bruised under foot. She was reminded of summer parties that had overflowed out here, filling the night with low laughter, the clink of glasses, the glowing tips of cigarettes; music in the background and the smell of night-flowering stocks. And all of a sudden, unthought of for years, the memory of being kissed by someone other than Henry; a long, expert and sexy kiss that had boosted her morale for days afterwards.

All very erotic, she told herself, and hardly in keeping with her day. She viewed the last hours of it coldly, feeling a fool amongst other things for not having foreseen the obvious. It was, after all, a natural outcome, Louisa with her loveliness in just the frame of mind to exploit it, and Tom in limbo and susceptible. When she had finally joined them in the kitchen, trying desperately to look careless, she felt as if she was breaking up a conspiracy.

The tiredness had been ironed out of Tom's face. He had taken off his sweater and lounged against the dresser in his shirt sleeves while Louisa busied herself with a pan of milk. She was slightly flushed and her eyes glowed. The mood of a wet afternoon was behind her. There were apologies, of course, Tom clapping a hand to his forehead.

'Rachel, I'm so sorry. Please forgive me, I'm only working on one cylinder. Look, I have your drink ready.'

Charming, rueful – was that the word? – he left her with no option but to force a smile.

'Tom's suggested we have dinner out,' Louisa announced, shaking the baby bottle vigorously. 'What's that new Chinese place like, Ma?'

'I've no idea. I don't much like Chinese food.'

'I suggested we should all go,' put in Tom hurriedly.

'Someone has to stay with Robin,' pointed out Louisa.

'Can't we take him with us in a carry-cot? Or a pushchair?'

'He's too big now for the carry-cot. Anyway, he'll probably grizzle.'

'I'll stay,' said Rachel firmly. 'I've got masses of letters to write.'

'Sure you don't mind, Ma?' Louisa asked unconvincingly.

Rachel caught Tom's eye and looked away quickly. He had the air of a man for whom things had got out of hand.

Sitting at her desk she had started a letter to Christian.

'Darling Christy,' she wrote. 'It was wonderful to get

your long letter. I'm so relieved about your decision to leave the Army. I never felt it was for you. As for the Church . . .'

Do what you must but please don't disappear from my life entirely, dear darling Christy.

She was quite pleased by the way she had carried it off when they left – 'Off you go. Have fun' – pretending to busy herself with her writing, giving nothing away. The front door closed behind them; a fine-looking couple, the dark and the blond. Rachel's pen dropped to the desk. One definition of loneliness was being the wrong side of a closing door.

My own fault, she told herself, her feet now chilled by the damp grass; my own bloody fault for allowing myself to hanker after a younger man, to teeter clumsily on the brink of falling in love. 'Fancying' someone, Louisa would call it, thus putting it in its undignified place. How Phyllida would laugh at the truth of her own predictions; Rachel's face burned in the darkness as she switched off the garden lights.

Piano music drifted suddenly from the open windows of the drawing-room, played softly. Louisa; so they had returned. Rachel locked up quietly, feeling disinclined to meet them. But the drawing-room was empty as she passed. They must have gone to bed; to whose bed, she wondered before she could stop herself.

In fact, Tom and Louisa creaked and whispered their way past her door an hour later. Rachel did not hear them; she had taken a sleeping pill, and the significance of a piano played without visible assistance went unmarked.

Chapter Six

Letter from Lisa Kincade to her friend, Gladys.

Norfolk. October 1942.

I'm sorry your mother is seriously ill. I know you're fond of her. I try to put myself in your place, imagine how I would feel if it was my own mother. And the answer is, I wouldn't give a damn. It's a dreadful thing to say but it's true. But I hope yours gets better, I really do, and that you're able to come back soon. The farm isn't the same without you, there's no-one I can talk to, and I do need to talk which is partly why I'm writing. If I don't tell someone what's happened I'll burst.

I've been to bed with Nat. There, it's down on paper and it looks wonderful. I know you're not like me, Glad, you think of sex as a sort of joke, don't you? I wish I could be like that, always laughing about it, because it wouldn't hurt like mad when someone gets taken away from you. Nat has been posted, he told me last weekend, I don't know where, of course, but I can make a guess. We had forty-eight hours of Heaven; he only told me just before the end about the posting. I'm happy we made love before I knew. Oh God! How I miss him.

It was my birthday on Saturday. It didn't start at all well. Nat was quiet, sitting in an armchair reading while I played the piano. He didn't seem to want to talk. We only just avoided a row and I knew it was because I'd never slept with him. I'd been holding back, frightened I suppose, and guilty about being unfaithful to Robbie in case he's still alive. And, of course, Nat felt it was his last chance before he left for God knows where, but I didn't realize that at the time. I know it sounds as if he was only after one thing, what you'd call 'having it off', but it wasn't like that. There was much more to it, I wish I could explain.

It was a strange evening. He was taking me out to dinner at a rather expensive restaurant, and I don't think he's got much money, but he insisted. We wanted to dance and they've got quite a good band. But there was a muddle over the table. When we arrived they said they'd over-booked and there was no room. It was an excuse, of course, they're prejudiced against Americans like Nat. It made me very, very angry, it was so hurtful and I let fly at the manager. Nat hustled me away saying it didn't matter and laughing because he'd never heard me swear before. He tried to pretend it was funny, but I had this extraordinary feeling that I was responsible for him, it was as if he was my child. All I wanted at that moment was to protect him.

When I'd calmed down he took me to a jazz club where nearly everyone was black. It had a marvellous atmosphere, alive and swinging, making the usual old places seem dull as ditchwater.

We talked a lot. He wants to be a lawyer, did I tell you that? But the war has interrupted his exams, he'll have to start at the beginning again when it's over. I think we drank rather a lot, and Nat got up and played the saxophone so beautifully he made it sing. Then we danced. Dancing with him was like swimming down river with the current, weightless and part of an effortless rhythm. I can't tell how long we were there, we lost all sense of time. At some point it seemed the right moment to go home and after that, well, you know the rest.

Mother was away with her current lover. We had the house to ourselves except for Codie who took a liking to Nat and left us alone. We spent most of Sunday in bed and she turned a blind eye. I know I shouldn't talk about this to anyone, but I feel so alone and there is no-one but you. What happened between myself and Nat was different from anything I had known. I never understood until now what people saw in making love. It wasn't Robbie's fault, I realize now it wasn't either of our faults. We were both novices and there was no time to practise. With Nat I don't need practise, it's like dancing, and if I get out of step he puts it right. It's like music too, the great crescendos and then the peaceful bits. And when he slips away from me, I'm terrified I've lost him and he won't come back, that it's for the last time. Does any of that make sense? I don't expect you to understand because what I feel for Nat is unbelievable even to myself.

The strange thing is, I'm no longer loaded with guilt over Robbie. I have this odd feeling that wherever he is, alive or dead, he wouldn't mind about us. Maybe that's wishful thinking, but I can remember him in peace now instead of pushing him out of my mind. But if the same thing should happen to Nat, I just couldn't bear it, I'd kill myself. We plan to marry one day and live in America, however long it takes and whatever the opposition. He gave me this little black cat before he left, a toy, to bring me luck. It's sitting on the table by my bed while I write. Speaking of luck, you forgot to give me back the packet of contraceptive gels, so luck is what I'll need. You can't have used them all, surely?

Come back soon, Glad, it's already winter here and Norfolk seems the coldest, bleakest place in England when you're unspeakably lonely.

Chapter Seven

The telephone woke Rachel from a drugged sleep full of disturbing dreams.

'Muriel Drummond speaking. Is that you, Rachel?'

'Yes, it's me.' Blast the woman; she could have done with another hour's oblivion. 'How nice to hear from you,' Rachel added insincerely, hoisting herself up on the pillows.

'Have I woken you?'

'Well—'

'Sorry, my dear. I'm one of the world's scourges, an early riser. It seems like midday to me.'

'Don't worry. I had it down to ring you, in fact.'

'Really? Well, I'm the purveyor of some rather extraordinary news. Are you still interested in the Rumbold family?'

'Yes, I am,' said Rachel, surfacing instantly.

'As I thought. Actually, this doesn't concern them directly; it's to do with Lisa's husband, Robert Kincade. I thought you would like to know, however.'

'Heavens, yes. Do tell—'

'I can't abide the telephone. Come and have tea, any day this week, and I'll give you the details then.' The receiver went down abruptly. Rachel realized she would be pleased about this call in about half an hour, after a couple of cups of coffee. It was a propitious moment to have her mind diverted. She closed her eyes, reluctant to get up and set the day in motion. Sun sliced through a gap in the curtains; there was the stillness of early summer. She lay ignoring it, weighed down by dark thoughts of yesterday. In her own eyes, she had made a fool of herself and the fact had an adverse effect on her temper. If she was not careful, she would lug her mood through the day with her, making everyone suffer. She swung first one leg, then the other heavily to the floor.

The kitchen was deserted. It was early; too early for Tom to have left for work. Piling toast and coffee on a tray she carried it back to bed, Morecombe trailing behind stiffly. If those two were embarking on an affair, they might as well get used to seeing each other at breakfast, preferably with Robin spitting out his porridge. She hoped this was not going to be a long-lasting relationship. There was Vijay to be considered; she was fond of Vijay. It was devoutly to be wished that Louisa would go home and decide to compromise: for many reasons. Rachel snapped the toast in two, watching a pair of pigeons flap madly about the acacia tree in clumsy foreplay.

Positive thinking seeped back slowly. Pushing her tray to one side, she searched amongst bedside clutter for her diary. The week appeared quite social by her standards; a drinks party, dinner with Renton and an assignation with Phyllida at the Royal Academy. It had been in her mind to cancel some if not all of these commitments. She stared at her scribbles thoughtfully before going to run a bath. In a wakeful moment during the night she had wondered fleetingly about asking Tom to leave; but on what pretext? The truth would be painfully obvious. Drastic measures were not necessary. There was hardly the need to set eyes on him if she organized herself properly.

I have too much time on my hands, she thought, getting dressed. Other women sat on committees, did good works, interested themselves in local politics. Idleness breeds inefficiency, her mother's voice reminded her from beyond the grave. There was a host of minor jobs to be seen to; the letter to Christian to be finished, stamped and posted, and a promised call to Emily amongst them.

In the end she attempted none of them. She put on a bright yellow dress and went straight to the butcher. Whistles from the scaffolders at number ten pleased her more than she cared to admit.

Mr Lambe was arranging trays of offal.

'So how's the book coming along then, madam?'

'Slowly, thank you,' said Rachel, allowing him his illusion. 'I wondered whether you had any idea of the whereabouts of Miss Codie, the Rumbold's cook?'

'Mrs, she was, or so she said. I had my doubts. No oil-painting, she wasn't; them pebble glasses, and a club foot.' He shook his stately head. 'Never heard of her since she left. After the fire, that was.'

'She had relations in Cornwall,' said Mrs Lambe from her cubby-hole. 'A sister, I believe.'

'So she might have gone down there to live?' One needed patience to make headway with the Lambes; God help the police if they were ever called as witnesses, thought Rachel.

'Not straight away, she didn't. She stayed on with Mrs Rumbold, that I do know. They moved to a flat, as far as I remember. Sloane Street way.'

'Word had it Mrs R took to the bottle,' said the butcher, *sotto voce*. 'Needed a minder.'

'She was a heavy drinker, always had been,' said his wife with conviction.

'Mrs Rumbold died,' said Rachel. 'So it's a matter of where Mrs Codie went to live afterwards.'

The shop was filling up. A woman behind Rachel heaved deep sighs.

'Just one more question, Mr Lambe. Would she be likely to be alive today?'

He made some silent calculations, then nodded. 'It's possible, but she'd be getting on a bit. Around thirty she were then, I'd say.'

Not a very satisfactory outcome, Rachel reflected, but only as she suspected. Florence Codie might be anywhere, in one of a thousand old people's homes or with her sister in the West Country; or, most likely of all, lying peacefully in some rural churchyard.

On getting home, she wrote out an advertisement and placed it in *The Times* and the *Telegraph* under a box number. She felt justified in spending the money. There was no other way of finding the woman that she could think of, and to find her, a prime witness, was imperative. Prime witness! I am beginning to act as if a crime had been committed, thought Rachel in amusement, and wondered how many of her actions served merely to give her a sense of purpose.

Louisa had decided to return to Vijay. She had telephoned him and, never one to rest on a decision, started to pack immediately. Rachel, who only that morning had wished her gone, felt perversely miserable. She wandered around the nursery collecting

105

objects about to be left behind and preventing Robin from rolling under his mother's feet.

'It would be easier to sit him in his chair while you finish.'

'Don't worry, Ma. I can see him.'

I am in the way, thought Rachel, picking up the ozone-friendly hairspray and dropping it in a carrier bag.

'Have you decided to take the West Indies job?'

'No. It really wouldn't be fair to Robin, being away so long. But the agency have come up with a brilliant week's work in Milan. I can take him with me if I don't get a nanny.'

'I'd always look after him.'

'I know you would, but you're supposed to be having a break.' Louisa, reconciled with Vijay, was full of virtuousness. 'Not that you seem to be taking one, exactly, what with Tom, and more research than ever.'

'Tom's no problem,' said Rachel firmly, shutting her mind to reality.

'Talking of ghosts—'

'Were we?'

'Research, ghosts, what-have-you. This should interest you.' Louisa stuffed a rolled-up sweater in the suitcase and lounged on the bed. 'When I came up here, the cupboard doors were open.'

'Darling, your cupboard doors invariably are.'

'Not this time. I shut them before going downstairs to make room for the suitcase; I remember doing it. Not only were they open when I got back but someone had gone through my clothes.'

'How could you tell?'

'I may live in a mess,' said Louisa, 'but I put my

106

clothes away in strict order; pale colours to the right, dark to the left.' She looked at Rachel. 'They were all mixed up.'

Rachel gathered together scattered papers, pamphlets and begging letters from Greenpeace, Save the Elephants, Seals and Whales and prepared to drop them in the waste-paper basket. 'Sounds as if the nursery spirit was doing some tidying up,' she said.

'I don't think so. Don't throw those away, Ma. I haven't sent them any money.' Louisa grabbed them. 'I suppose that's what you do with your appeals; chuck them away unopened.'

'It depends,' said Rachel, chastened. 'You can't help everybody.'

'Every little counts. Anyway, whoever opened the cupboard wasn't the child-minder. The landing positively reeked of scent, the heavy, musky sort.' She waited for Rachel's reaction. 'You don't seem very interested,' she said.

'Oh, I am. I'm interested in them transferring themselves to the top floor, and the reason why. It's just that I am trying to keep the investigation factual,' she added, 'not let myself be waylaid by psychic research. Ghosts are so intriguing they can become a subject in themselves.' She gazed out of the window at the trees already in full-summer foliage. 'It's Lisa. I can't help comparing her—'

'With me? Well, as long as you don't foresee my imminent death.'

'Don't be ridiculous,' said Rachel. 'Have you finished? We can start taking this lot downstairs.'

Louisa wound down the car window. On the back seat,

barely visible, sat Robin strapped in his chair, a small beaming Buddha amongst mountains of baggage. They might have been staying for months.

'Bye, Ma. Bless you for having us.'

Rachel kissed her, suppressing tears, bad at good-byes. 'I've loved it,' she said, not quite truthfully. She had run through the whole gamut of emotions that weekend, thanks to Louisa. 'I do hope it works out for you both,' she added.

'Of course it will,' said Louisa blithely as on other occasions. 'According to Tom, it's lack of communi-cation that's our problem. Well, I've made the first move by being nauseatingly creepy-crawly over the telephone to Vijay. It worked like a dream; I feel quite holy about it.'

'So it was Tom—?'

'Who drilled some sense into me, yes. Otherwise I might have stayed for ever. Lucky I don't fancy blond men, isn't it?'

Louisa looked up at Rachel innocently from under black lashes curly as a child's. 'Don't get too bound up in the past, Ma. Life is for living, remember. And give my love to Tom, by the way.'

There is an ambiguity about that last statement, Rachel thought, suddenly too relieved to care. Louisa started the car while her mother, watching the finely drawn profile, wondered how anyone could refuse it if it were offered.

'Drive carefully,' she said. 'This Japanese thing looks like a biscuit box on wheels.'

She waited on the steps until the car had swerved round the corner and disappeared, Louisa's hand waving perilously. The climbing rose on the front railings was in bud and about to burst into pale pink bloom.

Tom picked a yellowing leaf from his plant and watered carefully from the long-spouted can that Rachel had lent him. Twice a week he did this; the plant was undemanding. This was the second time since he had arrived; he had been here six days.

He changed out of his suit into light-weight trousers and a shirt. Shortly he would pour himself a drink and go downstairs with the tin of baked beans. As a rule he would walk down the road to one or other of the cheaper restaurants for supper. It had become a routine, like that of someone retired. But not tonight; tonight he would eat in, occupy the kitchen for a while in the hope of catching Rachel.

Leaning his arms on the window sill, he looked down on the garden, half-expecting to see her there. It was deserted. Rachel was conspicuous by her absences. He had, he realized, put his foot in it. He also knew exactly how to put things right and was preparing to do so if he could find her. He knew she was getting ready to go out; he could smell her bath oil drifting up the stairs.

Looking directly downwards gave him mild vertigo; space, emptiness. If one jumped, the earth would end all that with a crunch. Rather like his life, constantly trying to fill a vacuum and ending up a bloody mess. And more emptiness, and so on and so forth, *ad infinitum*.

There was always a chance of putting a stop to the cycle. One should always hope. He moved away from the window and touched a leaf of the plumbago gently with one finger. Lucky little bugger with its feet planted firmly in the soil. Picking up the baked beans tin, he glanced briefly in the looking-glass and saw the normal face of a man verging on middle age; extrovert, good-humoured, balanced. As always, he found it surprising.

By Thursday Rachel was exhausted. Used as she was to a steady routine of bed with a book by ten thirty, going out every night had taken its toll. She was due to dine with Renton and did not even have the energy to cancel.

Tom had kept to his promise. She hardly knew he was there. In the morning he left the house before she got up and in the evenings she had managed to be absent. She had no idea what he did with his spare time. There were no signs of his preparing a meal for himself, not a cup nor a plate on the rack beside the sink. The only sounds of his presence were the gentle opening and closing of the front door, and the muted creaking of floorboards above her bedroom. This was ideal, this was how she had hoped it would be and she had no business to feel disgruntled. They met only three times that week, she remembered afterwards; once in the hall, once on the stairs and finally now in the kitchen where she was pouring herself a drink. She did not hear him coming and jumped as he spoke, spilling whisky.

'Will I be in the way?' he asked. 'I'm planning on eating in and getting an early night. Sorry, I startled you.'

'You're very light-footed,' she said crossly. She glanced at the tin in his hand. 'Is that all you're having?

There's cold meat in the fridge, and half a quiche. Do help yourself.'

She was aware of her voice sounding absurdly formal.

'Thank you, but I'm not really hungry.'

'I hope you're all right here,' she said, relaxing a little. 'I'm afraid I've rather deserted you. It's been one of those weeks.'

He smiled, pulling out drawers in search of a tin-opener. 'It seems it still is. You look very nice.'

'Thank you.' She wanted suddenly to collapse, to tell him how weary she was of running round corners to avoid him. She found the opener and handed it to him.

'Don't worry about me,' he said. 'I'm very comfortable in my room. It's an extremely pretty refuge.'

'Refuge?' She frowned.

'After a day at the MoD, that's how I picture it.'

'Do you dislike it so much? The work, I mean?'

He punctured the tin and sliced off the lid swiftly. One of those tall, loose-limbed men, she thought, who are surprisingly deft.

'Dislike is too strong a word. But it doesn't compare with the previous job I was doing.' Baked beans slurped into the pan. 'I'm allergic to four walls and a lot of paper work, is what it amounts to.'

'What a pity you had to change.'

Watching him, she would not have guessed soldier-ing as his profession. There was not enough unyielding military briskness about him; nor about his haircut. Hair the colour of dark honey covered the nape of his neck and curled at the ends. 'Were you really made redundant?' she added.

'Did I say that?' He opened a cupboard. 'Where

111

would I find plates?' She bent down and extracted one. 'Thank you. It is partly true about the redundancy, but there was no immediacy. I applied for a transfer, in fact, for personal reasons.'

'Ah.'

'I needed to see more of my family,' he explained. 'Hana complained that I was hardly ever there, and she was right. Work took me away for long stretches at a time. So I decided a move was necessary. That was while the marriage was still saveable; by the time I got around to it, it was too late.'

'I'm sorry,' said Rachel; sorry not only about his life but her own behaviour. She would have liked to explain that her skin became sensitive when he was in the same room, a mass of prickly nerve-ends as if she was running a temperature; an impossible confession.

'It seems doubly unfair when you are good at mending other people's relationships,' she added brightly. 'I gather I have you to thank for persuading Louisa to go home. I'm grateful; she might have dithered for weeks.'

'I don't think I had much to do with it,' he replied, putting the saucepan on the cooker. 'She is obviously mad about her Vijay; she talked of nothing else. All she needed was a push in the right direction.'

'Mothers can't push, it goes down very badly. That's where you came in so useful.'

'It was no problem. She's a lovely girl; that amazing profile. And she made me laugh. I enjoyed the evening.'

Rachel picked up her glass and took a deep breath.

'Yes, Louisa is very lovely,' she agreed carefully. 'Well, it's time I was going.'

'Have a good evening.' He eyed her seriously. 'That's a stunning dress.'

'Thanks.' She felt suddenly shy, not knowing how to leave gracefully.

'By the way,' he said, 'I shan't be going away this weekend. I hope you don't mind.'

'Of course not.' She minded very much; there was a limit to making herself scarce, behaving like a displaced person.

'I've been given tickets for Covent Garden on Saturday. The ballet.'

'Oh, how lovely! What are they dancing?'

'*Giselle*. Not exactly new but I was wondering if—'

'Marvellous. I envy you. Heavens! Look at the time. I must dash.'

'I was wondering—'

'Tell me in the morning,' she said, grabbing her handbag. 'Good night, Tom.'

After she had gone, he poured himself a drink and stared dubiously at the contents of the saucepan. He stood like that for some time, thinking there was little need for his attempts at being unobtrusive; she was making a good job of it herself.

Eventually he emptied the baked beans into a plastic bag and dumped it in the dustbin. It crossed his mind to throw in the theatre tickets as well, but at thirty pounds each it seemed a criminal act. Then he took himself to the local pizza house, where the staff were beginning to know him as well as he knew the food; and where the majority of customers looked young and street-wise, as if they had life all sewn up.

He will have to go. The words repeated themselves

113

over and over in Rachel's brain as she sat huddled in a corner of the taxi. Tickets, he had said. That meant a woman. Only gays accompanied gays to the ballet, and he wasn't one, more's the pity. Of course there was a woman, women plural probably, and why not? Why should he be expected to live like a monk?

But it could not got on. She could not stand it; she had tried and failed. Some sort of excuse had to be found, a convalescent relative needing care and the use of his room. An emergency. She could not imagine him gone. To her horror a tear trickled down her face and she fell to silently cursing fate and the Ministry of Defence for conspiring to unhinge her.

They were passing the second half of Sloane Street, Cadogan Gardens on one side and the long line of blocks of flats and elegant offices on the other. Behind one of those upstairs windows, according to Mr Lambe, Lilian Rumbold had drunk herself into oblivion, whether from misery or guilt or alcoholic addiction it was impossible to tell. Rachel craned her neck, half-expecting to see Lilian's face hanging like a pale moon through glass. Her deep interest in the family had been pushed aside by the problem of Tom; she could not even appreciate the crucial piece of knowledge passed on by Muriel Drummond. But she did feel a fleeting empathy for Lilian in her drunken despair.

Earlier in the week Rachel had kept her appointment with Muriel, and discovered her living in an Edwardian red-brick square adjacent to Earl's Court. Overgrown plane trees, the tips of their branches within inches of the windows, effectively blocked out the light. Muriel, unaffected by this subfusc atmosphere, poured tea into bone china cups and cut the cake while launching straight into a monologue.

'I've just sold a house in Scotland,' she announced, 'and guess who's bought it? People called Kincade. Hold out your plate.' Rachel received a slice of sponge. 'I was beginning to despair of getting rid of it. It's a typical Gothic horror. My brother lived there for years before he died a few months ago. Never married, completely gay but rather a darling. Anyway, it's been on the market since his death and hardly a nibble. Not surprising what with the interest rates and the prehistoric central heating. And then suddenly, out of the blue, these Kincades pop up and give me the asking price without a murmur. It was the stretch of river that decided them. More tea?'

Rachel shook her head and waited for Muriel to come to the point.

'I knew I had heard the name, it's not a usual one, and I couldn't think when or how. And then I remembered our conversation, and your telling me that the Rumbold girl had married a Kincade; the husband presumed killed. Well,' said Muriel triumphantly, 'he wasn't. He's alive and living in France.'

'So is he related to the ones who took your house?' Rachel asked.

'He's an uncle of the man who has bought it. The family are fishing mad, apparently. I came clean about why I was asking; said it was on behalf of a friend trying to trace the Rumbold family. They hardly know Robert Kincade, but they couldn't have been nicer or more helpful.' Muriel heaved her bulk from the depths of an armchair. 'I've written down all the information I gathered,' she added over her shoulder. 'Now where did I put it?'

She returned from rummaging in an untidy desk. 'There. I've jotted down everything. The address is a village somewhere in the south, I believe. And he's remarried to a Frenchwoman. Her family hid him until almost the end of the war. Amazing. I'll let you read it for yourself. Have a piece of cake,' she added, flushed with enthusiasm.

Rachel ran her eyes down the writing, folded the paper and put it in her bag.

'This is wonderful, a giant step forward. Thank you.'

As she was leaving, Muriel had asked, 'Shall you go over there and hunt him out?'

Rachel, who had not even considered it until that moment, answered, 'Why not?'

She considered it again now, as the taxi turned down Renton's street. Her mind dwelt briefly and wistfully on hot sun and Pernod, old men playing boules in a shady village square, and picnics with huge crusty sandwiches and cold white wine. She cut her thoughts abruptly and paid the taxi. Holidays such as these were definitely designed for two.

The house was in darkness except for the hall light when she let herself in at midnight. There was a note on the table recording telephone calls from both Simon and Christian. She hated missing Christian; she could scarcely remember the sound of his voice. There was a postscript to Tom's message: might he talk to her as soon as possible?

'What is Mother up to?' demanded Simon of Louisa

over the telephone. 'I tried three times to contact her and all I get is this man. You must have first-hand news.'

'She's absolutely fine,' Louisa assured him. 'And the man is absolutely fine, too. Just the sort she needs,' she said, tongue in cheek.

'And what does that mean exactly?'

'Nothing. He's reliable, will look after her.'

'How old is he?'

'Younger than Ma, older than me.'

'Humph,' said Simon. 'Well, I shall see for myself. Camilla wants me to pick up some clothing which Emily left behind her. If I can't get her on the phone I'll just drop in.'

'I shouldn't do that.'

'Why not?'

'Not much point if she happens to be out,' said Louisa, yawning audibly, 'The lodger can't be expected to know where Emily's clothes are.'

Simon could be incredibly boring.

Rachel, plodding in Phyllida's wake from room to room, regretted agreeing to the Royal Academy. There were too many people, too many paintings hung indiscriminately. Her own suggested choices, the Courtauld Institute or the ever-restful Tate had been shot down, and because she felt in need of distraction, she put up little resistance to Phyllida's iron will. Standing in what must be the twelfth room of their viewing, in front of a large canvas painted entirely red with a slash of black across it as if it had been vandalized, Rachel's feet throbbed. She sank back on the central leather seat and stared at people's backs instead, Phyllida's amongst them. Hers was, as ever, an elegant back-view, her Bruce Oldfield skirt just above the shapely knees. Catalogue in hand, neat blonde head slightly to one side, she seemed to be seriously considering that ridiculous daub. Rachel knew otherwise. Phyllida came to the Summer Exhibition not for art's sake but in the hope of bumping into friends. Out of the corner of her eye she was raking the crowd for someone she knew.

We have grown apart, thought Rachel. Years ago our aims were roughly the same. Even our senses of humour have gone their separate ways. As girls, that picture would have had us shaking with laughter. She bullies me; yet we still seek each other's company. For security, for confirmation that at least some things do not change. We have chased after different values and I'm not sure either of us has found what we were looking for.

'What's your gut reaction to that painting?'

Phyllida sat down and arranged her legs neatly.

'I don't usually have them. But in this case my gut tells me to haul it off the wall and put a foot through it.'

'Do I detect a caustic note?' Phyllida raised an eyebrow. 'You look tired.' I look old, Rachel translated. 'Are things not going well at home? Beginning to regret the man in the house?'

'Tom Crozier is fine, no trouble at all,' said Rachel stiffly.

'Ah, so that's the problem,' murmured Phyllida sympathetically; and then, before Rachel was able to say something rude in reply, leapt to her feet and flung herself at a pink-faced, grey-haired man shrieking, 'Tony, darling!'

Rachel rose, smoothed the crumpled skirt of her linen dress and tapped her friend on the shoulder. 'Goodbye, Phyllida.'

'Darling, you're not going?'

'I am.'

'But – oh, if you must. Don't forget dinner Thursday next week,' shouted Phyllida at Rachel's retreating back. 'Bring someone.'

Silly cow. Rachel pushed her way into the fresh air and from there on to a number 9 bus, immediately regretting her bout of ill-temper. It was a hot yet sunless afternoon with the sulphurous yellow light that often precedes a storm. She stared out of the window at the Ritz, drawing comfort from its solid and unchanging air of affluence; a great deal more reliable than herself or Phyllida.

Sudden compulsion moved her to jump off the bus at Green Park and walk across the grass to stare up at the dining-room windows. She could see rows of conically folded napkins dotted behind the glass like tiny white spearheads. She was reminded of tea beside potted palms, treats as a child after the dentist; and the last time, vividly, with Henry after it had been confirmed that she was expecting a third child. She had not wanted it; the remembrance flooded back to her in shame. Somewhere after Louisa and before Christian she had discovered about Henry's women; everyone else had known for ages, apparently. Much too trusting and naïve to search out lipstick-stained handkerchieves and hotel receipts, she had been living in happy ignorance. And later, when it became obvious that Henry had no intention of stopping, she learnt to live in pretended ignorance. But it took time and immense effort to grow a second skin; the last thing in the world she wanted was another baby.

She could not think how they came to be having tea at ridiculous expense amongst the well-dressed shoppers; a celebratory gesture from Henry, who was delighted with himself? He was not given to such gestures; his socialist pretensions covered a certain meanness. She hated him for making her pregnant; she recalled with great clarity glaring at him furiously across plates of delicious cucumber sandwiches and little iced cakes, unable to eat a mouthful because of feeling sick.

It should have put her off the Ritz but she still felt an affection for it. If I was dressed suitably, I would go in right now and indulge myself, she told herself. She walked back to Piccadilly and took a taxi homewards, her mind on Christian, so unwanted by her and afterwards so much loved. Could a baby sense that, growing inside you? she wondered. He was more sensitive and vulnerable than the other two. By the time he was born, Henry had grown bored with the thought of him, and she was immediately besotted. Louisa had been the only one of the three to claim Henry's affections. Watching the trees coloured ochre in the peculiar light, she closed her mind to the memory. Dangerous ground; and too late to accuse him of incest now, or of anything else, for that matter.

The taxi jerked away from the lights and Rachel jerked with it into the present, anxious to be home in case Christian should call again. She thought of Tom's note asking for an audience and wondered if she crept in quietly, he could be avoided.

The telephone was ringing as she put her key in the lock.

Tom, halfway down the stairs, saw her run through the hall, heard the bright expectancy of her 'Hello'; then a long silence before she spoke again. Her voice was muted, asking questions. It was some time before she came slowly from the drawing-room to the foot of the stairs, as if she sensed he was there, and looked up at him, her face blank and quite drained of colour.

'It's Christian. He's been injured.' She sounded puzzled. Her hands grasped the banisters for support.

He reached her two steps at a time and put his hands firmly under her elbows.

'Come on, upstairs. I'll make you some tea.'

'I feel sick,' she mumbled.

'Shock,' he said, guiding her upstairs.

He suspected it was not going to be an easy evening and his assumption was right. One could never foretell the behaviour of someone in a crisis unless one knew them well. He was prepared and willing for his shoulder to be wept upon; but it was not necessary, nor so simple.

Before he had time to boil a kettle, Rachel joined him in the kitchen looking pale but self-contained and asked in a practical voice whether he would be in for supper, and did he like scrambled eggs. She showed no signs of being pleased or sorry when he said 'yes' to both questions. He knew something about shock and found this composure far more alarming than a show of hysterics.

His offer of tea was rejected. She poured herself a brandy. 'I can't stop myself shaking. Stupid of me.'

'Let me get supper. I'm quite capable.'

'I'm better with something to do, thanks. You could open the wine.' During the meal she told him the outline of what she knew, which was not a great deal; three men blown off the road by a booby trap near a check-point. Christian was thrown clear and was in hospital with concussion and other relatively minor injuries.

'The sergeant, the driver, was killed. If Christian had been driving . . .'

She spoke without emotion, as if it was just another tragedy that had nothing to do with her. But she hardly ate, possibly because of the tremor in her hands.

Watching her endlessly rotating the stem of her wine-glass, he said, 'Thank God he wasn't seriously hurt.' An obvious remark scarcely worth the utterance. 'What you have to realize is, the initial shock is the same.'

'I feel as if I have been personally violated,' she said quietly. Getting up, she started to clear the table, separating cutlery at the sink with exaggerated efficiency. He took the plates from her one by one and fitted them in the dishwasher, feeling useless. She should have a member of the family with her instead of a comparative stranger against whom she showed signs of bearing a grudge. When he suggested contacting Louisa, she shot him a look verging on dislike.

'Tomorrow,' she said shortly. 'No point in worrying her tonight.'

'Right,' he said. 'May I have that plate, Rachel, please?'

She took no notice. 'They should pull the Army out of Ireland,' she said with sudden intensity. 'Poor devils, neither side wants them.'

Whatever he said now would precipitate an outburst; perhaps it was all to the good.

'That would ensure a blood-bath, and whatever the North may want, they're supposed to be a part of us; our own people.'

Staring at him, she said with quiet fury, 'Christian is *my* own person. Or doesn't he count, along with dozens of others like him?'

'I don't really think this is the moment for a political discussion.'

'Because I'm in a state of shock so I can't see straight, is that it? When I've calmed down I'll see the sense in what you're telling me?' Two bright spots of colour appeared on her cheekbones. 'And Christian will mend, and the other wretched man will be buried with honours, and the whole God-awful process will continue *ad infinitum*.'

Tom regarded the dishwasher in silence. She needed to rant at someone; in that he at least served a purpose.

'Tomorrow there will be a short announcement on the radio,' she said, 'and it will go unnoticed. People won't even hear it because it's just one more incident in a thousand like it. And they won't catch the sods who have done it.' Her hands were shaking violently. 'Shooting is too good for them. They should be blown to bits, the fucking bastards—'

The plate she was clutching smashed to the floor, fragments scattering in all directions. She stood looking at it in surprise, then turned away, her passion all washed out. 'Dustpan,' she muttered dully.

'No, you don't.' He caught her firmly by the shoulder. 'You're going to get into bed and take a sleeping pill.' He gave her a gentle push. 'Go on.'

In sweeping up the bits of china there was relief in doing something positive. For some reason he felt illogically angry with her. He clattered the debris into the waste bin with a satisfying rattle and a sense of being in control at last.

She was standing by the window when he brought her a hot drink, staring out at the acacia tree etched black against a pale night sky.

'Hot sweet tea?' she asked with a touch of irony, taking the mug from him docilely.

'I found some camomile. It's supposed to be sleep-inducing; probably what you should have had earlier on instead of brandy. No sugar.'

'Good,' she said. 'I can't stand it.' Turning back to the window, she added, 'Funny how different everything looks to you when you feel shattered. I love that tree, especially at night. Now it seems menacing.'

He understood; only his visions were of shadowed streets, and shadows within the shadows.

'All I can think of is catching the first plane out there to be with him. Do you think they would allow that?'

'I'm sure they wouldn't stop you. But I should wait a day or so before deciding anything. They are bound to give him sick leave, in any case.'

'How sensible,' she said, as if it was a fault. 'I broke that plate on purpose. Very ungrown-up.'

'And very natural.'

'And I gave you a bad time. It was a horrible evening; I'm sorry.' She smiled faintly. 'Anyway, you won't have to face another like it tomorrow.'

'Tomorrow?'

'You're going to the ballet.'

124

He watched her put her mug on the bedside table, withdrawing from him.

'I suppose you wouldn't like to come? Under the circumstances, I expect you won't feel like it. But I've been trying to find the right time to ask you, when you were in one place for long enough.'

'But I thought . . .' She looked at him blankly. 'May I let you know in the morning? Perhaps it would take my mind off things.'

Her face told him nothing. 'Try to get some sleep,' he said.

As he left the room she called to him. 'Thank you for being here and – everything, Tom. I'm very grateful.'

This time she sounded as if she meant it.

I wish she'd bloody cry, he thought as he climbed to his room. The flash of unexplained anger was turned inward on himself now, for wanting her so badly at a totally inappropriate moment.

Rachel lay with her eyes wide open in the darkness. She was thinking that only yesterday she would have given a great deal for Tom's ministrations. Now the whole of her was concentrated on Christian, willing him to be all right. There was no energy left for misplaced emotions. He had slipped backwards in her mind to the age of six and dependent on her comfort. She had failed to protect him and was drowning in illogical guilt as a result. This had always been her reaction; the fact that he was a man fighting a war made no difference.

She gave up any hope of sleep, switched on the light and tried to read.

*   *   *

Tom dreamt his recurring dream. It ran darkly just below the surface of consciousness; the chase through a network of tunnels, feet slipping on the slimy surface, his breath rasping painfully in his chest, his back pressed suddenly against a blank wall, knife raised and driven upwards with expert precision, the dreadful soft feel as it met its objective. And finally seeing that the figure sliding slowly to the ground was Hana, and the scream that was never uttered; only in the dream did he wake with his mouth open and the sound of it echoing in his ears.

The aftermath was always the same, a sense of relief that none of this was real; the benison that follows nightmares. Then the sick shock of truth, the realization that he had merely dreamt a twisted version of what in fact happened; substituted a knife for the gun, put Hana in the place of the man he had shot. There was no chase; the running was over and they were so very nearly there. The guard had appeared almost casually from the shadows of a branch turning in the sewers. He had a girl's face, smooth and hairless, gormless and startled; young, very young, no more than a boy. He never knew what hit him.

Sweating, Tom groped his way to the bathroom and drank a glass of water. In these isolated moments, he missed Hana. For all her neuroses, or perhaps because of them, she had been understanding towards his fears. He wondered whether the new man in her life ever asked for succour and decided, from what little he had seen of him, that he was self-sufficient, reliable and quite without imagination. In other words, he was suitable for Hana, who needed someone straightforward, so she had told him repeatedly: 'You complicate

126

things, Tom, I never know where I am; I never know where you are. I want now the simple life.' Well, he had done his best, settled her in the country where everything was said to be less stressful. It was a mistake. She hadn't fitted in with the close community existence of a village.

He returned to his bed, feeling defeated. There was no sound from Rachel, but he was conscious of her lying sleepless in the room below him.

An account of the IRA's latest atrocity appeared in the morning papers, and the *Mail* carried a photograph. Rachel took one appalled look at the tangled wreckage and put the paper in the waste basket, her stomach churning. Louisa telephoned, followed immediately by Simon in answer to her messages.

'Poor old Chris,' he said. 'Have you had any news?'

'Only that he's comfortable, which means no change.'

She had spoken to the Sister in charge, pleasant but brisk, who suggested that Rachel should ring back at six o'clock when there would be a house registrar available to answer her questions. She did not know how to live through the day. 'I'll know more this evening,' she said.

Simon was harassed on his own account. 'Camilla's had to go into hospital, she's having contractions.'

'But surely the baby isn't due for ages?'

'That's right. I hope it's just a false alarm but it's rather worrying.'

'Why does everything happen at once?' said Rachel hopelessly.

'Will you be all right on your own, Ma? I'd come round, but I really ought to be with Camilla. I suppose you wouldn't like Emily for the day to take your mind off things?' he asked tentatively.

'I need to catch up on sleep,' she told him.

When they had finished, she took a kneeling-mat and started to weed the garden. It was only ten thirty. Grubbing in the warm earth brought a certain peace. Simon had called her 'Ma', a rare sign of affection which for some reason made her tearful.

Sleep was impossible; stretched out on her bed in the afternoon, she merely achieved a light-headed doze full of apprehension. She wondered whether she would have benefited from a husband right now, putting a hand flat on the sheet beside her as if testing the idea. Consolation would be a fine thing; arms to hold her, words of tenderness. Henry did not fit the picture, and she was dubious about Renton whom, she remembered, had asked her to marry him for the second time. That was the night before last; it seemed like a century ago. But no; emotional scenes would embarrass him. She was after all better off alone.

In fact, he had embarrassed *her* by uncharacteristically pouncing on her. Thrown, literally as well as mentally, objecting to being sprawled over, she was not particularly kind. Now possibly, they were not even fairly good friends, which was how she viewed their relationship. The thought depressed her; friendship should last where marriage did not.

Through the open window came the sound of Tom mowing the lawn; the sound of summer. He had been the soul of tact, leaving her to her own devices, sensing she wanted solitude. Thinking about it, she realized that everything he had done in the last twenty-four hours had been an act of friendship. She would settle for that, too tired for anything more. The lawn-mower stopped; her eyes closed. There was silence. What a quiet man he was, appearing and disappearing noiselessly.

She stretched out a hand for the alarm clock, set it for ten to six, and slept.

In the stalls bar, the ten-minute bell rang for the second half of *Giselle*. Rachel watched Tom struggling through the crowd, holding a plate of sandwiches high above head level. She sat on prickly red plush, cradling her glass, a little drunk on three glasses of champagne. Tom had insisted on it; after all, they were celebrating, he said.

Christian had regained consciousness, the doctor had informed her when she had telephoned promptly at six.

'I never knew he was unconscious,' she said to Tom.

They had given him a brain scan; all was well, no permanent damage, no fracture. He was sitting up and talking. The two broken ribs would mend of their own accord, and in a day or so she would be able to speak to him herself.

The things they did not tell you until they were certain; the same things that had plagued you in ignorance. Now she knew, Rachel experienced a moment of terror at what might have been; all her hours of fear exposed. It was like whisky on a bad tooth, the relief of knowing.

'I'm so glad,' Tom had said, watching her move restlessly about the room chattering, unable to relax.

'We have an hour before the ballet. Would you like to go?'

'Shall I?' Her eyes were bright, a little feverish.

'I'd like it very much if you did.'

She dressed in a hurry, pulling on the same Renton-rumpled dress because there was no time to pick and choose; realizing, when she looked in the mirror, that she had not touched her face since yesterday, and her hair needed washing. She drew it back in combs and added pearl-drop ear-rings, lipsticked in her mouth, squirted scent liberally on wrists and neck. A botched-up job; but Tom did not seem to notice. He looked at her seriously and then smiled, as if what he saw both pleased and amused him.

The Covent Garden stage mist cleared, the *corps de ballet* floated into the trees, and Giselle and her lover were left to dance out their hopeless passion. Rachel could not count how many times she had seen it; white arms rippling, outstretched and pleading, a dance of despair, backwards, forwards, together, apart. And in the background, the tomb to which the girl must return, leaving a pathetic scattering of flowers behind her.

The figures blurred and melded in Rachel's vision. She was susceptible to emotional scenarios; it did not take much to start her eyes pricking and her throat constricting. But not the deluge of tears that poured down her face now, quite uncontrolled. She had no idea why she was crying, which was odd. It was completely automatic, like a tap turned on and getting stuck, and once having started, she found it impossible to stop. She sat still and helpless in her seat, hoping Tom would not see, while water dripped steadily from cheeks and chin and on to her programme, despoiling the front cover.

* * *

The dawn chorus woke her, dragging her upwards from the depths of sleep like someone half-drowned. She seemed to be paralysed, unable to move a limb. Consciousness seeped in slowly, awareness of an arm flung across her, a leg pinning her to the bed and his body curved round her back. Twisting her head, she had a close-up of his face beside her, eyes open and watchful. In the semi-darkness she put out a hand and touched his chin. It rasped with a night's growth; he was real.

'How did we get here?' she mumbled, not entirely awake.

'The way most people do.' He bit her ear gently. 'We pulled back the covers and climbed in.'

'Very droll.'

There had of course been more to it than that. Fragments of what they had done floated through her mind in disbelief. In the taxi coming home he had pulled her to him and allowed that extraordinary silent flood of tears to soak his shirt front. Holding her face between his hands, he had kissed her, his mouth travelling over eyelids, forehead, nose, cheeks and finally lips, where the tears and all positive thinking stopped dead.

Lying together in her bed seemed the right and natural outcome. How they came to be there was quite irrelevant.

'Are you full of regrets?' he asked, leaning over, trying to gauge her expression in the dark. 'Do you want me to leave you?'

'No. Please don't.'

'That's good, because I hadn't any intention of doing so.'

He kissed her, stroking the silky inside curve of her thigh.

'I want to sleep now, Tom.'

'Of course you do.' He moved his leg to set her free. 'That better?' But there was no answer. She was gone; and soon he slept also, leaving the hand where it was.

According to Rachel's mother, one could always tell when a girl had lost her virginity; there was something about the eyes. This statement was hardly applicable to Rachel now, thirty years on, but all the same she wondered whether traces of the night before showed in her face, a kind of glow, transforming her into someone desired. She need not have worried; peering in the looking-glass she saw merely the reflection of a tired, middle-aged woman, a fact endorsed by Simon when he arrived to collect the missing clothes with Emily.

'Poor Ma. You look knackered,' he said, giving her a peck on the cheek.

'Simon!'

'Sorry, I was trying to sympathize. Now, is there anything I can do about Chris?'

'Write to him, he'd like that. He's going to be all right,' she said, smiling, her face losing its tiredness. 'I expect to get a letter from his CO on Monday or Tuesday. They're bound to give him sick leave, according to Tom.'

'Tom?'

'Tom Crozier who is lodging here.'

'What does *he* know about it?' asked Simon suspiciously.

'Quite a lot, probably, since he's in the Army.'

She switched quickly to the subject of Camilla who was leaving hospital the next day, still pregnant and with strict instructions not to eat hot curries. Tom appeared, introductions were performed and Emily bobbed a curtsey, to Rachel's astonishment. They stood around, an awkward little group in the garden, until she could bear it no longer and made a craven retreat to the kitchen.

Emily was slicing cucumber unevenly to put in the Pimm's.

'What was the curtseying about?' asked Rachel. 'I'm not complaining, but you've never done it before.'

'Because he's an actor, isn't he, that man—?'

'Tom is his name.'

'Tom, then. He was in an old film about a jackal. It was on telly at Christmas, only I wasn't allowed to watch much of it.'

'Edward Fox?' Rachel followed the thread with difficulty. 'Goodness no, but I can see what you mean.'

She poured Pimm's into a jug and reached for the lemonade, wondering if Tom would be flattered by his mistaken identity.

'He's got sort of a face like a bloodhound; all droopy.'

Rachel giggled. 'Be that as it may, why the curtsey?'

'You always do with actors,' Emily informed her gravely. 'I've seen them all lined up for the Royal Performance.'

'I believe it's the stars who curtsey to royalty.' Seeing Emily's disbelieving expression Rachel added, 'Never mind, it looks nice. We're ready for the cucumber.'

'Granny, you never rang me.'

Rachel paused; the accusation produced a stab of guilt. It made her realize how radically her life had changed in a matter of days. This was understandable in Christian's case. But long before that crisis, while she was busying herself with the mechanics of research, her mind had been elsewhere.

She had forgotten the complete selfishness of falling in love; nothing else existed. How to explain the inexplicable to a child of eight?

'I'm sorry, darling. I didn't forget but life has been very full with Christian and his accident.'

Emily dropped slices of cucumber into the jug and stirred thoughtfully. 'You're going off the Rumbles, aren't you?' she remarked, pushing her glasses up her nose and shooting Rachel a look of disappointment.

Only temporarily have I lost interest, Rachel wanted to reassure her; just until the world stops spinning. Soon, reason will put a spoke in it, and I shall be staggering back to normality. She searched for a sop.

'I have discovered about Lisa's baby,' she said. 'There was one.'

'I knew there was,' said Emily triumphantly.

'But it did not die in the fire. I believe it was adopted. So there are no ghost babies in this house,' Rachel said firmly. 'When you come to stay, we'll work on it together again, right?'

Emily's face lit up. 'Can we?' As an afterthought she said, 'Our baby was nearly born yesterday. That gave me an awful shock.'

Her dislike of the future sibling was worrying; Emily's attitude did not augur well for its early years.

Simon put his head round the door and asked

impatiently what had happened to the drink? Emily carried the jug of Pimm's out to the garden where she poured a glass for Tom with the air of a handmaiden, and left the others to help themselves. When her unswerving scrutiny of him became an embarrassment, Rachel suggested she go in search of her clothes.

'It wasn't too bad, was it?' Rachel asked.

'Emily will go a long way. No man will be safe with her,' Tom predicted.

'She's in love, for the first time. How did you get on with Simon? I hope he was nice to you.'

'Fine. We talked about the City of which I know nothing, and about the Army of which he knows little. And about our children, of course.'

'He told me you had been in Military Intelligence,' Rachel said. 'I might have known you would wind the poor boy up.'

'I certainly did not,' he said seriously.

She peered at him. 'I don't believe you.'

'That's the beauty of coming out with it casually. Nobody does believe you.'

'I still don't know if you're lying,' she said with a slight frown. He smiled in that way that he had, as if she inspired both love and amusement, and put his arms round her. 'Let's have dinner out. Early.'

'All right. But dinner only,' she said, trying to be firm. 'I need a good night's sleep.'

'Of course,' he said meekly.

There were adjustments to be made, she discovered as the days that followed turned into weeks. Not just emotional ones but the practical as well which she had not even considered; such as the fixing of Tom's bed to make it appear slept in, to avoid shocking Consuelo.

For a limited space of time she found a new enthusiasm for cooking, taking trouble to prepare complicated dishes until she discovered Tom's favourite food was sausages and mash and his appetite was negligible in any case. He insisted on raising his rent to cover the costs. Sometimes she felt he was embarrassed by her efforts on his behalf; it wasn't in the contract, he said, half-serious. Neither was sharing his landlady's bed, she pointed out; so what?

Occasionally he went out for the evening. He would usually explain where and with whom, careful to show lack of enthusiasm. She found herself acting like a suspicious wife, not in front of him but secretly; watching the clock, listening for sounds of his return. At moments such as these she grew wary, remembered the importance of independence, contacted neglected friends. The spasms never lasted longer than a day or two. She suspected him of a different kind of caution; a fear of commitment.

All these subtle changes shifted and settled themselves. None of them mattered. They were as nothing compared with the joy of falling asleep imprisoned by arms and legs grown heavy in relaxation. From the first, the strangeness inherent in lying welded to another's unfamiliar body had not existed for her. It was as if they had done this before, knew exactly what the other wanted, anticipated all the moves and nuances without effort. It was as near bliss as she could imagine, and a little frightening in its addictiveness. She struggled without much success to maintain a sense of balance.

*   *   *

As Christian recovered, she put through daily calls to monitor his progress, until there came a day when he telephoned Rachel to tell her he would not be coming home on sick leave.

Wandering aimlessly about feeling wounded, she wondered whether this was a kind of just retribution for climbing into bed with Tom. If she knew the reason for Christian's decision, she might be able to accept it more philosophically. The reasons he gave were valid enough; but he was hiding something, he never managed that successfully. Spending time in England would made it harder to go back, he said; he wanted to get back to work as soon as possible – before he loses his nerve, thought Rachel miserably.

Surely, she asked, some sort of convalescence was a good idea? Against a cacophony of hospital noises his end of the line, she heard him say something about friends, and a house by the sea. Before they rang off, he added a little urgently how important this was for him; would she please try to understand? He would write, tell her more in a letter.

What friends? she asked herself. What possible chance did he have of making any in that God-forsaken island? The Catholic church was behind this, busy manipulating and converting, sucking him into their clutches while he was at a low ebb. She let the hurt spill over into muttered obscenities about the system and, having demolished it to her satisfaction, climbed the stairs to Christian's room and stood amongst the relics of adolescence; a picture painted on wood of a stork carrying a baby, a guitar with no strings, a poster of Madonna, a pair of trainers with holes in the toes.

Breathing in the stuffy smell that went with them, her sense of proportion slowly returned. He might have been killed, might never be coming home. She ought to be full of gratitude instead of self-pity. This room was a better communicator by far than the disembodied telephone. Feeling better, she crossed to the window and opened the lower half with a jerk, letting in the scent of stocks.

Behind her, someone turned swiftly and left the room: she knew it as surely as she had known the invasion of the drawing-room. This time there was a draught of air, and the flick and swish of a skirt against the door. She could not be certain afterwards whether she had seen or heard it, or whether it was merely an impression.

It was shortly after this that she decided finally about France.

There had been no response to the advertisement for Florence Codie's whereabouts. She was not particularly surprised, nor disappointed for that matter. Robert Kincade's address lay in her desk, and in her mind an idea had been taking shape for some time. She needed a holiday, so she had been told, and at last she was inclined to agree. Christian's defection had tipped the balance, left her feeling rejected. Images of France under a July sun beckoned appealingly and Robert Kincade provided an excellent excuse. She would find it easier to persuade Tom to spend two weeks away with her if there was a motive; she was filled with an almost unbearable pleasure at the thought.

She wondered what sort of man Kincade was; irascible and embittered, or extrovert and contented?

He might hold as many answers to the Rumbold saga as Florence Codie but be unwilling to divulge them. She tried to imagine how he had felt, returning to London as the war ended to find this house a wreck, and his wife dead; ignorant of her having given birth to a child in his name. Presumably he had already fallen in love with the French girl he subsequently married. Whatever his feelings over Lisa's death, his return to peace must have been as traumatic as his war.

This was not the sort of enquiry to be conducted over the telephone, she assured herself, while her mind's eye travelled down one of those straight white roads in Northern France lined with poplars, in anticipation. Besides, there was no telephone number included with the address. A tactfully worded letter asking permission to call had to be the first step. Then, if he replied in the affirmative, she would be committed.

The more she thought about it, the more she was consumed by the longing to have Tom to herself without the gentle but insidious intrusion of the family. A vague idea haunted her that being alone, the two of them, in a different setting would clarify things; what things she did not quite know, but suspected it was some sort of assurance about the future. She realized it was an unreasonable demand; he was young enough to remarry, start again, have more children. There *was* no future for her where he was concerned. Easily forgotten in bed, the fact only crept up on her at odd moments.

She pulled writing paper towards her and sat, pen in hand intending to rough out a letter but starting instead to doodle Tom's head. I am no good at affairs, they are so transitory. (She had said that to someone quite recently; who was it?) And I fall in love, she added to herself; that is not in the rules, not the way you are supposed to play. I should take a leaf out of Phyllida's book; learn to lie back and enjoy it while it lasts.

She shaded in the hair at the nape of Tom's neck so that it curled nicely, filled with jealousy of the past and future of his life, the women he had loved and those he might yet love. Even his wife, Hana, who seemed to lurk in sinister fashion on the fringe of things. Giving her shoulders an impatient jerk, she took a clean sheet of paper. 'Dear Mr Kincade,' she wrote in a determined hand. 'You will not know my name . . .'

Tom opened the baggage hold above his head, taking the opportunity to scan the lines of heads down each side of the cabin. He took his time, peeling off his jacket slowly and folding it away beside the over-night case.

The plane to Berlin was not full; the first enthusiastic rush of British hordes to see the Wall in the process of destruction was long over. His request for an aisle seat at the rear had been no problem; the check-in girl merely pointing out that since he held a Club Class ticket, he had the right to travel in comfort. The tail end was the safest, he told her, smiling ruefully and charming her out of her cool efficiency.

He thought, as he buckled himself into his seat, how tired he was of the smile and the charm, and the lack of substance that lay behind them. Once they had proved a surprising help in oiling him in and out of sticky situations. They were no longer necessary, these personal tools of the trade; any more than it was necessary for him to sit with no-one behind him and a clear view in front. All were habits and harmless in themselves; it was when they developed into phobias that you had to watch it.

As the plane became airborne, his mind turned unwillingly to his mother-in-law, Eva, with whom he was having dinner that evening. Duty apart, he had a favour to ask of her, if an offer to spend two free weeks with her daughter in England could be called a favour. Hana was becoming an increasing worry, showing signs of the familiar depression. A furtive search of the bathroom cabinet when last he visited the children had revealed an alarming supply of pills. Her temper was volatile, and he was fairly sure she was drinking too much. There was an ominous absence of the lover which might easily account for the relapse. Whatever the reason, it had come at a bad time. Tom felt uneasy about leaving her alone with the children while he spent a fortnight in France. And fourteen days abroad with Rachel had grown from a good idea to an obsession, slightly unnerving him by its importance. Eva was a trying, beady-eyed woman, both timid and obstinate, who bore him an ill-concealed grudge for abducting her daughter from East to West. Doubtless, because of the divorce, the grudge would have doubled. But right now she was a solution to a problem; he could think of no other.

The drinks trolley drew alongside and he ordered a vodka and tonic, passing a half-bottle of wine to the girl in the window seat. She was eager to start a conversation, to take advantage of this slight courtesy; he could tell by the way she smiled, twitching her skirt surreptitiously higher up her thigh and recrossing her legs. He opened a paperback and pretended to read, in fact thinking of tomorrow's schedule without enthusiasm. The reunification of Germany had brought about its own inevitable problems; bribery, corruption and political activism bubbled beneath the new democratic surface. He had been sent on a fact-finding mission to advise rather than to get involved; to keep him busy, most likely. (Find Crozier something to do; get him off his ass for forty-eight hours.) The project bored him; he was happy with involvement. There had been a time when he believed there was some good in the work he used to do; that in a convoluted way he could be said to be saving lives. Now, he doubted its purpose; the excitement, the feeling for the giveaway gesture, the hidden nuance and coded word seemed suspiciously like a meaningless game. There remained a certain nostalgia for it, that was all. Just as well it had given him up; he doubted his ability, and once that happened, it was curtains.

His eyes ached. He closed them, conjuring up peaceful, escapist visions of open country, downs, trees, rivers, meadows; then Rachel. Just thinking about Rachel gave him the beginnings of an erection. He could not remember when last a woman had had that effect on him. He crossed his legs in embarrassment, away from the girl in the window seat. The plane dipped and started its slow descent, and almost immediately his hands grew clammy with the usual irrational and uncontrollable fear. A lot of people felt this way on coming in to land, followed by direct relief at a safe touch-down. He had to be the only one who dreaded leaving the safe haven of the cabin, walking down the steps on to the tarmac and into the night, unprotected.

Rachel knew very little about Hana and she had not asked, just as Tom did not probe about Henry. They were both observing the unwritten law of reticence where past relationships were concerned, she imagined; a kind of loyalty. But it had the effect of heightening her curiosity and glamorizing Hana who certainly did not need it, judging by her photograph in Tom's room. Rachel would have been happier if her likeness was no longer in evidence and knew that to be unreasonable. You did not shove people into drawers simply because you could not live with them.

'You remind me of her,' Tom had said. They were in his room at the time, Rachel snooping round examining all the things he had introduced; a music centre, a pile of books, photographs, a portable typewriter, a teddy bear wearing a red knitted coat, a small tape recorder and 'Fred' the plant.

'You must be joking,' she said, nevertheless feeling pleased.

'It's not so much the features, more the way you hold your head; tilted slightly when you talk, like a bird eying a worm. A certain expression when you smile, too.' He had added, 'Not that she smiles much at present.'

She said coolly, 'Yes, well, most people have a type,' not really liking the analogy of birds and worms.

When Hana telephoned, she happened to be on Rachel's mind, giving her an uncanny feeling of having conjured up the woman by process of thought.

'This is Hana Crozier. May I speak with Tom,

143

please?' The voice was muffled and accented.

'I'm afraid he is away at the moment; coming back tomorrow night. Shall I give him a message?'

'Yes, please.' She has been crying, thought Rachel. 'Will you ask him to talk with me when he is returning?'

'Of course.' How should one address her; Hana or Mrs Crozier?

'You will not forget? It is important.' There was a pause. 'He is going away soon, abroad I believe, and there are things we must discuss before . . .' The voice trailed away hopelessly.

'I'll tell him, I promise, Mrs Crozier,' Rachel said reassuringly, and replaced the receiver feeling an amoral bitch.

Tom had said Hana was inclined to be neurotic; nothing about her still being in love with him, which sounded probable. That wobbly, querulous voice did not match the smiling girl in the photograph. It was a sophisticated face, made slightly Mongolian by the upward-slanting eyes and high cheekbones. She was dark. Rachel, before she saw the picture, had imagined her to be fair; the darkness of her made her illogically more of a threat. Her hair was cut like a boy's, short back and sides and slicked flat. None but the beautiful could get away with that, thought Rachel, and sighed.

She wondered when and how the first cracks in the system had come about. Talking to Hana had brought her into focus as a human being with problems, and Rachel found herself sympathizing with her reluctantly. If Tom had behaved like a shit, she did not want to know or even accept it as a possibility. It is no business of mine, she told herself firmly, and returned to what she had been doing before the call; searching for a decent suitcase amongst the stack of battered luggage. But Hana remained at the back of her mind, not so much a shadow now as an emotional threat.

The sun filtering through drawn curtains made a pattern of watered silk on the ceiling; liquid, constantly shifting, like the sea over sand. So it occurred to Rachel, who lay watching it from under hypnotized lids. She wondered if it was possible to make love in the sea. Perhaps she would find out before long.

Tom said, 'The doorbell has rung twice,' his voice a deep rumble beneath her head.

'Leave it. It's bound to be the Jehovah's Witnesses.' She closed her eyes. 'Or some poor unemployed boy selling dusters and dishcloths.'

'You don't want a bible or a duster?'

'Not just now, thank you.'

'Think what a splendid doorstep sermon could be preached around our behaviour. Bed in the afternoon.'

'It was your idea,' she mumbled against his skin. 'Personally, I think it's decadent.'

'You didn't say no, Mrs Playfair, you connived.'

She rolled over on her back, paused before saying, 'I wish you wouldn't call me that.'

He turned his head to look at her, surprised. 'Then I won't.'

He did not ask why, but put a pillow behind him and sat upright. The spell was broken.

'Shall we have a cigarette and be unhealthy as well as decadent?' The pattern on the ceiling had changed. A breeze had got up, spoiling its lazy flow, making it jiggle. She could not think what had got into her, being disagreeable and bringing the first-ever note of discord.

'Do you always joke afterwards?' she asked, making the same mistake. He was silent for a long time, so it seemed to her. Now I've hurt him, she thought, I've spoilt everything.

'Not always, no,' he answered eventually. She heard him open a packet of cigarettes and the click of his lighter. 'I suppose it's a sort of nervous reaction,' he added.

'Nervous?' she said, amazed. 'Nervous of me?'

'Why do women always imagine nerves to be their prerogative?'

'I don't. But you must be sure about me. You must know—'

'When you've made a nonsense with one person who matters, you're scared about doing it a second time. Simple psychology.' He was silent a moment; a trickle of smoke wafted towards her. 'In other words, I only try to be funny when I'm serious, I suppose. Quite contrary of me, isn't it?'

She let the words sink in, making sure of their meaning. A mixture of incredulity and jubilance flooded through her; the room was very quiet. She wanted to tell him what it was like to be loved by him, with imagination and patience, but the words stuck. She remained silent, just as she made love silently and with great concentration, even when she came; no moans or shouts of triumph. Perhaps this was her biggest mistake of all.

She reached out and took his hand, lacing her fingers between his.

'Next time,' she murmured, 'ask me if the earth moved. That's a joke, by the way.'

Presently he put an arm round her and pulled her against him.

'Do you mind about us being in this bed?' he asked.

'No,' she said, surprised by the question. 'Should I, do you think?'

'It's the marital bed, presumably. I wondered, that's all – you might have inhibitions, memories. I don't know, I've never been—'

'Bereaved?' She supplied the word with irony. Plenty of memories, she thought, no inhibitions. The good memories had been desecrated. When she did look back on them, they were blotted out by a picture of Alison sitting up naked, clutching the sheet to her with a vacuous expression on her face; a clichéd example of being caught *in flagrante delicto*. There was a time when Rachel had wanted to get rid of the bed after that, felt she could not bear to sleep in it again. But she had not done so purely because she was fond of it. Now it was hers alone, to share with whom she chose, and she hoped Henry could see what was going on, wherever he was.

'I don't mind in the least,' she said, 'for various reasons.'

'Ah. I thought it might have something to do with your objecting to being called Mrs Playfair.'

'No,' she said sadly. 'That really is because of an inhibition.'

'Which one?'

'It makes me feel old. I am in any case nearly old enough to be your mother. I don't want to be reminded.'

147

'For an intelligent woman, you really can be incredibly stupid. It doesn't matter to me, I never think about it and neither should you.'

'I didn't mind until now. Everything either droops or wrinkles, I hate growing old all of a sudden. Most of all I hate my stomach.'

'It's a beautiful stomach. Show me.'

'No, I won't. Stop it, Tom! Oh, don't do that, there isn't time to start again.'

'All the time in the world,' he said, rather firmly for one of a nervous disposition, which was her last coherent thought for the next half hour.

Later, kissing her, he said 'I love you,' and she wondered whether she could allow herself to believe him.

Simon had forgotten to ask his mother if she would have Emily to stay for the night of the office dance. He had intended to mention it while collecting Emily's clothes, but what with one thing and another, and one in particular – meeting the smooth bugger who was lodging there – it slipped his mind. Camilla, vast in a blue tent-dress, was standing at the sink.

'You were determined to dislike him,' she pointed out with unusual perception, 'whatever he turned out to be.' Shifting her weight from one ankle to the other she added, 'You worry too much over Rachel; it's absurd. She's perfectly capable of looking after herself.'

This was such a turn-about on Camilla's part, who was the first to write off Rachel as scatty, that he stared at her in hurt silence and then retreated to the telephone. When he returned, she was still peeling potatoes with a martyred expression.

'Surely Françoise can do that?' he said.

'She's got the evening off, like most evenings.'

'I don't know why we bother to have an au pair. You give her too much free time.'

'If I don't, she sulks. I agree, she's useless; hopeless with children, Emily can't stand her. And she's constantly on the phone to her mates. The bill will be astronomical.' She dried her hands, feeling more cheerful after a good grumble. 'What did Rachel say?'

'She can have Emily.'

'That's good.' She sat down on a stool and sighed, staring at her bulging front. 'Though why on earth I'm going to a dance, God only knows.'

He kissed the top of her head. 'You're coming because I'd hate it without you. I promise we won't stay late.'

'Darling Sim, you're rather sweet sometimes.' She wrinkled her nose at him, acknowledging her grouchiness. 'What else did Rachel say?'

'Nothing much. Oh, she's taking a holiday. France, apparently.' He frowned. 'I wonder who she's going with? Can't think of anyone she knows who has a villa there. In fact, she hasn't gone away for more than a few days since Father died.'

'Perhaps she's planning to take the smooth bugger.' Camilla yawned, wondering if a glass of wine would give her heartburn.

Simon stared at her, appalled. 'You can't be serious. He's thirteen years younger than she is.'

'Then bully for her if she is,' said Camilla. 'I'll drink to that.'

He uncorked the bottle and pondered the strange effect of pregnancy on some women.

Chapter Eight

Letter from Florence Codie to her sister.

October 1942.

Well, now we're in the soup, good and proper. The girl's pregnant, knew it the moment I seen her when she come home last Friday. 'I'm frozen, Codie, is the water hot? I need a really hot bath,' she says.

'You won't get rid of it that easy,' I tells her sharpish, and her mouth drops open, wondering how I cottoned on. She slumps down in a chair and says, 'I can't keep it, can I?' sort of hopeless like.

'Have you told him?' I asks her, and of course she hasn't since he's thousands of miles away and she don't want him worrying over her. 'He's got a right to have his say,' I says.

So I keeps quiet then, reading the paper so's she can work it out. And she goes on sitting there, holding her hands to the fire and easing her shoes off her feet, and talking about everything under the sun 'cept the question in hand. 'Needs doing up in here,' she says.

'Well, so it do, but you need to get your priorities right, girl,' I tells her. 'Time waits for no man and babies gets bigger, and all you can think of is a bit of decorating.'

Wished I hadn't sounded harsh then, as I sees the look on her face. 'I've thought of nothing else but the baby for the last month,' she says, quiet like.

I asks more gentle, 'Would you want to keep it, if things was equal?'

'Oh, Codie,' she says, and her voice were that tired and desperate. 'Oh, Codie, things aren't equal, are they? How can I bring up a child on no money and nowhere to live? Can you see my mother welcoming an illegitimate grandchild? Where is she, by the way?' she asks. 'I'll have to tell her.'

'Shouldn't do that,' I warns her, 'not before you're sure what you want.'

'I'll have to,' says Lisa, and she tries to sound all hard and careless.

'She'll know where to go for an abortion. And I'll have to ask her to lend me the money.' Then she leans towards me and asks me whether *I* knows anyone who does that sort of thing.

I tells her no, and what kind of company does she think I keep? Well, matter of fact I do, but I wouldn't let the girl go there 'cept over my dead body. It'd be *her* dead body, more like. 'If that's what you're set on,' I says, 'best get your ma to fix you up in one of them posh nursing homes, it'll cost a packet but you'll be safe enough. And you haven't answered my question, for all that,' I points out.

She shuts her eyes for a minute, and I can see

there's a tussle going on inside of her twixt tears and anger, and then the anger wins, cos it's my belief she's wept more'n enough in the last few weeks. Anyways, she lets fly at me – 'Damn and blast you, Codie! Of course I want it. Satisfied?'

After which she puts a hand in the pocket of her coat and pulls out half a bottle of gin. 'But we can't always have what we want, can we?' she says in a fair mimic of her mother's voice, and holds out the bottle. 'As recommended by my good friend, Gladys. A mine of information on all sorts of subjects, is Gladys. I might as well enjoy myself as a murderer. Come on, Codie, fetch the glasses and have one on me.'

'Never touch it,' I tells her flat, knowing what'll be the upshot of this game, a lot of mess and nothing else.

'All the more for me,' she says, gets a tumbler and pours out enough gin to knock a navvy cold.

'Won't do no good,' I says. 'Your Gladys has been filling you up with old wives' tales.'

She takes no notice, just says, 'The water must be boiling now. Thanks, Codie,' in quite a cheery sort of way. But she stops when she gets to the door. 'If I'm not down in an hour or so, be an angel and check on me, would you?'

'You'll make yourself sick, that's all,' I tells her. Course I was right and no mistake. More'n that, she come close to losing it, near as dammit. There's yours truly trotting up and down stairs with hot bottles till I was fair worn out, what with the worry and all, and when it were over, I let her have it.

152

'Of all the fucking stupid things to do. You could have lost it,' I says, which were daft of me cos that were what she were aiming at. And you know what she says? 'Oh, Codie! I believe you want it as much as I do.' I could have slapped her.

'Don't talk daft,' I snaps at her. 'Who's just tried to get rid of it?'

She says, 'I know. But I'm terribly glad I didn't now,' and she turns her head to one side and the tears start sliding down her cheeks. Well, I never was one to hold on to me anger. 'One thing's for sure,' I tells her, 'he's a determined little bugger, hanging on like that.'

She gives a hiccough as if laughing and crying at once. 'He's a part of Nat,' she says, and a second later she's asleep.

When she were better she goes down to face her ma, which must have took courage. Funny, but she seemed calm like, as if nothing could touch her. Not like Lisa at all, feared of her own shadow as a rule. I won't say I listened to what went on, just let's say I got meself near enough the door so's I couldn't help but overhear. Enough to know how madam was taking it. Starts all quiet and persuasive, she does, on about nursing homes and doctors and the like – reckon she knows first-hand about them – and then the voice gets high and cold as ice when Lisa tells her she means to keep the bairn. All hell were let loose, I can tell you. 'Do you realize what you're planning to do to us? How it will affect *me*?' she says. Lisa says, cool as a cucumber, 'It needn't affect you at all, Mother. I'll go on working until a month before the birth, and afterwards, I'll go back to the country as soon as possible. I don't want to stay here,' she says, and you could tell she were smiling. 'No-one will know I'm here for that short time. I shan't make any difference to your life. When have I ever done that?' she says, fair piling it on.

Then madam says something about adoption and Lisa slaps that down, and her ma says, furious now, 'Who *is* the man? The least he can do is bloody well marry you.' And Lisa says, 'Oh, he will eventually, but you won't be thrilled when he does.' That's when she gives her ma the facts about Nat. And a short time after that madam slams up to her bedroom and Lisa come up to me, her face white as a sheet, it having took it out of her more'n she knew.

Well, the die is cast, and that's why I'm writing this letter, Gert, to put you in the picture. Cos I'm asking as to whether you'd take the girl after the baby's born. I know it's asking a lot, but your heart always were in the right place, and Lisa can't stay here, for sure. She'd thrive in the country, so would the child, out of the way of the raids. And she might be a help more'n a hindrance since she ain't feared of hard work, farm work, that is. Wouldn't be for ever. She'll marry her Nat being that he come back, God willing. Won't be easy for her, she's chose a rough path, but I'm that fond of her and for all her silliness, she's got a mind of her own, and guts besides.

'You know, Codie,' she says to me before she

leaves, 'I thought I was going to die at one point. I wouldn't have minded dying if I'd killed Nat's child.' Then she says something odd. 'Poor Robbie,' she says, 'I hope he can't know about any of this, ever.'

One thing she refuses to do, that's write to Nat, telling him. Got enough on his mind, she says. I'd be obliged, Gert, if you'll give me your answer pronto. Reckon it'll be born end of June, she'd be coming to you around mid-July if that suits. I'd be that grateful, I can see her now, walking on them Cornish sands with the bairn, if the sun shines. Hoping this finds you as it finds me . . .

Chapter Nine

It was raining when they reached Calais, a steady drizzle that changed to a deluge on the *auto-route*. Visibility was poor and all that Rachel could see through the rain-streaked window was an unrecognizable France punctuated by billboards advertising aperitifs and sun oil. None of this bore any resemblance to her original imaginings; they should be travelling down that straight road in sunlight dappled by poplars. This was the quick route, according to Tom. But where was the hurry? Glancing once at his profile, she saw it wore the grim implacable look of someone climbing Everest. The clock told her they had been on French soil for two hours. He asked her to wipe the mist from the windscreen in a voice that suggested she might have offered; an alien tone that lowered her spirits another notch. Inside her head, her own voice screamed, I want to go home, like a small child.

Queuing up for yet another toll, she collected the correct coins in silence, mutely annoyed that he had refused to let her drive; she longed to do something positive. He had sounded amused at the request, as if she were not competent. But there was no argument since they had brought his car, larger and faster than hers. He turned to her now and smiled the old desired smile, oblivious of her feelings, and she felt like hitting him.

'Are you all right?' he asked curiously.

'Fine. Why?'

'You're quiet, that's all. I just wondered . . .'

They moved forward once more, gathered speed against the monotonous music of hissing tyres and squeaking windscreen wipers. I don't know this man, thought Rachel in a flash of claustrophobic panic. We've been lovers for a month but I don't really know him.

She realized suddenly the extent of her tiredness. There had been so much to remember; she had forgotten the organization a holiday entailed. Arranging for Louisa and Vijay to house-sit and look after Morecombe, searching for suitable clothes to take, having Emily to stay the last weekend, passport, tickets, maps – the list had been endless. When they had arrived, she had told herself, once there was no going back, she would start to unwind. She shifted in her seat, the safety belt chaffing her uncomfortably between the breasts. 'Can I open the window; just a crack?'

'Twiddle that knob in front of you, it should let in cold air. No, not that one.' He leant over impatiently and a luke-warm draught blew in her face.

There was no denying that the cause in part of her exhaustion was Tom, through no fault of his own. She was too old to love distractedly. The whole of her, dormant for so long, had been drastically brought into action, like a superannuated engine suddenly asked to do a hundred. She closed her eyes, desiring nothing more than twelve hours uninterrupted sleep; separate rooms, a bed all to herself. In an hour or two they would be claiming their double-bedded room in a country house hotel – recommended by Phyllida – and the reception clerk, his or her expression professionally blank, would suspect she was sleeping with her son.

You love him, she cried silently. But would they ever have become lovers without the incentive of Christian's accident? She did not want to be loved out of pity. The prospect of two weeks in each other's company had become all at once daunting, and the journey already interminable. Staring at the runnels of water on the window, she longed for a minor hitch, a slow puncture for instance that would set her free if only temporarily. She loosened the safety belt from its socket to ease constriction and felt, in the same moment, the car veer outwards. There was a nasty sound of tearing metal, they bucketed violently and her nose came in sharp contact with the dashboard, while a red Porsche passed like a missile, dousing the windscreen with muddy water. Her prayer had been answered.

'Shit!' growled Tom. 'Fucking French.' He lowered his speed to a crawl. 'Look out for a service station, can you? I'll have to find out what the stupid bastard's done to us.'

She did not answer for a moment, busy searching for something to staunch the blood dripping copiously on to her trousers.

'For Christ's sake, Rachel, what's got into you? For the last hour you look as if you're going to a funeral and now you won't even speak to me. What the hell have I *done*?'

'If you had let me share the driving,' she shot at him

furiously through a wad of tissues, 'this wouldn't have happened for a start.' It was a splendid row.

Beside the service station there was a steep embankment, from the top of which Rachel could see the mechanic knocking out the buckled front wing. Tom stood watching, shoulders hunched dejectedly.

The rain had eased a little. She was past caring, grateful for this interlude, her T-shirt sticking to her with an inappropriate sexiness. When the work was finished they would proceed in silence, she supposed. Not a word had passed between them since their spat. Lighting a cigarette defiantly, she thought of better times such as the day they had gone in search of Lisa's grave, taking Emily with them. A day when the sun shone fitfully between high-flying cotton-wool clouds, and cow parsley grew thickly beside the twisting lanes; and Tom had been a different, sweeter man.

Emily had lost none of her single-mindedness. Sprawling on Rachel's bed while she sorted things for packing, Emily begged to be taken on this next leg of the quest.

'I won't be any trouble, Granny; really, promise.'

Rachel pointed out the drawbacks; constant picnics, wasps, hordes of ants, everything that Emily loathed, while her heart contracted at the sight of Emily's face in disappointment. A Sussex churchyard was a poor substitute for France, but the only one that Rachel was able to think up to distract her. There was nothing positive to be gained from Lisa's place of burial beyond the satisfying of curiosity.

It was a pretty churchyard on an incline, and shaded by beech trees. While Emily busied herself amongst the oldest gravestones, Tom and Rachel wandered onwards to the top where the memorials were white with newness, or of a sparkling granite grey. They sat on a bench surrounded by wilting offerings of flowers in jam-jars, and watched Emily in the distance hopping from one moss-covered stone to the next, peering at faded inscriptions.

'She won't find Lisa down there amongst the seventeen hundreds,' murmured Rachel sleepily. 'I must tell her eventually.'

'What will you do when you have completed Lisa's story?' Tom asked. The hairs on his arms were bleached like the scythed grass at their feet. She smoothed a hand over them, feeling a sacrilegious yearning.

'Go back to earning some pocket money, I suppose. I shall find it tedious; nothing will be as engrossing as this.'

'The fascination of Lisa,' he said thoughtfully. 'Even Emily has caught the bug. What is it exactly?'

'She lived and died in my house; and she seems to have had such a dreadful life. Tragedy is gripping; I can't help feeling her death was unnecessary,' she said, half to herself.

'How do you work that out?'

She hesitated, watching a small blue butterfly that landed on her knee.

'The baby was saved,' she said. 'It was tiny; they must have been sleeping near to each other on the top floor. But only the mother was trapped. Why?'

'Anything can happen in a fire,' he pointed out. 'She may have died trying to save the child; overcome by smoke fumes or hit by falling ceilings.'

'It's a feeling I have,' she said obstinately, 'not a logical deduction.'

She had never mentioned ghosts to Tom, wary of meeting with a repetition of male scepticism. It came as a surprise when he asked quite seriously, 'And do you hope to exorcise her by learning the truth? Lay her spirit to rest; that sort of thing?'

She was saved from thinking of an answer by the arrival of Emily, scudding up the gravel path, her face pink with exertion. Grown bored with searching, she demanded help.

'You're looking in the wrong place, clot-face,' Tom told her. 'So Rachel says.'

Emily lolled against his knee in a rare gesture of affection. They set off together hand in hand, Rachel remaining behind because she liked to see them like that; trying to imagine Simon in Tom's place and failing. Simon was waiting for a son; Emily would always come second.

They found Lisa's headstone, leaning askew like a rotten tooth and covered in lichen. 'In Loving Memory', read the inscription, and underneath, 'They Shall Grow Not Old.' In whose memory, wondered Rachel? Who was there left to remember apart from an ex-husband; did he spare her the occasional thought?

Emily said, 'Isn't it funny to think she actually lived in our house?'

Poor, sad Lisa, who still slipped from room to room.

Because Tom had shown some interest and not gone into guffaws of derision on the subject, Rachel asked him eventually about the ghosts, but he had noticed nothing. An occasional smell of burning, he said, which worried him slightly, that was all; but then, although he had an open mind on psychic matters, he did not think he was the sort to be aware of such things.

The smell of burning had alarmed her and she had the wiring checked. It was around this time, and probably because they were freshly in her mind, that she realized the absence of her ghosts. She had come to accept their presence and lately to ignore it, her interests totally transferred to Tom. It was almost as if they had left out of umbrage.

'Rachel.' Tom was climbing towards her, hair plastered to his forehead. He looked tired and ordinary, less attractive, more vulnerable. 'He's nearly finished. We can leave in five minutes.'

'Oh. Right.'

'You're soaked.' He looked around. 'This is an extraordinary place to choose. It's covered in thistles.'

She said nothing. He hesitated, then sat beside her, his expression resigned.

'How is the nose?' he asked neutrally.

She touched it. 'All right. Sort of stiff.'

'It might be broken. Maybe we should get you X-rayed?'

'Don't be ridiculous. It was a small bump, that's all.'

'You shouldn't have undone the seat belt.'

'Oh, shut up, Tom,' she said wearily. 'If it comes to that, you shouldn't have swung out of your lane.'

They sat staring into space. A slow trickle of water ran down the back of her neck and inside her shirt.

'Would you prefer it if we went home?' he asked. 'Called the whole thing off?'

Her heart froze. 'Is that what *you* want?' she said, tossing the ball into his court.

'If that's how I felt, I wouldn't have come in the first place.' He flattened a thistle with his foot. 'But you've had second thoughts, haven't you? Unspoken ones. You were sending them up like smoke signals; I began to feel I was abducting you against your will.'

She gave a feeble giggle.

'You had better tell me,' he added.

'I had a sudden dreadful feeling of inadequacy,' she told him.

'Silly Rachel.'

'It was as if the next fortnight were some kind of test which I might not pass. And if I didn't, at the end of it you would have stopped loving me, and I would be further in love with you.'

'It never occurred to you that it might happen the other way round?' He stared intently at the squashed thistle.

'No, it didn't. Besides, you were in a bloody awful mood.'

'Likewise.'

They stared at each other in disbelief at this juvenile exchange, their faces pale and unbeautiful; Rachel's in particular, still streaked with dried blood and her nose red with dabbing. He started to smile, then gave a hoot of laughter and suddenly they were convulsed, rocking backwards and forwards on the wet grass like abandoned children, drunk with the relief of it.

They sobered up at last and he kissed her. 'I want to make love to you. Here and now. What on earth are we doing here, anyway?'

'That's what *I* wanted; for you to stop the car

and ravish me by the roadside, to reassure me.'

'You need a lot of that, don't you?'

Below them in the forecourt the mechanic had stopped hammering and could be seen bending over the open bonnet.

'Perhaps I'm just not used to happiness on this scale,' she said simply, searching in her bag for a mirror. 'Oh my lord! No hotel is going to let us through the front door in this state.'

Some time later, he said out of the blue, 'I suppose Henry has a lot to answer for.'

'Such as?'

'Such as your low opinion of yourself.'

'Not entirely. *Is* it low?'

'Rock-bottom.' He slowed down to change lanes. 'We turn off at the next exit, thank God. You don't talk about him much; Henry, that is.'

'Nor you about Hana.' But she did not want to think of Hana.

'We're busy doing other things. Perhaps we'll get around to them one day.'

It had stopped raining and the sky was divided into two distinct bands of colour, one of dove grey, the other gold where the sun was trying to break through.

'Would you like to drive?' he asked her innocently.

'No, thank you. The offer comes too late.'

'Meaning—?'

'I no longer need my mind occupied.'

'Your mind is unfathomable, my darling, but I love you.'

Louisa picked up the mail from the front doormat and wandered to the kitchen for breakfast. She quite enjoyed having the family home to herself. It was an unusually good summer and the garden a blessing for Robin. He had started to crawl, venturing to the edge of the rug and pulling at the grass with an experimental fist. Vijay had bought a paddling pool where the baby sat splashing naked but for a sun-hat. Occasionally she remembered to water Rachel's plants, and rather less often, Tom's plumbago.

In a few days' time, Vijay would leave for America to direct a film. Although they were going through a good phase, the idea of being without him did not worry her. Secretly she found the effort of being constantly reasonable a little wearing; and besides, she would not be entirely alone. There was Robin; and there were the ghosts. Whilst staying with Rachel a month ago, she had not noticed their existence, apart from the one incident of her clothes being moved. This time she was not only aware of them, but their activities had doubled in comparison with Rachel's original account of them. Doors opened and shut of their own volition, the drawing-room smelt powerfully of Turkish tobacco and pockets of exotic scent hung in the air in widely varying places. The piano was played while she was in the garden or the kitchen, and one evening she watched in fascination the keys being depressed silently, straining her eyes to make out some form, however wraithlike. They remained obstinately invisible.

She started to write down these manifestations, a kind of diary for Rachel on her return. Her mother might claim that psychic phenomena merely distracted her from her purpose, but Louisa did not entirely believe her. This insurgency was so sudden and insistent she felt it was worth recording. A peculiar impression had been stamped on the house, of people preparing themselves for an event; whispering behind doors, calling to each other noiselessly down the stairwell.

Vijay noticed nothing; she found that hard to believe. 'Honestly? I was certain you would be tuned in. Indians are spiritual people.'

'Maybe,' he answered with dignity, 'but we no longer swing from trees or practise voodoo. I'm surprised at you, Lou.'

She left it at that, changing the subject quickly instead of arguing, as she undoubtedly would have done before Tom's lecture. Neither was it worth mentioning to Simon, who telephoned as she was drinking her coffee. A card had come in the post from Rachel; a picture of a medieval village against an impossibly blue sky. She wrote lyrically of scenery and places they had visited; no word as to her personal happiness. Louisa hoped genuinely it could be taken for granted. Simon, it appeared, did not share her sentiments.

'Has she actually gone with this man – Tom what's-his-name?'

'She has,' Louisa bristled. 'Anything wrong?'

'She never said anything to me.'

'Why should she? Perhaps she knew you'd get po-faced about it.'

'I'm not. But you must admit it's rather extraordinary going off with a man young enough to be her son.'

'Thirteen years younger. Don't exaggerate, Simon, she wasn't a child bride.'

'Is she serious about him?' Before she could answer,

he added, 'God! I hope not. I don't fancy him as a stepfather.'

'For your information,' she said coldly, 'he's an extremely nice man.'

'Well, I only hope he's not after her for the money and the house. I hope she doesn't do something stupid.'

'And *I* hope she has a fantastic time whatever happens. She deserves it; all those years coping with Fa.'

'Father must be turning in his grave,' said Simon gloomily.

'Fa never gave a damn in his lifetime; I don't see why he should mind now. Anyway, he has no right to object since he screwed anyone remotely nubile who came his way.'

'You don't know that for certain. You're very hard on him.'

She had reason to be. But Simon did not know that; no-one knew. There would never again be a man in her life like Fa. She loved him, hated him, missed him, and rather regretted maligning him.

'I'm merely worried she'll end up miserable,' Simon was saying. 'The trouble with you is, you're blinded by sentiment, Lou.'

'Oh, piss off!' she told him.

He retired hurt, wondering why no-one would ever credit him with an altruistic motive, and why Louisa's language grew steadily coarser ever time they communicated.

A black cloud had descended on Louisa's day. The painful bits of growing up had been pushed to the back of her mind and ignored for years. Remembering them only brought impossible feelings of shame and doubt. She put Robin in the paddling pool and tried to forget their unwanted resuscitation.

Rachel had arranged an appointment with Robert Kincade for the eleventh of July, leaving them a week to reach his village in the Tarn and time afterwards to go where they wished.

As they moved steadily southwards, with Rachel acting as map-reader, she lost her fear of booking in at strange hotels and became adept at searching the *Michelin* for the right places, counting the number of knives and forks with a sharp eye. Contented now to be a passenger, to sit and watch, her faith was restored by the country unfolding before her. France had not changed after all, except for an increase in traffic. Farmland was still divided by neat hedges, small rivers snaked idly through meadows, hamlets clustered round modest little churches; there was the blue rise of distant hills and fields scarlet with poppies. Indistinguishable from England at first glance, there were the subtle differences which made it unmistakably France and which Rachel noted with nostalgic pleasure. Narrow-shuttered windows on the houses, for instance, and the tinny sound of church bells which she much preferred to the sonorous peals of the English variety. Even the scent of open country was foreign, made up of wild thyme and garlic and other less definable sources.

They bought paté and peaches for picnic lunches, and her arms and legs turned brown in a matter of hours; a gipsy shade quite different to Tom's honey blond. His hair bleached in streaks, like designer highlights, she pointed out in amusement. Their silences were comfortable ones, her initial attack of misgivings a dim and faintly funny memory. She liked to choose a hotel where they could have dinner out of doors, on a terrace or in a garden. In some ways, it was the best part of the day; the pleasure of food chosen carefully and eaten slowly, the smell of honeysuckle, the gently insidious effect of the wine. A process that either drew them into somnolence or sent them up to bed rekindled, depending on what they had been doing beforehand.

'It's such a sensible hour, five o'clock to six,' Rachel commented. 'I wonder why it seems suitable here and not at home.'

'The French organize their work round their love lives, and the English the other way round, that's why.'

Tom ran his finger down her stomach, tracing a pale line of scar. 'What's this one for?'

'Caesarian. Christian. He was lying the wrong way. His limbs were at funny angles, an arm here, a leg there. He's always been gawky.'

She no longer minded about her body, nor about her age.

'It's funny with children,' she said. 'They are born exactly how they continue to be. And you can tell their characters by the expression in their eyes as babies; that never changes. Were yours the same?'

'I haven't thought about it,' he admitted. 'Perhaps women notice things like that.'

He paused, and she sensed she had touched on a raw nerve for some reason.

'The trouble is, I don't know them well enough. Being away half the time – they're fairly undisciplined and very affectionate,' he added, swinging his legs out of bed.

She watched him at the window, rubbing his hair thoughtfully, his mind elsewhere.

'You're not decent,' she said. 'People will see over the sill. What's our view like?'

'An orchard, and a meadow to one side with horses. Hills in the distance, downland, I should imagine. Oh, and right below us a walled courtyard and tables laid for dinner. What's the time?'

'Half-past six. What's today?'

'I haven't the least idea.' They laughed. He had returned to her. 'Why ask such difficult questions?'

'The days and nights here seem to run into each other, they seem endless—'

'I hope you don't mean that?'

'In the best possible way, I mean. Time standing still, and reality too far away to matter.'

'This is real,' he said, 'and this and this.'

'Oh, yes,' she said. 'Yes.'

There was silence, broken only by the evening murmur of wood pigeons.

She slept, in between times, as she had not slept for years, sinking to an untramelled dreamless depth.

Tom's sleep was not always so untroubled. He shifted and turned and occasionally flung out an arm, mumbling. Waking confused, he would touch her carefully, comforted by the warmth of her oblivious body. For him, reality could not be so easily ignored.

Every other evening he slipped away at the end of dinner on some pretext or other, to telephone home. He had not told Rachel, reluctant for his motive to be misconstrued. Standing now in the glass kiosk by the reception desk, this furtiveness struck him as mad. Rachel must be put in the picture; the trouble was, he disliked the idea of discussing Hana. It was his problem; Rachel should not be bothered with it. It wouldn't be fair to lumber her, he told himself, knowing perfectly well she would be understanding and probably constructive. It was he who did not want their present existence disrupted, wanted the warm flow of it to continue; needed this period of false tranquillity to think. He dialled, got the engaged tone, hung up and waited in the airless cubicle.

Recent conversations between Hana and himself left him with a sick sensation of *déjà vu*. Tears and incoherences, bringing back memories of the bleak corridors of the psychiatric ward where she had been confined for three months. Deep depression, according to the doctors. The unpredictability of his work, her East German upbringing, the stress of settling in a strange country, a genetic instability; any of these could be the cause. They did not know. She recovered, or appeared to, with the help of medication and analysis. Damn the cause; his sense of failure was the same.

He wondered whether the fact that he had killed on her behalf disturbed her more than she would admit. They never discussed it now. Perhaps that was a mistake. He no longer loved her, although he had been, must have been, desperate for her once. Emotions should not evaporate that easily; it showed a weakness in him that might be repeated. He imagined a falling away of his wanting Rachel, and lifted the receiver from its socket hurriedly.

Through the glass he suddenly caught sight of Rachel's eyes, pale grey in her small, tanned face, looking at him in clear contempt; only for a second, before the imagery resolved itself into the receptionist, wearing her habitual expression.

A child's voice answered; Cassie, his eldest, impatient to get back to the television. 'Mummy's asleep. D'you want to speak to Granny?'

'No. No, not really. Is everything all right? Is Mummy all right?'

'Yes, of course. Daddy, I'm missing a spooky film.'

'You should be in bed.'

'Kate is. Mummy said I could watch. Can I go now?'

'Yes. Good night, darling. Lots of love—'

The line went dead.

Rachel was reading when he returned to the table. 'Tummy trouble?' she asked, smiling across a bowl of clove-scented pinks.

'No. I was asking at the desk about things to see, places of interest and so on.'

She put the book in her handbag. 'Ah. Only I wondered. You wander away quite often.'

'I'm fine.' He covered her hand where it lay on the tablecloth, very brown on pristine white. 'Just tired. Let's go to bed.'

The Loire Valley formed a demarcation line in Rachel's mind; the place where the first stretch of their journey was almost over and, with it, complete and unquestioned happiness. This was how she looked back on it, later. At the time it was merely the Loire, somewhere she had always wished to visit and never had. It remained side by side in her memory with a lunch, the best of the entire holiday, eaten on a river bank.

They had come upon it by accident, Tom having grown irritated by the same car sitting on their tail for the past half-hour.

'I'm going to lose him,' he muttered, swinging off the road and on to an unpromising cart-track flanked by nettles. 'Lunch,' he said firmly.

'What, here? Tom!'

It led to better things. The river, a tributary, trickled haphazardly over round white stones. Weeping willows leaned towards the water and curtained off the sun. There was the flip-flap-splosh of moorhens and rising fish. There were flies.

'Nothing's perfect,' he pointed out, picking huge dock leaves to use as fans.

'We could cool the wine in the water if we had some string. Do you have any string?'

'No, darling. Any more than I have a Swiss army knife or the SAS survival handbook. How about you?'

'No call for sarcasm,' she said and, taking the bottle, slid down the bank to the river's edge. 'At least I have ideas.' She wedged the wine amongst the reeds, standing calf-deep in shock-cold water.

'Ooh, that's lovely.' The river eddied around her legs, mud oozed between her toes. 'You should try it.'

'Come back. I'm lonely.'

She took a step, slipped on one of the smooth stones and sat down with a splash.

'That settles it,' she said, while Tom rolled about laughing on the grass above. One by one she removed skirt, shirt, pants and bra and flung them at him in a sodden bundle.

'Spread them out to dry, when you've finished

mocking me,' she shouted, 'callous bastard,' and lay back to let the water flow over her.

'There's someone coming,' he teased her.

'Don't care.'

'Very refreshing,' she said, clambering back to him eventually with difficulty, clutching the wine bottle. 'Open it. I'm longing for a drink.'

'Are you having lunch like that?' he asked, as she lay stretched out to dry alongside her clothes.

'I have no alternative. Any complaints?'

'None, except I can't promise to concentrate on the food.' He leaned on an elbow watching her. 'You look like a siren of Lorelei. Very beautiful and more tempting than a ham sandwich.'

'When are you going to open that bottle?'

Sun falling like coins on the water and beneath the willows, the cold sharp taste of wine, tiny creatures crawling over bare feet, Tom's hand resting warm against her cool skin; memories building themselves up in her mind, layer upon layer.

'Amazing having this to ourselves,' she said after a while, lighting a cigarette to keep the midges at bay. 'Almost too good to be true.'

He did not answer. He was looking across the river to where two stationary figures, a man and a woman, were staring from the opposite bank, seemingly mesmerized. He out-stared them, and they faded hurriedly into the camouflage of trees. Rachel giggled.

'Obviously they've never seen a naked woman and a clothed man sharing a ham sandwich. I've shocked them. They look ultra-respectable.'

Tom said without smiling, 'They're the couple in the Volvo, the one that tailed us for miles.'

'Really?' She reached for her dried clothes. 'Oh well, I don't suppose we'll see them again. I hope not. It might be a bit embarrassing.'

He grunted, and she saw he was not with her any more, he was not listening. Some of the joy had drained out of the day, for no particular reason.

She supposed it was inevitable that the voyeurs from the wood should land up at their hotel; as if on purpose to annoy rather than coincidence. She had chosen the hotel so carefully, too, for its situation and its load of knives and forks.

Tom seemed to be developing a fixation. There was no sign of the Volvo during the afternoon's driving, but he glanced constantly in the mirror, his eyes inscrutable behind dark glasses, so that she began to feel as if she was taking part in some corny film. The charm of their bedroom, when they finally reached it, had a soothing effect on both of them, and after a shower and a drink from their supply of whisky, he was back to normal.

She put on the white crêpe dress that he liked particularly, and wandered to the window; and there below her in the courtyard was the wretched car. Too late to guide Tom away; he was by her side, looking down.

'Will you do me up, please?' she asked, and he turned slowly and closed the zip on her dress, saying, 'It's a German number-plate. Berlin,' as though it was explanation enough.

It was no use getting cross. 'Yes, darling, so I saw. What of it?'

'Typical of the Germans to follow one round like fucking sheep.'

'Oh, come on, Tom. They're tourists like us. They probably feel the same way about the British.'

She stared up at him, rubbed his cheek to get the tautness out of it, worried despite herself.

'You're spoiling everything,' she said. 'It's ridiculous. Can we please forget it?'

'Sorry,' he said, and put his arms round her, and she felt him pretend to relax.

They had dinner in a garden which lived up to her expectations. Fuchsias and lobelia spilled over the sides of terracotta urns and a small fountain splashed peacefully in the centre of a lily pond. The Germans were seated at a fair distance, late-middle aged and unremarkable, intent on their food. Tom's surreptitious surveillance of them stopped after Rachel kicked him fairly gently under the table, fixing him with a warning stare over the rim of her glass. He had learnt to respect that expression. Her eyes changed colour, turned dark and steely, and lost their amazing clarity. It was not difficult to switch his thoughts over and concentrate on her in the low-cut dress, her slim arms the colour and texture of a brown hen's egg. Nevertheless, that night he went to bed more than a little drunk.

The tour of Dutch and English moved slowly from room to room of the château. They gazed obediently at pictures, at the fine double staircase and the mouldings of the ceilings, listening to the bored spiel of the guide. Tom excused himself, left Rachel to complete the course and drifted by devious routes into the grounds. His head ached.

Lawns sloped expansively and gently towards the

river, more or less hidden from view by giant cedar trees, their lower branches sweeping the springy grass. He sat himself down on a stone seat and lit a cigarette, watching two peacocks demolishing a shrub for lunch. He thought of Rachel. They had talked about a lot of things last night; he wished that one of them had been the cause of his fears. They must seem irrational, verging on the insane, without an explanation, but he found the words impossible to utter.

Rachel, I think you should know I killed an East German border guard some years ago. I shot him at point-blank range and left him lying in a Berlin sewer. I hope this won't make any difference to our relationship. For Christ's sake! How could one say that in cold blood? (Cold blood; what a pun.) He would have to break down completely, sob on her breast.

Not a killing in the course of duty. A civil crime. A murder. And he was young, Rachel, very young, no more than nineteen . . .

It was unlikely he would ever tell her. He was sweating; he wiped his palms on the rough stone.

The boy would not have hesitated to shoot him first had he been given the chance. The border guards were murderers themselves on a grand scale; they had forfeited the right to be pitied or regretted. Strange that these facts had no power to reduce his guilt. He shouldn't give a toss. Yet the enormity of what he had done had taken years to seep up in him, and with it an obsessive fear of being found out. Perfectly feasible, if someone took it into his head to investigate; detection had become a sophisticated art. He looked unseeingly towards the grey elegance of the château's façade.

A way must be found to live with all this. He could

not continue to jump at shadows, seeing menace in each bloody tourist with the wrong number-plate. It was ironic to fear the law rather than old adversaries put out of business by the collapse of the Cold War. He wished he had a faith so that he could shift this load on to someone else's shoulders. He wished, but not strongly enough to do anything about it, that he had not let Rachel become more and more a necessity in his life.

At least she knew now about Hana. Last night he had made his way unsteadily towards the telephone booth and Rachel diverted him, pushing him giggling up the stairs and on to the bed.

'I shouldn't ring her tonight, while you're pissed.' She pulled his shoes off. 'You've only missed one night, after all.'

This sobered him. 'You know, then?'

'Of course.' She shot him a look of pity and went downstairs to fetch black coffee.

'I'm wide awake now,' he said after two cups, 'and I can't make love. I'd be an abysmal failure.'

'It's not something we have to do,' she said calmly. 'Why did you make such a secret out of ringing her?' she added, lying beside him on the bed.

'I was afraid you would read something into it that wasn't there.'

'You mean, I'd be jealous?'

'Roughly that, yes.'

'I'm jealous anyway,' she said. 'Telephoning her doesn't make much difference.'

'You have no reason to be. I don't love her; I'm sorry for her.' One day, she thought, he may say that about me.

'I mind about any woman in your past,' she

said, 'especially one with a face like Hana's.'

He took her hand, held it lightly in his. 'Silly Rachel.'

'You're worried about her,' she said, making a statement, 'worried she's having a crisis.'

'On the verge, yes.' He sat up and reached for the coffee pot. 'Do you want any more of this?'

'No, thanks, it's cold.'

He drained his cup and made a face.

'The trouble is, the current lover has walked out, I believe.'

'Did she love him?'

'I don't know. But he represented stability; a rock in her life, he seemed that sort of man. Obviously I got him wrong.' He grinned. 'Rodney,' he said inconsequentially.

'That's his name?'

'Mmm. Rod-the-sod.'

'We shouldn't laugh. Poor Hana.'

Breaking a moment's silence, she asked, 'How did you meet her?'

'Behind a check-out till at a supermarket in the Eastern Bloc. Sounds like consequences, doesn't it? I went in to buy cigarettes—'

'What were you doing there? Surely, based in the West—'

'Various things took me over the Border every so often. She gave me the wrong change,' he said. 'She was ill, had a bad go of flu. I got hold of some antibiotics for her . . .'

Rachel imagined the pale, lovely face, the hollow eyes, the cough; like Bohème.

'And so on,' he said vaguely. 'One thing led to another.'

'Marriage, obviously.'

'Not for some time. I had to get her out of the East first of all; little things like that.' His voice was tinged with irony. 'Her mother didn't like it, the only child running away.'

'And then?'

'That's it, really. You know the rest.'

'You haven't told me how you got her across the Border.'

'Forged papers, the usual thing. There's nothing much to tell.'

Or nothing more that he is prepared to give away, she thought. It can't have been that simple.

'It's an unusual way of starting off a life with someone,' she said. 'A great deal more romantic than Henry and myself.'

'Is that how it sounds? It didn't continue; look at us now.'

'Perhaps,' she said in neutral tones, 'you shouldn't have come away if you're riddled with anxiety.'

He turned his head to look at her. 'And stayed at home riddled with misery instead?'

He pulled her towards him so that her head rested on his shoulder.

'I couldn't have managed that,' he added.

'Are you going to go on worrying about her for the rest of the holiday?'

'No,' he said. 'Not if you don't.'

That was the moment when he should have told everything. There might not be another opportunity.

Someone was calling. He raised his head from contemplation of his shoes and saw Rachel walking towards him across the lawn, her blue shirt brilliant against the grey of the château walls. She looked about seventeen at a distance, making him feel years older.

She kissed him, running a finger down the folds of his cheek.

'Come up on the ramparts with me. The view must be terrific.'

Louisa wondered whether she had imagined a false note in her mother's voice, over-emphasizing how marvellous everything was. But then, it had not been a good line, nor an ideal moment since she had asked people to supper, the nut roast was due to be removed from the oven and her hair was still wet. She tried not to hustle Rachel, but neither did she encourage a lengthy discourse. She felt slightly guilty about it afterwards.

It was a spur-of-the-moment party. She missed Vijay more than she had bargained for; and there were contributory factors. She had started to find the atmosphere in the house increasingly oppressive. There was a sense of being pressurized, hemmed in as by a crowd. She would wake in the night unable to breathe, once or twice leaping out of bed in a panic, imagining something to be wrong with Robin, only to find him sleeping peacefully on his back like a starfish. Until recently, she had been relaxed about living amongst ghosts, and feeling slightly superior that she could sense and accept them while others could not. Now it had ceased to be amusing.

Searching through the desk she found Rachel's research notes. One of the first entries was the date of Lisa Kincade's death; the seventeenth of July, nineteen forty-three. Forty-nine years ago almost to the day, it now being the ninth of July. She sat chewing her thumbnail and debating the significance, if any, of this information. In any case, there was nothing to be done about it until Rachel returned and her obligations were over.

The house was silent. Robin was having his rest. Even Morecombe showed a distaste for the drawing-room these days and preferred his basket in the kitchen. She felt very much alone, yet aware of being watched, and got up abruptly, seized with the longing to have a noisy, live crowd of friends round her, who would drink a bit too much and laugh at their own stupid jokes. She had been solitary for too long; had not spoken to anyone for days except Consuelo and Robin, and their conversation was limited. Two hours on the telephone arranging everything brought definite relief. The lot she had invited could be relied upon to shatter the worst of atmospheres.

She was right. Standing next morning surrounded by dirty glasses and heaped ashtrays, she felt lighter, as if a space had been cleared for her. She threw open the french windows and breathed deeply; her mouth tasted foul but it was a small price to pay under the circumstances. Putting as many glasses on to a tray as possible, she paused before staggering down the stairs to the kitchen. The room smelled disgustingly of old wine dregs and stale smoke, but there was not a trace of Turkish tobacco or musk-laden scent.

'Quite right, too,' she muttered aloud. 'Whose house is it anyway?'

There was no saying how long this exorcism would last, but even a day without them was a relief, and Rachel would not be gone for ever.

She remembered her mother's telephone call as she washed up, and wished now that she had not been in such a tearing hurry to get rid of her.

Some days just did not have the right aura; whatever one planned went flat, Rachel decided, as she peeled off her clothes and waited for Tom to finish his shower. He had disappeared to the bathroom in the same subdued mood that had accompanied him for most of the day. It was a side of him she had not seen before. But wasn't that the whole idea behind this journey, getting to know one another? She fished the bottle of whisky out of the cupboard and eyed it with a certain longing.

It was partially her fault. She had been mistaken in dragging him hither and thither, thirsty for history; first to view the château, and in the afternoon *les caves* with their wall paintings. He had hardly glanced at them, standing beside her in the vaulted dimness one moment and vanishing the next. She found him outside in the sunlight, pale and sweating. Claustrophobia, he had said, enclosed spaces; stupid, but there it was.

Even lunch, at a promising little café in a village square, was a disappointment with its tough steak and surly proprietor. And last of all, the lovely but dilapidated house she had taken it into her head to wander around, having see the photograph in an estate agent's window.

'Oh Tom, do let's. Please.'

The house reclined in the sun, long, low, graceful like a faded beauty, its windows mirrored in an ornamental lily pond. They explored the twelve bedrooms and the ballroom, peering under dustsheets at pieces of furniture left behind to rot. Damp patches showed through once elegant wallpaper of grey and gold. There was a strong smell of decay, and their voices and footsteps echoed under the high ceilings. Outside they sat on the steps of the terrace flanked by chipped and crouching lions, and looked down a deeply wooded valley steeped in shades of green. In the near distance a lake lay motionless and solid as a silver tray.

'How would you like to live here?' she asked; and then wished she had not because it sounded too much like a serious invitation.

'Live here?' he repeated. He found a stone and flung it far out over the lily pond in an arc. 'It's infested with dry rot for a start. It would cost a bomb to put right—'

'I thought it was rising damp.'

'Whatever.'

'It's very beautiful,' she said, 'you must admit.'

'Very. But it happens to be in France. England is what I want when it comes to putting down roots. I've had enough of abroad.'

'In that case,' she said coldly, 'why did you bother to come?'

She got to her feet, dusting crumbs of cement from her skirt briskly as if about to leave. He grabbed her arm.

'Don't walk away, Rachel. I wasn't talking about holidays; they're a different matter altogether. This one in particular is – special,' he said diplomatically.

She subsided against one of the lions and stared away from him.

'You could have fooled me,' she said.

He moved, sat down on the rear end of the lion and put his arms round her.

'I'm sorry, darling. I know I'm about as much fun as a clockwork mouse without the key at the moment. It won't last, I promise.' She snorted and relaxed against him.

'I was only fantasizing over the house. Playing games. You like that as a rule.'

'I know, I know—'

'Henry . . .' she said, and stopped.

There was silence. She felt his arms loosen.

'Well, go on. What about Henry? Are you making comparisons?'

'Of course not.'

But she was. Henry had swum in and out of her thoughts several times during the last few days. It was inevitable; she had been doing exactly the kind of things they had once enjoyed together. He was at his best on holiday; it had always amazed her that someone so restless and intolerant should manage to relax completely when given no choice. For those two or three weeks he reverted very nearly to the man with whom she had fallen in love, so that even when the love had turned to something close to hate, she understood why she had married him. Tom's metabolism seemed to work in reverse, winding itself up with each passing hour.

She heard the click of the lighter as he lit a cigarette.

'Go on,' he repeated. 'Let's hear about Henry.'

'You're cross.'

'I'm not; just resentful of anyone who had you to himself for years – in every sense.' He stood up, taking her by the hand. 'I'm getting a sore bum. Let's walk.'

They skirted the low wall of the pool, walking in the direction of the lake. Long feathery grasses, the overgrowth of what had once been a lawn, brushed against her bare legs. Butterflies hovered above wild flowers; poppies, scabious, meadowsweet. There was a continuous murmur of bees, and the scent of thyme, and another, more pungent smell that possibly came from the lake itself.

'Henry would have been in his element here,' she said. 'That's why I thought of him. He was a different person on holidays; quite liveable with, really.'

'And at other times?'

At other times he was Henry, successful darling of the academic fraternity, faithless, cruel and possibly perverted. A bastard.

'Look,' she said, pointing. 'There's a gazebo on the bank opposite.' She bent to pick a blue flower and fixed it through a buttonhole.

'I do find it difficult to talk about him,' she added.

She had gone on loving him for a long time; long after there was any reason for doing so. Hanging on to the last shreds of that original bliss until Alison liquidated it once and for all. All she had left was a mistaken integrity over maligning him in death.

'When you think about him,' Tom said, 'and refuse to tell me a thing, it makes me uneasy. I'm left to imagine—'

'Imagine what?'

'Superior intellect, looks, expertise; a man who made you so gloriously happy you can't forget him; ever.'

She burst out laughing.

'What's funny?'

'You're hopelessly wide of the mark. Do you think we could get through that undergrowth to reach the gazebo?'

'I shouldn't think so . . .'

But she had already started, wandering off towards the fringe of the lake where the grasses grew waist high, interlaced with all manner of other vegetation, and he had to hurry to catch her up.

'Rachel! Will you stop being enigmatic?'

'We can still talk as we go,' she said over her shoulder, 'only it'll be easier if we're side by side.'

The grass now sprouted from large, hidden tussocks against which he kept stubbing his toes.

'Shortish, thin, dark, a face like one of those stone gargoyles we saw on the roof of the château,' she said rapidly as if wanting to get rid of the words. 'And pointed ears. Pointed ears are supposed to be a sign of unreliability, according to my mother. But she told me too late, I'd already married him. Expertise in his chosen field: excellent; Victorian novelists and poets, that is – and in everything else, pretty poor.' To mention the exception would be tactless. 'Women were mad about him, and he made the most of it.' She drew breath. 'There you are; a thumbnail sketch of my late husband.'

A right little sod, thought Tom.

'And you'd include yourself amongst those women, I suppose?' he asked.

'I was far more deluded,' she said, frowning into the sun. 'I married him. I think I could have been quite a good historian; but I don't regret the children.'

The lake at close quarters no longer looked undisturbed. The surface was broken by tiny circles where fish were rising for insects. She stopped to watch, saying conversationally, 'I found him in bed with someone. Our bed. I wanted to kill her, but not Henry. Odd, really.' She turned and smiled. 'Lucky I didn't have an offensive weapon to hand or I'd be serving a life sentence. She was called Alison. I never did like the name.'

'What did you do?'

Privately appalled, Tom could not think of a sensible or comforting remark.

'I stood there looking ridiculous. Henry thought I was spending a day and a night in the country, but it was cancelled. I'd been shopping in Peter Jones and my hands were full of carrier bags, pillows I'd bought in the white sale. I suppose I could have flung those at her, but it would have been too much like a dorm romp.' She sighed. 'My nose needed blowing, so I dropped the bags and blew it. That's all. Then I left the room and went and made myself a cup of tea. I felt numb; the reaction came later,' she told him, 'delayed shock.'

Tom waited, saying nothing.

'My only consolation was, Alison looked even more idiotic than I did; pop-eyed and speechless.'

'And Henry?'

She considered. 'He lit a cigarette and stared at the ceiling as if nothing had happened. He was good at that sort of thing, ignoring disasters.'

Tom in silence contemplated the inexplicable attraction of the complete shit.

'It was quite funny, really,' she said. 'You've got to laugh.'

'But you're not, you're crying. Rachel darling—'

'Not much.'

He cupped her face in his hands, kissing at the tears.

'Why didn't you leave him?'

Why not? She could not explain. It seemed easy enough in retrospect, with two of the children adult enough to be absorbed in their own lives; and Christian, who at fourteen was frightened of Henry and would have blessed her for the decision. But she lacked the guts. Bad marriages were no different from good ones in that they provided security of a sort.

'I lost my nerve,' she answered. 'No-one and nowhere to run to; simple as that.'

'No-one?'

'Not without involvement and I wasn't capable at the time. And there was the house. I was frightened of losing it for good.'

The significance of the house slotted into place in his mind; ladybird, ladybird, fly away home, your house is on fire and your children all gone. Had she also peopled it with ghosts for company?

'I should have been around,' he said. 'My timing was always dreadful.'

'Oh, I'm not so sure,' she said surprisingly. 'I might not have been ready for you.'

Unbelieving, he asked, 'Don't tell me that after all you actually miss him?'

She recalled suddenly, vividly, Henry slumped forward amongst the breakfast things, an overturned cup dripping tea on the floor and a bar of sunlight striking the back of his head like an accusatory finger. The words 'a merciful release' had repeated themselves over and over in her brain. She wanted to whoop and shout with the heady sense of freedom as it gradually seeped into her.

'I cried when he died,' she said, 'but that was from relief, I'm afraid.' She waved a hand at the gazebo. 'I don't think I can be bothered to go that far.'

As they slowly retraced their steps she said, 'It's a funny thing; there I was with freedom handed to me on a plate, and I didn't know what to do with it. I was afraid.' She smiled. 'Everything's changed since then, of course.'

'Of course,' he echoed, nervously aware of responsibility.

A heron rose quite close to them and flapped its way clumsily down the valley.

'The lake must be well stocked with fish; trout, perhaps. You don't see herons without a good feeding-ground near by.'

In the car on the way to returning the keys to the estate agent, he said, 'One could make a splendid trout farm out of that place.'

'Is that your secret ambition?'

'It is, as a matter of fact. Would you mind living on a fish farm, if I transported your crumbling mansion to Wiltshire?'

She laughed. 'Now who's fantasizing?' she said. But the ridiculous suggestion made her happy, all the same.

Her guilt over Louisa, and the sweeping under the carpet of those feelings, were not mentioned. Everyone kept something back during confession time. She was quite aware of Tom doing the same.

He came from the bathroom refreshed and smelling

of aftershave, and in a better frame of mind.

'Whisky. What a good idea.'

They sat drinking peacefully in the pretty bedroom with its golden sloping floors, its brass bedstead, its large blue-and-white jug of gladioli.

'I think we should start early tomorrow,' he said. 'It's a long drive.'

It occurred to her that he was relieved to be going, anxious to move on.

The owners of the Volvo left the next morning as well. Rachel stood at the window, cradling a cup of coffee and watching them load expensive-looking luggage into the boot. A prosperous suburban couple, seeing something of the world while young enough to enjoy it. Heading for Provence, so they had divulged at dinner in a last minute burst of garrulity; quite oblivious of the unexplained aggro they had caused.

Louisa no longer felt safe. There came a day when she was scared to walk downstairs. On the face of it this appeared absurd in a house where the sun streamed in through open doors and windows, and neighbours' gardens were alive with the sound of children at play. But inside there was no air, and the pressure had become intensely physical, as if she was being pushed by unseen forces. Sometimes the pressure would confront her so that she had to drive herself forwards; sometimes it came from behind, which was why she became frightened of the stairs, in case she fell. Night was the worst, waking abruptly, half-suffocated by a dead weight across her chest. Robin seemed to be affected also, grizzling during the day and crying at night, although the heat might be a possible cause where he was concerned. Ninety degrees was seriously hot for London. They spent as much time as possible in the garden, but meals had to be prepared, bathrooms used, beds straightened. Going indoors had grown to be a nightmare.

She thought of exorcism, and wondered how one went about it. To contact the local vicar was probably the answer, but since Rachel went to church only two or three times a year, it seemed presumptuous to call on him to provide this service. Louisa attempted to question Consuelo on the subject, but either she did not understand or did not wish to, and went about her work singing, oblivious to any abnormality. More-combe refused to be coaxed upstairs to sleep on Louisa's bed, where he would have provided some sort of comfort. He kept resolutely to the kitchen and the garden which seemed the only unpolluted areas.

Six days remained to Rachel's return. The limit to Louisa's endurance came on finding the toy cat with glass eyes lying in Robin's cot. Rachel kept it on her bedside table. Louisa opened her mother's clothes cupboard, flung the cat inside and locked the doors, pocketing the key. She sat down at the dressing-table, shaking, and stared at her face in the looking-glass. It appeared to have shrunk, to be pinched with nerves. I can't stand another moment of this, she told herself. The solution was obvious; pack up and go home. She had done her best, but enough was enough. The plants might die from drought, but Morecombe would not, she would take him with her. Arriving at this decision brought an instant flood of relief, and she marched upstairs to fetch Robin who was yelling his head off. He cried on and off for the whole afternoon while she threw things into suitcases and plastic carriers, impatient to be gone. She realized how lucky she had been to have a contented baby up until now; perhaps he was teething, those back molars which were said to give the most trouble.

When she held him he felt burning hot to the touch. She left the confusion of packing and took him downstairs to the paddling pool, removed his cotton shorts and lowered him into the water. He screamed, and went on screaming. Windows shot open and heads appeared, looking to see what the fuss was about. Louisa stopped making soothing noises, wrapped him in a towel and stuck her tongue out at the curious faces before carrying him out of sight. That evening Rachel's telephone call went unanswered. Louisa was sitting beside a cot in the Westminster Childrens Hospital, sick with worry, while her sedated baby slept at last, his temperature a terrifying hundred and five degrees.

Chapter Ten

Rachel stared into her wineglass, at a loss as to how to begin; sitting in Robert Kincade's garden, she was consumed with embarrassment. It seemed a gross imposition all of a sudden, to walk self-invited into this man's home and ask personal questions about his past. A particularly nice man, moreover, who was doing his best to put her at her ease; one of those rare people in whom you might automatically confide, given normal circumstances. She sipped at the wine and made a complimentary remark about its quality, clinging desperately to banalities.

Tom had gone for a walk; it would be less inhibiting for her to be alone, he suggested beforehand. Robert Kincade sat at right angles, presenting her with the ruined side of his face, the one puckered and distorted by the flames of his aircraft before he baled out. The eyelid and the corner of the mouth were drawn downwards in a permanent grimace so that full-face he gave the impression of two separate people, one optimistic, the other sad like a clown. She realized her expression had registered shock as they met, before she could stop herself; but he seemed unaware. Perhaps he was used to the reaction.

They had talked about his life here in Montmiral, of his wife Véronique who had died of cancer two years ago, of the antique shop he owned in the village, and his painting, and the restoring of furniture. They were running out of social exchanges. He lifted the bottle of wine questioningly.

'I wonder if you would like a whisky instead?' he asked gently.

'No, this is lovely, thank you.'

She could see as he turned to her, the unharmed bit of his mouth crooked upwards in a smile.

'You're nervous,' he said. 'I thought it might help. It strikes me you haven't done this sort of thing before; interviews and so on. That *is* why you came, isn't it?'

She nodded and sank back, trying to lose herself in the squashy cushions of the garden chair.

'I've decided it's impossible; an invasion of privacy. I should have realized . . .'

She could feel his eyes on her, summing her up as an idiot.

'I'll finish my drink if I may, and then we'll leave you in peace.'

'That would be a pity.'

'Why?'

'Because I'm enjoying myself,' he said. 'It doesn't upset me to talk about my first wife, if that's what is worrying you. If it did, I would have said so. You have to remember it's forty-nine years ago. Given that length of time, events lose their reality; they become in a funny way like someone else's story, d'you see?' In the same considering voice he added, 'I didn't quite gather from your letter. You're not a professional researcher, are you?'

'No,' she replied. Time for the truth. 'At least, I am in fact, but not at this moment. This is on my own account.' She smiled awkwardly. 'It's difficult to explain.'

He shifted his chair to face her. 'Why don't you start at the beginning?'

She had intended to give him a brief outline and found herself telling him the lot, things she had not told Tom, laying herself open to ridicule. Tales of the supernatural; hardly the stuff for realists, for men who had fought wars. He was a good listener, sat without stirring. An extremely still man, she thought, as she sat back and waited to be told it was ludicrous.

He merely said, 'I understand now. What you want from me is to fill in the gaps for you.'

He was not as she had pictured him. She watched him walk away to find a second bottle of wine, a tall, lanky figure younger than in her imagination, his dark hair hardly touched with grey. She had been circumspect about Lisa's baby; he might be ignorant of one having existed and she did not want to be the informant.

'Tell me more about Lisa,' she asked him as he pulled the cork from the new bottle.

'She was a beauty,' he said, 'which is quite different from being beautiful. Each decade has its prototype, and Lisa fell into the category of the time; blonde, even features, blue eyes. An English rose, in other words.' He tasted his wine. 'A perfect face but static. I never saw it light up; or at least, not for me,' he added.

'Were you in love with her?'

He considered. 'No,' he said. 'I thought I was at the time, no doubt. But later, when I met Véronique, I realized it was a fallacy. We were children, Lisa and I, grabbing at a bit of mutual comfort. A mistake; twenty-one, I ask you!'

He stared at his hands, folded before him on the table, one of them puckered and shiny like his face. Perhaps, Rachel wondered, the whole of that side of him – she shied away from the thought.

'I spent years worrying about how to tell her, if I survived. My one hope was that she wouldn't be able to cope with this.' He touched his face. 'It was quite likely I *wouldn't* survive. Véronique's family kept me for the remainder of the war, at enormous risk to themselves. There were some bad moments. Germans swarmed like bees in the area; and there were certain of the French who would have given up a British pilot only too happily to gain enemy brownie points.'

She tried to imagine the horrors, but sitting here in sun and purple shadow, the velvet lawn curving away from them, they seemed remote and improbable.

'Going home must have been difficult for you, after all that,' she said diffidently. 'And I suppose you didn't know that Lisa had died?'

'I knew before I reached England. I telephoned the Consort Terrace house to find the number no longer existed, so I got in touch with relatives. That was how I learnt about the fire.'

He was quiet for so long that Rachel began to regret all over again having intruded on him.

'I went to stand outside the house,' he said at last. 'I suppose it was a macabre thing to do; a kind of compulsion. There is something pathetic about a building that has lost its roof. I was full of conflicting emotions, pity, horror and, it has to be admitted, a guilty element of relief that I was free to marry

Véronique. I was deeply ashamed; it was a terribly inhuman reaction.'

He paused, indulging in some private reverie.

'So did you go back to France and pick up your life from there?' Rachel prompted him.

'Not at once, I spent some months at the "guinea-pig farm" in East Grinstead.' He glanced at her. 'You know what I'm talking about?'

'It's where they treated the burns cases, isn't it?'

'Right. They did what they could, but the damage was four years old. While I was there, I had plenty of time to think and Lisa's death weighed on my mind. I decided the least I could do before I left for France was to put flowers on her grave, and visit her mother. I didn't relish the thought of meeting Lilian, but it was unlikely I'd have to do so again. Besides, I wanted to know the full story, to be reassured she had not suffered. So that was what I did, and got two versions of what happened. Only one of them matters; that of Codie. She was the cook–housekeeper and solid as a rock.'

'Florence Codie,' said Rachel.

'Really? I never knew about the "Florence", she was always known as Codie. Unfortunately I had to listen to Lilian first. God! That was one of the worst half-hours of my life, hearing Lisa pulled apart by a vitriolic old woman. Lilian was always a heavy drinker. In my absence she had become an alcoholic and, which was far more alarming, seriously unbalanced.'

Rachel was chilled, seeing quite clearly in her mind's eye an ageing Lilian sitting in her eyrie in Sloane Street, deriving pleasure from hurting, while hands like talons gripped the inevitable glass. He must know then, she thought, Lilian must have told him. She waited.

Robert smiled, and she caught a flash of how he was before losing half a face; rather like a handsome bird of prey.

'So you see,' he said, 'I'm quite aware of all that happened in Lisa's life, including the child. You were trying to spare my feelings, weren't you?'

'Something like that,' she admitted.

'What a nice person you are,' he said. 'Shall we stretch our legs, wander round the garden? I can fill in the last bit for you as we go.'

Robert Kincade's house was situated outside the village of Montmiral, in a cleft of hillside that sloped steeply downwards to beech woods. The massive trees were widely spaced and the sun filtered through the upper branches, making filagree patterns across the glades and rides. A designer forest, Tom decided, treading on turf that made no sound; manicured to perfection for some medieval drama where hounds might at any moment come baying, followed by canopied horses and riders with hawks on wrists. There was a hollow silence, a cathedral hush; no rustling of small creatures, no bird-song.

He glanced at his watch, trying to decide if Rachel would have finished her interview. An hour should be sufficient, surely. He felt a mild resentment that someone else was claiming her full attention, which was illogical since it had been his own decision to make himself scarce. Getting up from the tree stump where he sat smoking and enduring the midges, he started slowly to retrace his steps. Three quarters of an hour was up; it would take at least another fifteen minutes to get back. He hoped he was going in the right direction. Bloody silly he would look if they had to come and search for him.

As he walked, he imagined Rachel in the bath, and then in bed, and looked forward to the reality of both.

The sun was sinking and the wood had darkened, the trees changing from majestic friendliness to monochrome, faintly menacing shapes. He quickened his pace automatically. Overhead the branches, laced together against the sky, created the roof to a tunnel. His trainers travelled noiselessly as on carpet. Heaven-sent for assassination, a place like this, he thought casually; no inkling of adversaries, slipping from shadow to shadow until they were at your back. With an effort he prevented himself from looking over his shoulder, until a shot was fired some distance away and a pheasant rose squawking and thrashing from nowhere, putting his heart in his mouth. Bloody bird; he saw that he had arrived at a junction where the paths divided, and he had lost all sense of locality.

Escaping eventually from the trees into the blessing of the evening sun, he stood for a moment at the foot of Robert Kincade's garden. His shirt stuck to his back with sweat. He had gone no distance and at no great speed. At this rate, he told himself, I shall end up in the funny farm instead of Hana. He felt for some reason bitterly ashamed, and when he caught sight of her sitting comfortably at the end of the lawn, unreasonably cross with Rachel.

'This place is haunted, by the way.' Robert paused by the cedar tree. 'A farm labourer murdered his wife a hundred years ago. I've never seen her but I know she's there.'

'Do you mind?'

'She's harmless enough; I suspect rather sad, and for good reason.' They fell into step again, slowly perambulating the walled garden past beds of lilies and hibiscus. Rachel thought of murder victims.

'My mother-in-law was made for haunting,' he said. 'Abominable woman.'

Rachel was about to say, 'I know', realized there was no plausible explanation for that, and asked, 'In what way?'

'Self-centred, dominating and tough as old boots. She was also brave, it has to be said; drove an ambulance during the war. She hadn't a nerve in her body. And she was good-looking, if you like the black-haired witch type. In fact, I managed to get on with her all right in small doses.' He smiled ironically. 'But then, she liked men and wasn't beyond a pass at a younger one.'

'Even one belonging to her daughter?'

'She didn't succeed,' he told her, laughing, and bent to snap off a sprig of lavender. 'But she made Lisa's life a hell; jealous of her, I imagine. Lilian was obsessed with her own looks. Old age was the only thing that terrified her.'

Rachel wondered whether he had married out of kindness; the protective instinct.

'Poor Lisa.'

'I believe,' he said, 'anyway I like to hope, that she found real happiness with her American; short-lived, but the real thing.'

'So he was American?'

'An airman, apparently. She loved him. I had the true story from Codie. She kept her pregnancy to herself, but after the baby was born, she changed her mind and wrote to tell him, wherever he was posted. Six weeks later she was dead. I wept,' he said. 'It seemed such an appalling waste.'

A criminal waste; the phrase occurred to Rachel and remained unspoken.

'And what was Lilian's reaction to Lisa's situation?' she asked.

'In keeping with her character. She was lethal enough about the pregnancy. But after the baby was born, she became paranoid about the child, refusing so much as to look at it. According to Codie, Lisa and the child confined themselves to the top floor for the last few weeks, there on sufferance, while it was arranged that Codie's sister in the West Country should take them in.'

'You would think,' said Rachel, 'that even Lilian would have relented towards the baby. I can understand the antagonism towards Lisa, but not the baby.'

'Ah, there was a very definite reason in Lilian's distorted eyes. The father was coloured, you see, and the child took after him.'

They fell silent. Many inexplicable things whirled round her brain and came to rest the right way up. In the forefront, Robin new-born, his skin smooth and perfect, the colour of *café au lait*.

'They never got to the country,' he said. 'The fire happened only a few days before they were due to leave.'

'And Lisa was killed and the baby was saved?' she said slowly.

'Yes.' He seemed to be thinking. 'I gather the child was sleeping in Codie's room. By Codie's account, Lisa was trapped; the door jammed, perhaps from the heat, I don't know.'

They had completed their circuit of the garden, arriving at the table without noticing.

'By the time they reached her, it was too late,' he ended abruptly.

'Doors don't jam that easily,' she said, and immediately regretted it. 'I'm sorry, I don't know why I said that.'

'I agree,' he said calmly. 'If the door didn't respond to a few kicks, then it was locked. It wasn't locked from the inside because no key was found there. If it was locked from the outside, then it was deliberate.' He topped up their glasses. 'I think we've both worked that out, and you were hoping I would come up with an answer. I can't; I can only surmise.'

Rachel shivered; shadows had lengthened across the grass.

'Is it possible—?'

'Possible that Lilian turned the key on her daughter and left her to die?'

'Yes.'

'Who knows?' he said. 'They say we are all capable of murder under extreme circumstances. And Lilian perhaps more so than most. She was quite unbalanced.'

'It is difficult to believe.'

'I spent a long time thinking about it,' he said, 'to begin with. Then I came to the conclusion that even with proof, of which there is none, Lilian had cheated punishment by dying.' He smiled to himself.

'Although if anyone knows the truth, it's Codie. I always had the feeling she was holding something back.'

'Do you know what became of Lisa's baby?'

'He was legally adopted by his father eventually, and brought up in the States by the grandparents. Codie kept in touch with them for years.'

'And Codie?'

'She's alive, living in a home near Windsor. We still exchange Christmas cards although she's almost totally blind now.' He sighed. 'She's a remarkable woman. I should make the effort to go and see her one of these days.'

'May I go?' asked Rachel. 'I could give her your love.'

'Would you? She has all her marbles, you know, and doesn't get many visitors, I suspect.'

He raised his head, nodded towards Tom's figure wending its way across the lawn.

'He looks ready for a drink,' said Robert.

And bad-tempered, thought Rachel, who had come to recognize the signs.

'You needn't have been so dogmatic,' she told Tom over dinner. 'How do you know I didn't want to stay on?'

'I wanted you to myself,' he said with disarming candour.

'Even so.'

Driving away in the dusk she had glanced back to see Robert silhouetted in his doorway, waving, and felt a sadness for him. He looked suddenly very much alone.

'Stay for supper,' he had suggested after showing them the interior of his house. 'Only an omelette, I'm afraid, but I've got them down to a fine art.'

Before she could open her mouth, Tom said firmly, 'Thanks, but we should be getting back. Rachel's probably tired you out as it is. Another time, perhaps.'

Robert accepted the refusal without fuss and with a cynical gleam in his eye. His sitting-room had white-washed walls and black beams, and enviable pieces of furniture amongst a bachelor's clutter; an overflowing waste-paper basket, discarded newspapers, used mugs. A large bowl of garden roses filled the room with their scent. Several photographs of the same dark-haired woman, Véronique presumably, were placed on well-polished tables.

He gave her Codie's address and his own telephone number, and asked her to let him know the outcome.

'I hope you'll come here again one day,' he said. 'It's been wonderful to meet someone outside this closed community.'

Tom had disappeared for a pee. She sensed the invitation did not include him.

'I'd like that,' she said. 'You've been very kind.' On impulse she kissed him as they said goodbye, standing on tip-toe to reach his cheek.

'You seem to have got to know him extremely well in one afternoon,' Tom remarked, driving too fast up the narrow lane.

Now, on the terrace of the hotel in Montmiral, she made a stab at togetherness.

'I learnt a great deal today,' she said. 'Shall I tell you, or would you be bored?'

'Tell me,' he replied. 'I hate to be left out of things.'

She dissected a grilled sardine carefully.

'No-one's leaving you out. You're being childish.'

It was the sort of remark she might have made to Simon.

'Sulking,' she added.

'I am *not* sulking.'

The waiter brought him a large whisky and he took a mouthful immediately.

'Ah, that's better.'

'Don't act like a martyr. You could have had one with Robert; you were offered it.'

He merely smiled without answering and said, 'Talk away. I'm all ears.'

But she had lost heart in the face of his ill-humour. She heard her voice droning on tonelessly, doubtful whether he was bothering to listen. Far below them, lights pinpricked the night like misplaced stars. Behind her eyes, tears pricked also as the change in him successfully doused her enthusiasm. For one awful moment, she regretted the entire conception of their love.

In bed before him, she hid herself behind a book and pretended to read while he undressed. The lamp shone on his skin in her mind's eye only.

As he climbed in beside her, he said, 'I suppose you'll keep in touch, you and Robert, now you've found a common interest.'

'Probably.' She snapped the book shut and switched out the light. 'Don't tell me you're jealous?'

'Why not? It's a compliment, isn't it?'

'Of someone of seventy-one with a disfigurement? What sort of competition does that present, for Heaven's sake?'

'Bad luck about his face, poor bugger.'

'Yes, it is,' she said with emphasis.

'Still,' he said, 'I dare say it acts as an attraction for some, don't you think? Like duelling scars.'

'That's a nauseating remark.'

'Rachel—'

'Don't bloody touch me.' Her eyes were a cold slate-grey. 'What's got into you?'

She turned her back on him and pulled the sheet over her shoulders as a barricade. Later he broke it down, and her arms went round him of their own volition. But there was no harmony. Whatever ensued was not so much a love session as a battle of wills, a settling of disputes; a thing of discord.

In the morning she felt used and bruised and unaccountably depressed. His sleeping face was unchanged; but she saw him differently, as if a layer of him had been peeled away to reveal a flaw.

Driving away from Montmiral he stopped to take her photograph standing in a field of sunflowers. The blue shirt, he said, amongst all that yellow would be wonderful. He was back on form, happy, elated as he always was when they were moving on, Rachel thought in irritation as she stood smiling foolishly beside the giant flower heads.

In many ways she would have liked to stay for longer at Montmiral. There was a quality of solid reassurance about its ancient walls. Centuries before they had repelled invaders. Now they basked, mellow under the hot sun like war veterans warming their bones, while the only invaders were tourists. And there was an abundance of flowers which should have appealed to Tom; hanging baskets, tubs, urns full of brilliant geraniums and fuchsias up and down the narrow streets where the upper stories of the houses almost touched.

But he did not feel the same way and any insistence on her part would have been misconstrued. She could tell by the way he spread out the map across the bed while they drank their breakfast coffee.

'We'll reach the coast quite easily in one day,' he said.

'No, we won't. I'm fed up with driving.' She kicked a leg out sharply so that the map crackled. It was her turn to be difficult. 'I don't care where we go as long as we get there by lunch-time.' She reached out for the *Michelin*.

'And it had better be *grand confort* because I've no intention of shifting until we leave for home.'

By the time he had finished shaving, and worked out the best tactics for soothing her down, she had chosen Auberge L'Hirondelle between Toulouse and Carcassonne; and by mid-afternoon they were having their first swim in the pool, where swifts darted down to drink in constant flight.

She nursed her frayed temper for a day, but it was no match for Tom at his most endearing. There was little point in pretending to be a block of ice when she could be melted in seconds. She lay in the darkness at peace and on the verge of sleep, and the night before had become, if not exactly erased, so smudged and blurry it was beyond importance.

She had doubts as to whether he would settle to days of complete idleness but she need not have worried.

208

The hotel boasted a miniature botanical garden which took a lot of his entranced attention. He wandered around it with a pocket book of plants, looking things up and reeling off Latin names.

'You should be a botanist, or a landscape gardener,' she told him. 'Much more rewarding than a trout farmer.'

'Not financially,' he said, bending over a wicked-looking cactus. The rest of the time they lay by the pool, reading, swam when the mood took them and ate lunch in the shade of an umbrella. There was not a château within miles, and even if there had been, she had no desire to find it.

'We should have done this sooner,' she said. 'I'd be happy with several weeks of this.'

'Holidays are like that. The best bit comes at the end when you need another. In any case,' he added, offering her a slice of his peach, 'Robert Kincade made the journey necessary.'

She frowned. 'You don't like him, do you?'

'I think he's charming.' His eyes narrowed to blue slits as he laughed at her. 'And I'm not going to start an argument. I behaved badly and I'm sorry about it, and that's that. Resentful was what I felt, excluded, messing about in those bloody woods.'

He put his hand over hers.

'As long as it was worth it, as long as you found what you wanted.'

She was quite proud of her success. If all research was as rewarding, she might be more inspired; but then, she was unlikely to have the help of a Robert Kincade in the future.

Tom said, 'It's an amazing story.'

'Lisa's? Not really. Quite a lot of girls got pregnant by coloured servicemen during the last war.'

'Not that,' he said. 'I was thinking of Louisa and Lisa, both with little brown babies. Doesn't it strike you as a coincidence?'

She ate a peach without answering.

'I haven't upset you again, have I?' he asked.

'No,' she said, 'but it has indeed struck me, and I find it faintly disturbing. Shall we go to the sea tomorrow? I'd quite like a swim in salt water.'

Tomorrow came, and the next day, and they were far too entrenched in their laziness to bother. For the first time he slept later into the morning than she, as if catching up on nights of disturbance. She would watch him reflected in the dressing-table mirror, the shutters closed so as not to wake him; one knee drawn up, his cheek resting on both hands. This was how he lay in deep sleep, the creases of his face ironed out, platinum eyelashes two white lines on sunburnt skin. Whichever devils plagued him, whether it was Hana or the one he had chosen not to divulge, they were dormant for now. It would be nice to think she had something to do with it, but nothing was certain; only that it hurt to love him so badly.

His skin smelt faintly of sun-oil even after showering.

'Is that all you can say?' he asked.

'I like it. In the depths of winter I shall sniff the bottle of Puiz Buin and it will remind me of you.'

'You won't need to be reminded,' he said. 'I shall be there for real.'

They never had their day by the sea. Two days later she was at Toulouse Airport, watching a plane take off, bearing Tom with it, while she waited miserably for the next flight.

She wished the telephone had not been invented. In weeks to follow she saw it as a kind of evil symbol that had divided them. If she had not decided to make a call to Louisa that evening, Tom might not have rung home to learn of chaos. Hana, it transpired, had swallowed a bottleful of tranquillizers or sleeping pills, and her distraught mother was beyond making sense.

Rachel had her own worries. No-one had answered the telephone at Consort Terrace and she was thrown into a state of apprehension. Tom, considering his crisis to be valid and hers non-existent, failed to understand.

'Louisa must have gone out for the evening and taken Robin with her. It's obvious, I don't know why you're bothered.'

Rachel watched him stuffing clothes into a suitcase.

'She wouldn't do that. She'd get a sitter who would have answered.'

'Then perhaps she's returned to her flat. There are many explanations,' he said shortly.

She was silent.

'Look, I'm sorry, but frankly I'm too fraught over the Hana situation to concentrate on supposition.'

Bloody Hana, thought Rachel. She said coldly, 'Why are you packing when you haven't found out about flights yet?'

He paused, ran a hand through his hair, stared at her.

'Because I'm still coming to terms with what's happened.'

211

He fetched the bottle of whisky from the cupboard and poured a measure for each of them.

'It's possible there's a flight tonight. I'll go down and ring the airport now.'

Alone, she drank her whisky standing at the window, trying to make her mind a blank. The night was full of moonlight and velvet warmth and cicadas and peace. Suddenly she wanted to run, longed to be opening the front door to her own home.

'I couldn't get us on the same plane,' he told her. 'I've booked myself on the nine thirty in the morning. Yours goes at four o'clock in the afternoon.' He glanced at her. 'You don't mind, do you, going on the later one?'

She shook her head. 'What shall we do with the car?'

'Oh, God, I don't know.'

He swallowed his drink at a gulp.

'We'll have to find a garage in Toulouse, is all I can think of. Leave here at the crack of dawn. I suppose,' he added, 'you don't feel able to drive home alone?'

'No, Tom. Please don't ask me.'

'All right, all right.'

She said, 'There's Robert. He might look after it for us, if he's willing to fetch it from the airport.'

He was pacing the bedroom, backwards and forwards, staring at the floor.

'You've got his phone number, then?'

'Yes. Why not?'

'Perhaps it's worth a try,' he said reluctantly. 'Perhaps you should ring him straight away.'

She searched in her bag and handed him a piece of paper.

'You do it,' she said. 'It's your car.'

He stood still and gave her a look unlike any she had received from him before.

'Are you being deliberately aggressive?' he asked quietly. 'It doesn't really help, you know. I'd have thought you might have some understanding of what I'm going through.'

'Likewise.' She hated the expression; it slipped through her guard. 'Where is *your* understanding?'

'Rachel, someone may be dying. Groundless fears are hardly comparable, for God's sake.'

'It may seem ridiculous to you,' she said, 'but I care about my children, adult or otherwise.' She took a deep breath. 'And it seems to me that Hana does not. I'm sorry if she's put herself in danger, but suicide is selfish, particularly when you have children. I suppose she's trying to get you back by emotional blackmail.'

He took a step towards her. For a second she thought he was going to hit her; it would have been preferable to chilled fury.

'Are you too bloody thick to realize it's the children I'm worried about? Left alone with a daft old grandmother who hardly speaks a word of English. As for Hana, you know nothing about her, so kindly leave her out of it.'

Rachel proffered the words 'I'm sorry,' but they got lost in his onslaught.

'You know the trouble with you, Rachel? Your children are *all* that matter to you, they and the house and your damned ghosts. You've buried yourself, and I should never have dragged you out because it's too late. You can't face other people's problems, let alone your own, you've forgotten how. The real world scares you. Well, I suggest you return to your cosy little nest, barricade yourself in and stop telling me how to run my life.'

She felt herself disintegrating at this gross injustice; anger and misery bursting inside her.

'That's hot, coming from you. Buried I may have been as you so charmingly put it, but at least I'm not running away. Talk about groundless fears. God knows what yours are but you're scared of your own shadow.'

She burst into tears.

He came to her and put his arms round her, rocking her like a child.

'I'm sorry, sorry, sorry,' he murmured into her hair. 'I'm a shit. I didn't mean any of it, darling. I'm so wound up I don't know what I'm saying; everything's falling apart.'

But the words stuck, his and hers, branded irreversibly on memory. They clung to each other in the night for mutual and impotent comfort. In the opaque light of very early morning, they paid their bill and drove to Toulouse where Tom boarded his plane and Rachel started the desolate wait for Robert. Collecting the car would be no problem, he had said. He would attempt to get there by midday; there would be time for lunch.

Tom looked grey, ill under his suntan.

'You will let me stay on with you? After I've sorted things out?'

'Of course,' she said through dry lips, past crying.

'I love you.' He kissed her hard and was gone. He had promised to telephone that evening, promised to let her know what happened; promised this and promised that. She watched the plane until it was no more than a bright speck of silver lit by the sun, and then turned away hopelessly.

The taxi-driver dumped the last of Rachel's cases in the hall and departed with a cheerful ' 'Bye, luv'. She stood listening, hoping to hear sounds of occupation; but the house had the stillness of desertion. Mail was stacked in neat piles on the table and the air smelt strongly of floor polish, denoting the recent presence of Consuelo. That at least was something for which to be thankful.

She sorted through the letters and bills in search of a message, some sort of clue to Louisa's whereabouts. But, of course, there was nothing; nobody expected this sudden return three days early. She yelled up the stairwell twice, waiting expectantly for an answer. Hot, crumpled and exhausted, she moved to the kitchen and filled the kettle, trying to stifle a growing premonition of disaster. Newspapers were folded on the dresser, today's uppermost. The date rang a bell but she could not identify it. Somebody's birthday, most likely, which she had forgotten.

Mug of tea in hand, she went round throwing open windows and outside doors, letting in turgid city air. The evening was sunless and heavy, as if it might rain. On the bureau in the drawing-room lay her own red exercise book of research notes, and a similar one beside it. Flipping through, she recognized Louisa's writing, large and extravagant. It appeared at a quick glance to be a kind of diary. The last entry was marked July the thirteenth and below it, as if to stress the significance: July the seventeenth, Lisa, underlined. Today was the seventeenth; not a forgotten birthday but a death. Rachel crossed to the french windows. On

215

the lawn below sat a red-and-white paddling-pool half-full of water; filled some days ago judging by the number of drowned insects floating on the surface.

On an impulse she ran downstairs to the washroom. Hanging over the rails of the dryer were various pieces of clothing; Louisa's shirt and trousers, and tiny T-shirts belonging to Robin. They were bone dry. Illness, an accident; she stopped herself. It was useless to panic, there was probably a perfectly simple explanation. If there were no clues in the nursery, she must call Simon, although he was the last person with whom Louisa would communicate.

Upstairs was unbearably hot, all windows sealed. She paused on the first landing to get her breath; overhead a floorboard creaked, then another. Her heart thumped uncomfortably. 'Louisa?' she called uncertainly, her voice croaking. Old houses creak all the time, she told herself firmly, climbing the last flight and turning the handle of the nursery door. She tried it once, twice, three times, pushing with her shoulder. The door was indisputably locked; she stepped back in panic, trying to get her mind under control.

Her immediate coherent thought was of burglars, surprised in the act by her arrival home and taking refuge up here. There was no sign of a break-in, but then there wouldn't be with professionals. She stood silent and listening, preparing to creep downstairs and telephone the police. There was an impression of someone close to the other side of the door, listening as intently. The skin on her back and the palms of her hands started to prickle, and at the same moment she had a clear vision of Lilian Rumbold standing where she was standing now, and Lisa inside the room

216

struggling to escape, while her mother quietly withdrew the key and walked away. Lines zig-zagged up and down before Rachel's eyes; intruders forgotten, she shouted out loud, ejaculated something which she could not afterwards remember.

The lock clicked back suddenly, the handle turned, the door slowly opened and there stood Louisa. Rachel, expecting by now an extraordinary mêlée of thugs and spirits, pushed past her daughter and slid on to the nearest chair, where she waited for the room to stop tilting.

'Why did you lock the damn thing?'

'You might have let me know you were coming back today.'

They spoke at once, the relief of finding each other manifesting itself in anger.

'I always lock myself in when I'm alone,' said Louisa. She would like to have added, Ever since Fa, but what was the point? 'You can see how sensible it is; you might have been a rapist. I thought you were, creeping around like that.'

'I tried to let you know. You weren't here. You can imagine how worried I've been—'

'I've told you for ages, you should have an answerphone,' Louisa lectured her. 'I've been here on and off to get some sleep. Otherwise I was with Robin; he's in hospital. Oh, Ma, he's been so ill. He's in a sort of glass cubicle; it's pathetic.'

'I knew something was wrong. What is it?'

'Measles. His temperature soared and I was terrified. I didn't know what it was so I rushed him off.'

She looks exhausted, thought Rachel with pity.

217

'Poor little boy. He's very young to have measles,' she said. 'Hasn't he been inoculated?'

'Yes, Ma, he has,' Louisa said wearily, 'but you can still get it. It's better than meningitis, which is what they thought in the first place.' She sank on to the bed, yawning. 'God! I'm tired. You woke me up.'

'You go back to sleep.' Rachel got up a trifle unsteadily. 'We'll talk later.'

'I have to get back to the hospital in a couple of hours. Could you wake me?'

'Shall I go instead?'

'No, thanks. They let me stay the night, you see.' Louisa raised her head from the pillow. 'Don't ever ask me to stay here alone again, will you?' she said.

'Because of what's happened?' Rachel was surprised; it was unlike Louisa to be dependent.

'No, not because of Robin. I'm too tired to explain. Some other time. I'm terribly glad you've come back, Ma,' she added, 'but why have you?'

'It's a longish story.'

'Are you and Tom all right – you know?'

'Fine,' said Rachel carelessly, 'fine.'

'Well, you don't look it,' said Louisa bluntly.

Ten days passed before Tom returned to London, during which time he managed to solve, temporarily, some of his problems. His daughters were taken to Greece by friends for a fortnight. He put his mother-in-law Eva on the first possible flight to Germany. He attempted to break down the silent wall of resistance between Hana and the outside world, and listened while the state of her mind was explained to him by two psychiatrists with differing opinions. He arranged for the cleaner to caretake the house while it remained empty. In the spare time left to him, he thought of Rachel with a sense of failure; the kind of desperation felt when, embarked on a journey, you discover something immensely important to you has been left behind.

It seemed to Rachel, as she chopped the ingredients for a salad, that she was suspended between two worlds and belonged to neither of them; an emotional refugee. There was the world that had ended abruptly and uneasily several days ago, and the old one in which she had led her own contented if unexciting existence. She felt equally at odds with both, and full of a lethargy which she suspected to be depression.

Fortunately she was given little time to indulge her feelings. Camilla gave birth to a son two weeks early. Robin was discharged from hospital and Louisa stayed on in the house with him until Vijay's return. Rachel was kept busy cooking, buying woolly toys, visiting the new baby and minding Robin while Louisa shopped. The demand for her attention was excessive, as if the fates had decreed she should be punished for her two weeks of unbridled bliss. On reflection, only a small part of it had been bliss; the first few days in which she and Tom had found complete harmony. The rest of it, she realized now, had been spent worrying about him.

Perhaps, she thought to herself, there were few people on an even keel; men like Robert Kincade, who had suffered and survived to possess an inner calm, a philosophy of acceptance. She sprinkled dill on the lettuce, thinking how peaceful an attitude it must be to live with. On that dreadful day at Toulouse Airport he had taken her to lunch and, although she had not intended to talk much about herself and Tom, he somehow invited confidences.

'Are you planning to marry him?' he asked.

'Oh, I don't think that was ever on the agenda.'

Or only on mine, she thought, staring at her delicious langouste without appetite.

'The age difference . . .' Her voice trailed away.

He did not say anything ridiculous like how marvellous she looked, and he would never have guessed. She knew how she looked. There was nothing like unhappiness for etching in the lines.

'I never thought that mattered,' he said, and then made a curious observation. 'You know, Tom reminds me of certain fliers during the war who lost their nerve. Lack of sleep and facing enemy flak night after night broke them down; it wasn't surprising. Friends used to cover up for them and most of them flannelled through. But they were terrified, and their fear made them ashamed, and shame made them difficult to live with.'

She frowned. 'You mean, Tom may have lost his nerve? But over what? Me?'

He smiled his crooked smile. She had grown used to his face, no longer trying to avoid it with her eyes.

'You're in a better position to answer that than I am,' he told her.

'But I'm not,' she said sadly. 'That's the trouble. I've come to the conclusion I don't really know him.'

She remembered watching Tom's broad shoulders – shoulders made to lean on, to cry on – as he fixed the curtain the very first evening. He had seemed the embodiment of dependability. She had jumped to conclusions. Tipping the salad into a bowl, she was aware of the self-consciousness which accompanied all such household tasks. Tom's words, accusing her of family obsession, served as a constant reminder, and she disliked him for it.

As the days passed without him, her attitude changed subtly. She had said some fairly unforgivable things in return, had goaded him, withheld her sympathy. It was not, after all, his fault that Hana had tried suicide. By the end of the week she had persuaded herself that she was largely in the wrong, and it was up to her if she did not want to lose him. She chose to forget that she had used just such placatory tactics in Henry's case without winning. The solitude of the double bed was no longer a pleasure. She tried to read, and found the ache of his absence intolerable.

A long, chatty letter arrived from Christian. The length and the chattiness were out of character. He had been passed fit for duty and was back with his unit. In September he would be coming home on leave, and he had a surprise for her; one that he hoped would make her happy. The announcement alarmed her. She could think of nothing surprising other than his acceptance into the Catholic faith; only his obvious cheerfulness raised her spirits.

'I've decided to marry Vijay.' Louisa broke the news at lunch as casually as if she intended to buy a pair of new shoes.

'Darling! That's wonderful.'

Rachel got up and kissed her. A moment's stab of envy came and went.

'I'm so pleased. Was it a sudden decision or one that grew on you?'

'Fairly sudden.' Louisa was smiling, something she should do more often, in Rachel's opinion; her face had become radiant as a virgin bride. Louisa, of all peope; no-one was immune, apparently.

'It was while Robin was so ill. I thought he was going to die and Vijay was the wrong side of the Atlantic. By the time I got hold of him, Robin was better. But it made me realize how much I needed him when things got desperate.' She looked at Rachel, her eyes glassy with tears. 'That's all,' she said. 'It may not work; he can be terribly boring when he's in one of his autocratic moods. But I suppose we've got as much chance as anybody else.'

'Of course you have,' said Rachel firmly. She sighed. 'I should have been here myself.'

'Ma, you can't look after us all of the time. You've got your own life to lead.'

'That's roughly Tom's opinion, too.'

'I'll bet it is.' Louisa fixed her with an accusatory stare. 'Is that what the trouble is about?'

'What trouble?' Rachel dissembled. 'I've explained why we had to tear home.'

This is what happened as you got older; it became the children's prerogative to bully and interrogate. Louisa changed her expression to 'you can't fool me' and let the subject go.

'Are you going to visit this Codie person?' she asked. 'Or isn't it worth it now you've learned almost everything you can from Robert Kincade?'

'Not quite everything,' said Rachel. 'I need to talk to her. Besides, I promised Robert.'

But not yet, not while her mind was elsewhere.

'Supposing,' said Louisa, 'you have it confirmed that Lilian was a murderer, what will you do? She's a bit beyond being brought to justice.'

'It will be a sort of justice having found her out.' Rachel lit a cigarette. 'And perhaps it will put Lisa to rest,' she said, 'to know that we know.'

'She already is at rest,' said Louisa. 'They've gone. Ever since I took Robin to hospital there hasn't been a sign of them. And I've worked out why. They weren't trying to terrorize, they were issuing a warning to leave the house. That's why they brought in the heavies, because they considered we were in danger. Ma, you're not listening.'

'Yes, I am,' said Rachel, 'and I think it's a very sound supposition.'

In fact she was thinking how relieved she was to have corroboration of her beliefs, that the ghosts were not entirely the figment of a lonely woman's imagination; and how seriously Tom had made her lose faith in herself.

'And when did you start smoking again?' asked Louisa.

'That's my business,' Rachel told her with asperity.

Rachel peered into the crib and saw for herself that Camilla's son was exactly as Emily had predicted; bald and pink.

'Where is Emily?' she asked after the usual admiring comments.

Camilla sighed. 'Reading, I expect. She's being pretty difficult.'

Rachel found her granddaughter on her bed, chewing

223

a strand of hair and deep in a book. For once she showed no aversion to a walk. They bought a box of Maltesers and ate them strolling in Battersea Park, while Rachel told her about France and a censored version of her talk with Robert Kincade. She felt mean leaving out the bit about Lilian; Emily would have revelled in the possibility of murder. In any case she lost her air of listlessness, stopped dragging her feet and asked endless questions as she used to do. But when they turned for home she fell silent, kicking up clouds of dust with her trainers. She did not mention the baby apart from asking, 'Have you seen him?'

Rachel nodded, and Emily's upturned face, her eyes despairing behind her glasses, said everything.

'You did say I could come and stay, Granny.'

Torn by the necessity to disappoint yet again, Rachel said, 'I did and you shall. But would you mind if it wasn't for a week or two? There's something I have to tidy up.'

'If it's the linen cupboard, I could help,' said Emily.

'I'm afraid it's not.' She wished to God it was as simple. 'Would you understand if I tell you I'm in a muddle and have to untangle myself?'

There was not much hope. Emily had been born orderly; she would not know what muddle was.

'I'll try,' she said in a small voice.

'Good,' said Rachel, sounding untypically bracing. 'And Tom will be back. I expect you'd like that.'

As they neared the house, Emily's face grew peaked and withdrawn, and Rachel's heart began to bleed for her.

'It's only a short time, but if you can't stick it out, ring me up; all right?' she said, and realized that sounded ridiculous. Emily was supposed to be a privileged child, not a deprived one.

Nevertheless, Simon and Camilla were behaving like idiots. Driving back slowly in the rush-hour traffic, Rachel recalled Simon, home early from work, bending over the muslin-drenched cot with a besotted expression; the au pair, sulky and in need of a hairwash, and Camilla, too busy to think straight, writing off Emily as 'difficult'. Not far off being deprived, poor child, Rachel considered angrily as she jammed on her brakes to avoid hitting the car in front.

She planned a special dinner for the evening of Tom's return, buying a duck and putting a bowl of roses in the centre of the table, flanked by candles. The candles were green and did not quite match. Why did one always end up with two separate colours? She folded the napkins into presentable cones, put the duck in the oven and went to run a bath.

Lying in warm water, she suddenly decided she was trying too hard. There should be no fuss made about this homecoming. Men loathed fuss, it made them uneasy, and there was a strong masochistic streak in all of them; the more churlishly they were treated, the more they responded. Leaping from the bath, she ran downstairs wrapped in a bath towel to drag the bird from the oven and stare at it dubiously. It sizzled slightly but had retained its pallor. She lifted it on to a plate, took a shepherd's pie from the freezer and submerged it in hot water. If we don't get salmonella from one or other, she thought, we'll be lucky. The napkins had unfurled; she flattened them ruthlessly. And that was how Tom found her, letting himself in and padding down the stairs, light-footed as ever.

'What are you up to?' he asked curiously from the doorway.

'Ooh-ah!' she gasped in fright. 'I could murder you for that.'

He advanced, taking in the odd assortment of food.

'Are we really having all that for dinner?'

'As a matter of fact, no. I decided I couldn't be bothered to cook.' She wrapped the towel firmly round her. 'We might have the wine, though, since it's here.'

He picked up the bottle and glanced at the label. 'Mm. Very nice. Why not save it to go with the duck when you *do* cook it?'

In the light from the window she could see him properly. He did not look well; he had lost weight which made him seem older and more vulnerable. She regretted her attempt at coolness. Instinct told her it was the wrong moment, and anyway she was not very good at it.

'How are you?' she asked, truly wanting to know.

'All right, just about.' He put down the bottle and took her hands between his as if they were cherished objects. She looked down on them joined together, still brown from the sun, and then up at his face. His eyes were bluer than she remembered and held an expression of something like sadness. It made her uneasy.

'Well, have I changed?' She laughed, a little nervously.

'No,' he said. 'It's funny, though; you worry that someone might, if you love them.'

She had imagined how their reunion might be, agonizing over it for days. But she had missed out this permutation; this hesitancy.

'That sounds very Chekhovian,' she said, trying to lighten things, and moved away to cover her disappointment. The moment had been right for him to kiss her, to bring on the violins. No violins.

'I can't think what to do with this now,' she said rather fretfully, poking at the shepherd's pie with a finger.

'Leave it,' he replied. 'Put it in the larder or something, along with the bird.' It was obvious that whatever else he had in mind, eating was not a priority. 'Rachel . . .' he began and then stopped. 'I had planned for us to have dinner out, if it doesn't upset you,' he added.

It was not what he meant to say, she thought.

'That sounds lovely,' she said. 'In that case, I'd better go and put some clothes on.'

'I've brought a bottle of whisky. I'd like a drink; how about you?'

'Fine. I'll have it when I'm dressed.'

'No, wait.'

She turned to him at the door, frightened by the note of urgency.

'We must talk,' he said.

'Well, of course we must,' she agreed, her heart plummeting down to her stomach like a lead weight. 'Over dinner, I should think, wouldn't you?'

'Perhaps,' he said, distracted. 'Why is it,' he asked in an odd, cracked voice, 'you always have to greet me in a bath towel?'

He put his arms round her, and the smell and the

227

touch and the warmth of him rushed back, unbeliev-
ably reassuring.

'It was a dressing-gown, the first time,' she muttered
into his shirt.

'Whatever, it stops all concentration apart from one
thing.'

'It wasn't intentional.'

'The effect is the same. Please may we go upstairs?'

'Are you sure we shouldn't get the talking over first?'
she asked, plagued by apprehension.

'Rachel, darling.'

'All right. I was only asking.'

A week passed, and Tom had gone to spend time with
Hana, a commitment he would be compelled to
honour for an unspecified period. Rachel understood,
telling herself she could afford to be magnanimous
since she had so much compared with Hana's bleak
nothingness. Who would begrudge her a portion of
Tom's care and attention? Rachel could and did,
despite self-admonishment. A day spent without him
was time wasted. For her, this second phase of their
love had a new set of values, as if it had been shaken
up and aired. She no longer felt precarious in her
happiness, or a compulsion to have the future cut and
dried. He had come back; that was all that mattered.

She did not know from where this feeling of security
sprang. There were more than enough worries for
Tom; what to do with his children, where to find
someone reliable to take care of them until Hana's
recovery, whether she would ever recover completely.
Rachel offered to take the children while things were
sorted out, feeling as she did so a mixture of pleasure

and doubt. A charming picture of Emily playing happily with Tom's daughters presented itself erroneously in her mind. According to Tom, his offspring were undisciplined, and Emily preferred the company of books. The idea was discarded and Rachel gave Tom's name to a number of domestic agencies. Involvement in his life added to her certainty.

His thinness troubled her. The appetite for food seemed to have been transferred entirely to making love, as if it was the sole thing that sustained him. In bed she could feel the tension drain away and leave him in peace. There were times when she doubted her ability to keep pace, began to feel her age after only one week.

'It's as if we are doing this for the last time,' she told him weakly.

He did not answer, or joke as he used to do, and she did not mention it again. There was a kind of resignation about him that had not been there before. He showed no bitterness over Hana, neither did he talk about her much, but then what was there to be said? The trout farm had become a far-fetched dream and it was no time for dreaming; he needed his job. In her mind she nurtured a firm resolve to help him achieve his objective; one day.

The house was deserted, empty of Tom, of family, of ghosts. She watered 'Fred', wondering what he saw in this rather dull plant until she noticed three tiny blue flowers, the piercing blue of his eyes, which had appeared overnight. In the afternoon she had tea with Phyllida, who was offended at being ignored for weeks. Tea consisted of a mug, closely followed by a stiff whisky; after which she thawed out and started to ask embarrassing questions. Nothing distanced you from your women friends like a happy love affair, Rachel decided; only an unhappy ending retrieved their affection.

Camilla had asked her to Sunday lunch; tender, garlic-stuffed lamb, crisp roast potatoes, real gravy. Whatever else was allowed to deteriorate in Camilla's household, it would never be the food. Halfway through the meal, Emily broke her total silence to ask, 'Are you still in a muddle, Granny?'

'Muddle?' queried Simon. 'What muddle?'

'Nothing, really. Just something Em and I were discussing,' said Rachel repressively.

'We haven't had a talk for some months. If it's something I can help over . . .'

Most muddles had a financial basis, in Simon's view.

'It isn't, thank you.'

In that case, it's the Man, decided Simon sourly. He cleared his throat.

'Anyone like some more?' he asked.

She drove home thinking of the strain of family relationships, and how unimportant everything seemed compared to the fact that in an hour or two she would be with Tom.

He telephoned before she had time to wonder what had happened to him. He was staying overnight; there were problems, he said, things that had to be ironed out. It meant he would drive up early in the morning, go straight to work and see her in the evening.

'Can't you tell me why?' she said calmly, cold with disappointment. His voice had the careful enunciation of one neither entirely sober nor yet quite drunk. She could not catch his answer, it was so low.

'Darling, I can't hear you.'

'Sorry. I said, not over the phone; when I see you tomorrow.'

'Are you sure you can't get away tonight?'

'Rachel, it's impossible.' There was a pause. 'For one thing, I've had a certain amount to drink. I must be over the limit.'

One could not argue with that. She wandered out to the garden, her spirits around her ankles. At midnight she went to bed and spent the night battling her way through a series of weird dreams; in the last of which Tom figured, entering the house carrying a plant that grew grotesquely as she watched. She woke abruptly, the sound of the front door closing left over from the dream. According to the bedside clock it was only six-thirty, but sleep, she knew, was out of the question. The faint mist over the garden promised another fine day. Her reflection in the looking-glass showed the ravages of a restless night as she pulled on a dressing-gown and went downstairs to make a cup of tea. Picking up the newspaper from the hall mat, she drifted towards the open door of the drawing-room to read the headlines.

Tom was slumped in one of the armchairs, unshaven and awake, his clothes as crumpled as if he had slept in a cardboard box. He looked at her without expression, devoid of hope, reminding her horribly of a long-term hostage. She found her mind had gone as dead as his eyes.

'Would you like some tea?' she asked politely, remote as a stranger. 'I was just going to make it for myself.'

He rose to his feet in a parody of good manners and nodded silently.

In the kitchen, much of the hot water went on the floor rather than in the mugs from her shaky manipulation of the kettle. She clasped her hands tightly together, sitting opposite him while he explained that he must leave her, that Hana stood no chance without him. It did not take long. She listened to the words: no option, could not live with himself otherwise, only chance of recovery, how bloody miserable he felt. But they appeared to be endless, these phrases, hitting at her ears and heart like drumbeats. It seemed unnecessarily cruel, because he was merely confirming what she already knew; had known since last night, perhaps for weeks past, if she was forced to acknowledge it. From the moment his plane had shrivelled into the distance like a burnt-out meteor, she had known and deceived herself.

By the time he stopped finally, she felt nothing but numbness which in itself amounted to a kind of peace. From this strange isolation, she watched him weep, and wondered, with complete detachment, what he had to cry about?

Chapter Eleven

On a fine September morning Rachel drove to visit
Florence Codie at a retirement home in Datchet. In the
back of the car, Morecombe sat with his nose pressed
against a crack of open window. A packet of sandwiches lay in the glove compartment, a bottle of wine
on the passenger seat, for her intention was a walk in
Windsor Park at lunch-time. One of the endurance
tests she had set herself; the first picnic since France.
Her life had come to be measured in terms of before-
and-after Tom, driving her quietly insane. The only
cure she could think of in her desperation was to
relive as many shared experiences on her own; a
painful but effective process. By the end of the day, the
catharsis would be completed and Tom's influence all
but expunged; in much the same manner as she hoped,
by this interview, to tidy away the last loose end of her
research.

'I can't hear you,' complained the old woman in a surprisingly strong voice. She had a Walkman strapped to
her ears.

Rachel leaned forward, gently lifted the earphones
from her head and turned off the volume. 'Is that
better?'

Florence Codie chuckled. 'The dratted thing, I forget

it's there. Going ga-ga in me old age.' She peered at Rachel through spectacles thick as reinforced glass. 'What's your name, dear?'

Rachel told her. 'I'm a friend of Robert Kincade,' she said. 'I saw him in France a few weeks ago and he asked me to visit you. He sends his love.'

'Robbie? That's nice.'

The old woman fell silent, seemingly unsurprised, her head turned slightly towards the stretch of lawn, although in all probability she could see no more than a blur.

'Lovely man, Robbie. Have they done anything for his face?' she asked, trying to refocus.

'The best they could, I think.'

'Shame, that, poor boy. Didn't have much luck, what with Lisa an' all. She died, you know.'

'So I gather,' agreed Rachel, treading cautiously. 'He told me the whole story; or most of it,' she added. 'You see, I live at number seven, Consort Terrace.'

'Well now, fancy that.' Florence Codie's face showed only mild interest. Perhaps, having reached one's eighties, events ceased to amaze one. 'That's a coincidence, isn't it?'

She lifted the rug wrapped around her, found a battered handbag and scrabbled about inside it.

'Got something here what might interest you. Where's it gone, now? There.' She held out a snapshot between knotted fingers. 'That's Lisa's boy, Robert.'

Rachel looked at the picture of a man who might or might not be coloured, arms folded, smiling into the camera. 'He's very good-looking,' she said.

'He was a beautiful baby, too. Well, his parents

wasn't what you'd call ugly. He's good, keeps in touch. Nice, that.'

'Robert – Robbie tells me the boy owes you his life,' Rachel said. 'I believe you saved him when the house caught fire?'

Florence Codie grunted. 'Just luck, that's all. Had him in with me that night, 'stead of his mother. She were the unlucky one, poor little mite.'

Rachel waited, but the old woman had drifted away again.

'Mrs Codie—'

'You can call me Codie, everyone does.'

'How was it that Lisa was trapped, Codie? Robbie mentioned something about the door getting jammed.'

'Some people are born to tragedy,' mused Codie, and Rachel had the impression she was evading the issue. 'Lisa was one of 'em.'

'I suppose,' suggested Rachel, 'the door couldn't possibly have been locked?'

Swift as a cloud over the sun, the expression on Codie's face changed. Her mouth tightened in an obstinate line.

'Couldn't say, I'm sure, ma'am,' she said tonelessly, reverting to class warfare without effort; the classic answer of the parlourmaid asked to explain a breakage.

For a second or two Rachel saw her own kitchen with startling clarity, transported back in time, and a younger Codie drudging away in the same resigned but stubborn manner.

'Was there a key,' she asked, 'on the outside of Lisa's door? Can you remember?'

The woman showed signs of irritation. 'That'd be a

daft place to have it, wouldn't it?' She sat up straight and her glasses flashed in the sun. 'All these questions. You're not from the papers, are you?' she shot at Rachel supiciously.

'Certainly not, I promise.' I am making a pig's breakfast of this, Rachel thought. 'It's only that I have grown interested in Lisa and everything to do with her because she once lived in the same house. But probably you don't want to talk about it, and I'm sorry if I pried.'

Codie relaxed slowly, sinking back into the confines of her wheelchair.

'No offence taken. But there's some things better left unmentioned,' she announced obscurely.

Rachel nodded silently. The old woman appeared to be thinking.

'Have you got children?' she asked at length.

'Yes, one daughter and two sons.'

'Well then, I 'spect that's why Lisa's taken your fancy, you having a daughter of your own,' said Codie, showing unexpected insight. 'Lisa never had what you'd call a mother.'

Rachel waited.

'There's some people what shouldn't have children,' Codie added, as if the pronouncement settled the matter.

This is one of those maddening conversations, Rachel told herself, an Alice-in-Wonderland situation full of innuendoes and no hard facts. We shall exchange words like this until it is time for me to go, and I shall leave none the wiser. Resigned, she started to talk of other things; of the garden where they now sat, and whether the home was satisfactory, and of

236

Robert's life in a French village. Codie's defences were gradually lowered. There was a connection in her mind, apparently, between Robert and Lisa's lover, Nathaniel; she had an unbiased affection for both of them. Watching her, a very old woman with a wiry beehive of white hair, practically blind and partially crippled, Rachel was amazed by her obvious penchant for men. She could never have been a beauty and there was not an ounce of envy in her memories of Lisa. It was quite humbling.

'You should have seen them together, Nat and Lisa,' she told Rachel. 'She so blonde and him dark; lovely colour, he was, sort of dark bronze.' She paused for a second, held in the past. 'Just the one weekend they had together,' she continued, 'but long enough to get them into trouble. 'Course, I knew what was going on. Locked themselves into the bedroom and hardly come out. Hadn't the heart to say nothing. Wouldn't have done no good and I didn't want to, neither. Grab a bit of happiness where you can is my motto.'

So there was a key to Lisa's room. 'It's rather my motto, too,' agreed Rachel.

She reached for her bag, preparing to make her goodbyes without the undue haste offensive to the elderly.

'Thank you for telling me so much about Lisa, Codie. I have to go, I've left a dog in the car and he'll be wanting his walk. But it's been lovely to meet you.' She got up slowly, held out her hand. 'Would you like me to visit you again some time?'

Codie said, 'That'd be nice.' Her mouth turned up at the corners ironically. 'Haven't told you what you wanted, though, have I? Not what you come for.'

'That's not true. I came to see you, and to have a chat, and I'm glad I did so.'

Walking away across the grass, she glanced back to wave at the wheelchair, lonely in its isolation on the broad expanse of lawn. Codie was already waving; beckoning and calling to her, and Rachel retraced her steps hoping whatever it was would not take long. She need not have worried; Codie did not beat about the bush.

'The door was locked,' she said tersely. 'Lisa's door.'

'You mean—'

'I mean what I say. It was locked. The firemen knew when they come that night. And it weren't from the inside 'cos there weren't no key found in the room.'

'So the key is still missing?' Rachel asked.

'No, it ain't,' said Codie. 'I had a good idea where it'd got to, and I were right. But I'm not saying where, mind.'

'No, of course not,' said Rachel hurriedly. There was no need now. 'Someone,' she added slowly, 'must have locked her in. What an appalling thing to do.'

'Well, it weren't me,' Codie said, 'and since there was only one other in the house at the time, it isn't difficult to work it out.' She glanced in Rachel's direction, her face stern. 'But I don't want it spread around. What's done is done and it won't serve no purpose, digging up past evils.'

'I shan't tell a soul,' Rachel promised.

'That's right. It's for your ears only.'

'Why,' asked Rachel, 'did you decide to tell me this?'

Codie pulled the rug more firmly round her. 'Because I've never said a word to no-one. It's been a burden, keeping it to meself all these years. I knew I'd

'I feel used,' she said tonelessly.

'Is it such a crime to want someone badly?'

'Perhaps not. It categorizes me as a tart, probably quite correctly.'

'For God's sake, Rachel. I want you in every way, in bed, out of bed, to share things, to love. Why do you have to read it as purely sexual?'

There was a pause before she answered, for she was crying now.

'Because I shall miss it,' she told him furiously, 'quite besides loving you. And that isn't a crime either.'

She had never been able to get angry without crying. It was a grave drawback; allowing Tom, in this instant, to hold her while she wept over him. He had got his weeping over and done with.

As in the aftermath of a death, she could remember nothing more about the morning until they were standing in the hall, washed and dressed like any normal day. He was newly shaven and wearing a suit, and looked exactly as he had the first time he entered the house.

'Where will you live?' she asked impersonally.

'Home, for the time being. I'll commute. Eventually – I don't know – I'll find somewhere to stay for a night or two during the week. I'd like it to be with you, but I imagine you want me out for good.'

She stared at him, shaken out of her anaesthesia, unable to believe what she heard.

'Oh, God,' he said, 'I'm not explaining properly. I shall have to spend a large proportion of time with Hana, but I also have to work.' He was speaking quickly, decisively, not giving her the chance to interrupt; looking directly at her as if to persuade her by eye-contact. 'If I am at home for long weekends it would be enough, once she gets better. The rest of the week I could stay in London.' He paused, fiddling with his wristwatch. 'Isn't that better than nothing? It is for me.'

The soft option, she thought in despair; half of him, three nights a week.

'Wife in the country, mistress in London?' she said sarcastically, while a drivelling part of her shouted out to accept. 'I don't imagine that will do Hana's confidence much good.'

'She need never know.'

'She will find out; people do. There's the small matter of my self-respect as well,' she added.

'I am not going back to her on those terms,' he said desperately. 'Merely as a friend. Everything else between us was over a long time ago; you know that.'

Liar: all at once she wanted him gone.

'I'm sorry,' she said, 'but no, Tom. I'm no good at sharing things.'

He had not spoken after that, just picked up his overnight bag and his brief-case and left, closing the front door behind him with a gentle click. The click she remembered most acutely; that, and the look on his face, she would never forget.

She must have fallen asleep for a moment; her limbs jerked involuntarily in the manner of a dog dreaming. There was a metallic taste in her mouth from the wine. She glanced at her watch, put out a foot to scratch at Morecombe's recumbent form.

'Come on, exercise,' she told him.

They walked slowly, neither of them enthusiastic,

242

the warm still beauty of late September filling her with melancholy and resentment. They came eventually to an enclosure where horses grazed. One of them hung its grey head over the fence, ears pricked inquisitively. She fed it the rest of the apple she had been munching.

'He is probably a royal horse,' she informed More-combe. 'The Queen often comes to give them titbits. We'd better turn back before you're eaten by a pack of Corgis.'

She realized that she had not thought of Tom for at least twenty minutes. The endless video of their few months together had suddenly ceased to run its way through her brain. This was encouraging, a small victory. She should cash in on it, concentrate on the people who were unlikely to bolt in and out of her life creating chaos; Louisa with her imminent wedding, Christian who had brought his surprise home on leave, and Emily who had run away. The family might be disruptive and contrary, but they were fixed stars, and caused a different sort of pain.

Christian had never thought it necessary to give warning of his intentions ahead of time. He was a dropper of bombshells, in this case the acquisition of a girlfriend whom he had asked home for a few days. Rachel, with only forty-eight hours to adjust to the news, was full of relief and mild panic about where they were to sleep. Did they expect to share a room, or hadn't they reached that stage? Christian had rung off cheerfully before she could ask. She was left to conjure up a picture from the scant amount of information he had given her; a nurse whom he had met in hospital – of course, didn't everyone fall in love with their nurse? – and her name was Kathleen. The nipped-in waist, the elfin face under the pert, starched cap, were so vividly embedded in Rachel's imagination that she almost laughed when the girl arrived. She was built on a large scale. Ushered into the hall by Christian, she towered over Rachel like a benevolent Amazon, smiling happily; a smile that was seldom to leave her face for the duration of her stay. In the midst of introductions, Rachel found herself crushed against a pillowy bosom.

'Chris's mother!' said Kathleen, setting her free. 'He's told me a lot about you altogether, Mrs Playfair.'

'Rachel, please,' said Rachel breathlessly. 'I'm delighted you're here, Kathleen. I'm afraid he's kept very quiet about you.'

'Isn't he the sly one?' the girl roared, digging a grinning Christian in the ribs. 'And please call me Kate. It's how I'm known.'

Kate was like a warm west wind bowling everything in its path into neatness and order. She had an inexhaustible supply of energy that demanded to be fed household tasks to keep it appeased. In those four days she turned out the linen-cupboard, cleaned and sorted the larder, mowed the lawn and hung two pictures while Christian stood by to hand her the nails. In between times she baked bread from a special recipe of her mother's and the house smelt deliciously of farm kitchens. Rachel ran out of new ideas to keep her occupied. At the end of it all, the place had never been so organized since they first moved in. Secretly, she wondered whether she would be able to find a single object in its old niche.

Watching the arms that had tended the wounded Christian, doubtless lifting and turning him like a baby, Rachel could understand the attraction. His eyes

244

glowed as they followed the girl everywhere. The day before she left, they announced they would marry after he left the Army next spring. Rachel congratulated them without the envy she had felt over Louisa. Her life had changed since then, had become empty of aspirations. Christian's plans had not altered. He was going to theological college to train as an Anglican priest.

'I'm pleased,' said Rachel. 'I somehow got the impression you were heading for the Catholic Church.'

Kate and Christian exchanged glances.

'He was thinking about it,' she said, 'until he met me.' They burst out laughing. 'I don't think your son's cut out for celibacy, Rachel. Besides, I'm a Protestant.'

'Isn't she lovely?' Christian said when they were alone.

Fond as she had grown of the girl, it was good for Rachel to have him to herself at last.

'Lovely,' she agreed, and meant it as she remembered the warm brown eyes, the cloud of dark hair and the exuberance. Kate would organize him gently and judging by her hips, bear him children with ease. It was to be expected he would find that sort of girl, Rachel realized; comfortable and uncomplicated, so different from herself and Henry. And she would make a better mother than Rachel, if her way with Emily was anything to go by. For Emily had chosen this moment to leave home and land amongst them, unannounced and determined to stay for ever.

Rachel, nearing the end of her walk in the park, remembered her granddaughter on another walk, dragging her feet under a cloud of depression. She had needed help and Rachel had denied it, put her off with excuses. She could not forgive herself for that, for allowing an obsession to blot out love for Emily.

She had arrived in a taxi early one morning, three days into Christian's leave. Rachel saw in astonishment the small defiant figure clambering up the front steps, complete with red suitcase, and opened the door to her. The driver hovered, perplexed, in the background.

'Have you got any money, please, Granny? I've only got a pound and it isn't enough.'

She was not as tidily put together as usual; brown hair escaping in wisps from a band and face suspiciously tear-streaked. It was not the time for an inquisition. Rachel paid the relieved driver, who obviously had not believed in her existence.

'Now,' she said when they were alone, 'let's find the biscuits and you can tell me about it.'

'I've run away.' Emily's voice was quite firm apart from a slight quaver on the last word.

'I can see that. Which would you like, chocolate or custard creams?'

'I'm not going back. Can I have one of each?'

A jumbled saga emerged of beastly baby, foul au pair and constantly being told to go away and play; the culmination of which was a row with her mother. Emily, in Camilla's words, had been unforgivably rude. Banished to her bedroom, she packed her case and left.

'What did you say?' asked Rachel, intrigued.

'I can't remember everything.' Emily hesitated. 'But I called her a bitch, and that's when she got really angry.'

'Ah. How did you know the word?'

'Daddy says it sometimes, about other people, not Mummy. I don't see what's so bad about it,' Emily said in grieved tones. 'It only means a lady dog.'

'It has a double meaning,' said Rachel, 'but I think you know that.'

She left Emily to her milk and biscuits, and went to telephone Camilla. Rachel, who had never crossed swords with her daughter-in-law, never interfered, made up for years of reticence. Without giving Camilla a chance to answer back, she delivered a broadside on the neglecting of one child in favour of another. Emily would stay for at least two nights while her parents had a long, hard think about a change of attitude towards her.

'But she should be at school,' protested Camilla feebly.

'That's your problem. Besides, she's in no fit state.'

Rachel thought, as she rang off, that Camilla might well be too stupid to get the point. She called Simon, to be told he was in a meeting.

'Then please fetch him. This is an emergency.'

When she returned, Christian had joined Emily at the kitchen table. She was asking him about his wounds and he was cheerfully describing them in detail. She looked at Rachel anxiously.

'What did she say? Is she still cross?'

'No. Just relieved you are safe.'

Emily stared at the floor. 'I don't want to go back. I want to stay here with you.' She added hopefully, 'You could adopt me.'

Rachel drew up a chair and sat down. 'I couldn't do

247

that, I wouldn't be allowed to. Besides, Mummy and Daddy would be extremely unhappy if you were taken away from them, believe it or not.'

'I don't,' said Emily stoutly. 'I wish I was a boy and Alexander was a girl. They only want boys.'

'Listen,' said Rachel. 'When you were born they behaved in exactly the same way. You were the best thing since sliced bread in their eyes, the most beautiful baby in the world. All parents are like that about their new-born babies. Later they settle down, remember that children are not always adorable bundles and everyone becomes a family again. And that's what will happen to all of you.'

'Is that his name, Alexander?' said Christian. 'How wimpish.'

Emily looked at him appreciatively.

'I bet I know what this brat's like,' he continued. 'I bet it's sopping wet and red and wrinkled and has a face like this.'

He drew his mouth up and his eyes down with two fingers, and squinted horribly. Emily shrieked with laughter and rolled about, suddenly a different child.

'I thought so,' he said. 'Well, I don't know what you're worried about, Em. You're prettier and bigger. You'll be able to sit on him when he annoys you, like Sim and Louisa did to me.'

'But not yet,' said Rachel hurriedly.

'Tell me about it,' pleaded Emily.

'Worse to come; Louisa shot me with a bow and arrow. Lucky I'm alive.'

'Christian!' warned Rachel.

Kate had come into the kitchen and was quietly gathering together the ingredients for her bread-making. Her normal ebullience was toned down tactfully in respect of a crisis.

'I could do with a hand,' she said now. 'But not you, Chris. It's a girl I'll be needing.'

Rachel left Emily to the therapeutic effect of digging fingers into dough. After that she trailed Kate wherever she went, and giggles could be heard coming from the linen cupboard as they put away the sheets. Rachel came upon them finally sitting in front of the mirror in Kate's bedroom. Emily had her hair tied in a knot on top of her head and was busy plastering her face with make-up.

'She doesn't think she's pretty, so I'm showing her how she'll look when she's older. It'll come off with cold cream,' Kate said. 'Isn't she beautiful altogether, now?'

'If they're still angry when they come to take me home,' said Emily before she went to sleep, 'then I won't go.'

'It'll be quite different, you'll see,' said Rachel.

'Promise?'

'Promise.'

'Where is Tom?'

'He's with his own children in the country.'

'He's taken all his things.' Kate was sleeping in Tom's room. 'He isn't coming back, is he?'

'No,' said Rachel, 'I'm afraid not.'

'Bother. And there isn't any research now, and Lisa's baby doesn't cry.' Emily sighed. 'I wish things didn't change so much.'

Rachel racked her brain for some pearl of philosophical wisdom but for the life of her could think of none.

It was Simon who came to collect his daughter; a subdued Simon, chastened and uncertain of his ground. He lifted Emily off her feet and kissed her.

'We're not going straight home,' he said. 'I thought you might like to see the dinosaurs at the Natural History Museum.'

'It's a step in the right direction,' Rachel told Christian when they were alone.

'Poor old Sim. He can be rather thick at times.'

The only relic of his injuries was a scar on the left temple. He was the same Christian outwardly, thin as ever; but he had broadened a little on the shoulders, he had lost most of his nervous gestures and his eyes had grown up.

'Show me the pictures of France,' he said. 'I haven't seen them yet.'

She was hoping to avoid this torture. She skipped through them rapidly.

'Not so fast, Mum. You took that last one away before I could look.'

And there she was, caught by the camera in a yellow sea of sunflowers; a happy woman with bare brown arms and a straw hat on her head.

He hugged her as he left. 'Don't worry, be happy,' he told her. He did not ask about Tom, but it was his way of showing that he knew.

Going into Tom's room was another torture also to be avoided, but on this occasion she had to remove the sheets from the bed. Tom had left behind nothing of himself but 'Fred'; one potted plant, a memento of desertion. It was time for it to be planted out in the garden, completing the withdrawal. She began to strip the bed ruthlessly, keeping eyes and mind on what she was doing. Suddenly the tears began to pour down her face and on to the sheets. She turned, picked up the flowerpot and flung it through the open window.

Tom's mind was also on change. At the precise moment that Rachel was picking up her mail from the mat on her return from Windsor, he was puzzling over the traumatic rate at which his life had altered within the year. It made him wonder whether, after all, there was not some Higher Being twirling the carousel and laughing immoderately when one fell off. The point being, dare one climb on again?

He was seated at his desk, turning a pen over and over between his fingers. Recently he had spent a couple of nights in Berlin, and at one of the inevitable lunches found himself sitting next to a police commissioner. It was not necessary to steer the conversation in the right direction; crime of every description was uppermost in their minds, from anarchy to corruption to mugging. His tentative enquiries concerning crimes of the past drew a certain amount of cynical humour from his neighbour. They had their work cut out dealing with the present, thanks to the population having doubled. Besides, the killings caused by the bloody Wall were a matter for the Military, not his department. But there were no records available; the deaths and the false papers were too numerous. The lunch companion filled Tom's glass and started to talk about matters nearer his own heart.

In the evening, Tom walked as far as the Brandenburg Gate, and as darkness fell, tried to find the place where he had stood with Hana, looking back in disbelief that they had made it alive. But the city was altered beyond recognition, no familiar landmark remained. That night he fell into a deep sleep under a new-found sense of security. The next day his paranoid behaviour was already beginning to make him blush at its absurdity; the fear of being followed. He had mentioned it to one of the psychiatrists at the hospital. A form of persecution complex, he was told, quite common, probably brought on by anxiety over his wife. Rachel had called it 'running away'. She had been nearer the mark.

It was difficult, sitting in this office, gazing at the russet tips of late September trees, to remember what extremes of emotion had enabled him to kill in cold blood. The idea of it now seemed so completely beyond his capabilities, making him feel physically sick, that surely it was the action of some other man? The same man, presumably, who had chosen a profession in which assassination figured inevitably at some time, and squeamishness was unheard of.

A feeling of emptiness crept over him, reminiscent of schooldays and thereafter throughout his life; a panic sensation of being outside his own body, searching for himself. 'Colourless' was the word that cropped up in his school reports; withdrawn, lacking in contribution to the team effort. Where is this boy's personality? Where indeed; everyone else could be typecast, classified as bully, swot, games-freak, good all-rounder. Alone he remained as grey and insubstantial as a wisp of smoke. Far more desperate to find an identity for himself than any of those who tried to mould him, he found in the end it was easier to become whatever people required of him, and discovered a talent for invention. It was not he who chose the profession, the profession had chosen him for his ability to blend into the background. An ignominious reason, he thought to himself, and a mistake, for he was totally unsuited for it in all other respects.

And he was no nearer self-discovery; he had acted too many parts for too many people. Women had never been a problem. He was blessed or damned with an exterior that appeared to please them, and after that, it was merely a matter of creating a suitable character. There was no conscious effort attached to this, it happened naturally; the macho hero for Hana, the straight, uncomplicated male for Rachel. But in Rachel's case, it was not so simple. He had foundered halfway through, dogged by anxiety. Gradually, unexpectedly he had fallen in love with her, and from then on it was as if she could see through him, see how little of him existed. The extraordinary clarity of those eyes seemed to act like an X-ray.

It was ironic that the decision to return to Hana was based on principle. One of the few attributes that Rachel should have admired in him had destroyed them. And even more ironically, Hana had discovered religion and a good man in one amazing stroke of fortune. Religion had become her solace in hospital; the man, in the shape of the newly appointed vicar, had followed on its heels, and they were to marry when Hana was free to do so. A widower and twenty years her senior; Tom's moral support was no longer needed. How they would square a divorced wife with the Church of England remained a mystery, just as the idea of Hana coping with parish duties defied belief. But already she was a changed woman, her make-up confined to pale-pink lipstick and a zealous gleam in her eye. They'll have their work cut out converting our heathen children, thought Tom, allowing himself a sketchy smile before his mind slid back to Rachel.

He stared into space, the pen still rotating as he weighed up the possibilities of Rachel taking him back. It was his secrecy that had hurt her, interpreted by her as duplicity. An unfair judgement; he had never set out to deceive her. At least she might give him a hearing. He would explain everything, there would be no more barriers between them.

There were no doubts in his own mind. All he wanted at this moment was to lay his head between her breasts and stay there. Beyond the love-making, beyond all else, he longed for the tranquillity she exuded, reminding him of a river, clear and unrushed. There was peace with her, and safety, such as he had never experienced. He understood now her desire to hide, for it was so exactly what he wanted; to get out of the glare and into the shadows. The need for her swelled and ached inside him so that he could barely breathe.

'Tea,' said a voice, and a cup was put in front of him, a regulation biscuit balanced in the saucer.

'Thanks.'

'Are you all right, Tom? It's late, nearly six o'clock.' His secretary peered at him sympathetically. 'Quite honestly, you look ghastly,' she said. 'Why don't you go home?'

'Thank you for your flattery.' He smiled at her dismissively. 'Just one call to make before I pack it in.'

Rachel ripped open one of two handwritten envelopes. The other bore a French postmark and she wanted to leave the most interesting to the last. Putting her feet up on the sofa, she drew out the letter to discover she was being offered a job. The writer was compiling a book on the evolvement of children's toys from the reign of Elizabeth I to that of Edward VII, and was in need of a researcher. Rachel had been recommended as a social historian. Now who on earth liked her enough to gild the lily to that extent? Reading on, she was astonished to find it was Phyllida who had named her. People were surprising. She had thought Phyllida to be too self-engrossed to give a boost to an old mate. She felt suitably remorseful and not a little flattered; a new-born historian, well, well!

The second letter was from Robert, spiky black writing on white paper; masculine and difficult to decipher.

'Dear Rachel,' she read, 'Tom finally fetched his car from my guardianship last week. I was beginning to think he had forgotten about it or had kindly bestowed it upon me as a gift! But I gather he has had a lot on his plate, and I understand.

'I am writing on two counts, one to thank you for your letter. It wasn't necessary; I did little for you that day in Toulouse apart from give you a lunch you were unable to eat. However, it pleased me very much to hear from you.

'Secondly, Tom told me he had returned to his wife (or ex-wife, as it may be). Doubtless he has perfectly honourable reasons for doing so. But my thoughts have been very much of you and your feelings, and it doesn't take much imagination to realize what they are. None of this is my business. I only wish to say that if you want a change of scene, there is always a bolt-hole here, and I would be delighted to see you at any time. Just call me up if you feel so inclined. I mean it, Rachel.'

The rest of the letter described the grape harvest, a particularly successful one apparently; almost certainly a vintage year. It was signed, 'Love, Robbie,' and as a postscript: 'No strings attached.'

The solitary evening had taken on a different complexion. She had a bath, poured herself a drink and prepared supper for herself and Morecombe buoyed up by these unexpected communications. She would accept the work. Toys were cheerful and light-hearted things in which to absorb oneself, and it would prevent her from slipping back into a rut; burying herself, to coin Tom's acid phrase. The payment was more generous than usual, enough to make escape possible if she felt like it.

She put the dog bowl on the floor and watched Morecombe slowly eating the contents, her mind on Montmiral and Robert. She thought of the convoluted series of events which had led to their meeting. Theirs was probably the only introduction via a ghost on record. 'No strings attached'; she had not regarded him in this light but he had obviously done so, and she found the fact uplifting. It made her realize how completely Tom had monopolized her fantasies, the very smell of his skin always in her nostrils. Coming to terms with the loss of him was like recovering from a long illness. An end to convalescence; it was time to get off her bottom and start afresh.

The telephone rang. It would be Phyllida trying to press-gang her into a dinner party she was giving the following week. Rachel had an obligation to her now;

she would have to accept. Lifting the receiver she said, 'Hallo,' and heard Tom's voice, tentative and enquiring, as if he fully expected to be cut off.

She hovered on the perimeter of the lounge bar, trying to locate him. It had been her idea to meet on neutral ground, refusing his plea to let him come to the house. Home was pregnant with memories and she did not trust herself, would not have agreed to see him at all if his insistence had not worn her down; the desperation in his voice. When their conversation was finished, she was shaking; that showed how easily all the hard work she had put into forgetting him could be undone.

The bar was dimly lit. He rose from a corner table, signalling, and she threaded her way towards him on legs like jelly, forcing herself to look him in the eye, kiss him coolly on the cheek and ask for a brandy and ginger ale, the first thing that came into her head. While he was fetching her drink, she tried to memorize the resistance speech she had prepared. It was like planning a campaign, except there were two adversaries, the most deadly being her other self; the one who was willing to risk being trodden on all over again. He had not said what he proposed, but presumably it was a second chance, a starting-up where they had left off. I dare not let him back into my life, she told herself. She clenched her hands, nails digging painfully into damp palms. It was crazy to have come, particularly to this chrome-and-marble horror of a place. They should have said whatever was necessary over the telephone. From a nearby table, a heavily bearded man in very white robes stared at her unblinking. She glared back.

Tom put a glass and a bottle of ginger ale in front of her.

'I made it a double with ice. I hope that's all right?'

She nodded a 'thank you', willing her hand not to shake as she drank.

'Funny sort of place,' he said, smiling at her. 'Rather like a sinister night-club.'

The smile had not changed, the same slow lighting-up of the eyes.

'I chose it in case I cried,' she replied, staring at her brandy.

'I hope I'm not going to make you. Am I?'

'I believe not.'

'Then perhaps I could switch on this awful little table lamp? I do want to see you, Rachel, as well as talk to you.'

There he was, suddenly coloured an artificial pink through the shade; the folds of his face and the hair that would never quite lie back, and the smile. All of him was as she remembered, so why did she sense a difference as if a part was missing?

'I've missed you so much,' he said predictably, putting a hand over hers, transmitting a wave of nervousness. 'There's a great deal I have to say, if you'll listen.'

Her heart sank. There ought to be a way of preventing this prolonged torture.

'You told me about Hana planning to remarry when the divorce is through,' she said, 'and I'm glad for you, if it's what you want. Tom—'

He broke in, saying, 'This is about you and me. I must explain. Please, darling.'

'All right,' she agreed ungraciously, withdrawing her hand and searching for a cigarette.

It was far more disturbing than she had imagined. Things came tumbling out of him as if he was in the confessional, many of them nothing to do with their joint lives; experiences, feelings, secrets that must have been fermenting inside him for ever. He kept sliding in references to themselves and then slipping back to some incident in the past. Rachel found herself losing track. Was he really riddled with guilt over an assassination, or had she imagined it? Revelations, she thought sadly, and all of them too late. She had once begged for confidences and been denied them.

Confused, she found that she was viewing him objectively for the first time; recognizing the obvious attraction and yet remaining unmoved, as if he was a complete stranger. The difference she had sensed in him belonged to her alone. Watching him lean towards her, his hands clasped earnestly, pledging his love in the form of some extraordinary curriculum vitae, she sat miserably silent. The whole of her defence mechanism had been made redundant. In desperation to prove herself wrong, she tried to summon up erotic memories of his mouth and hands and the pleasure they had given. It was no use. With a cold and empty finality, she knew she was no longer in love with him.

'A sense of belonging,' she heard him say, and realized she had not been paying attention.

'Sorry, I didn't quite catch—'

He sighed; a sigh of relief, she felt, rather than resignation.

'Does any of that make sense?' He took her hand again. She let it lie, flaccid and unresisting in his palm.

'Poor darling,' he said, 'always the good listener. God! I do love you. I'll get us a drink.'

'I don't really want . . .' she began, but he had already left, walking away from her with the optimism of a man who has just shed three-quarters of his burden and is confident of the outcome. She was momentarily annoyed. Tell all, and all will be forgiven; Henry had been the same, only in his case there was greater cause for absolution. And women went on bestowing it, as long as the sexual drive was strong enough. Was that all it amounted to? La question de la peau, the French called it; a natural fusion of skin types producing the right chemistry. Nothing would ever start without it. But it was the mind that destroyed it; the disappointments, the doubts, the words that should never have been uttered and were never forgotten. The eventual discovery that the person you loved was a myth, solely of your creation.

'There we are,' he said comfortably, setting down two full glasses. Hers would be wasted. Soon, very soon, she must leave, walk away without hesitating. She could not bear him to talk his heart out in ignorance.

'Tom—'

'Please,' he said, 'just one last thing.' She fell hopelessly silent. 'The sense of belonging I was talking about; you're the only person who has given me that, a feeling of complete certainty.' He looked at her, convinced also of her answer. 'I want to marry you,' he added, as if giving her a present of untold value.

She closed her eyes, angry at her devotion being taken for granted. It made what she had to say easier to pronounce.

'I'm sorry, Tom. It really wouldn't work.'

There was a fractional pause before he said, 'If you're worried that there'll be trouble from Hana, I can promise you there won't be. She's entirely contented now she's found a father-figure.'

Hana and the vicar, thought Rachel hysterically, sounds like a music-hall turn.

'If that's the problem—'

'It isn't.'

'Look,' he spoke quickly, 'I've rushed you, haven't I? Silly of me, jumping the gun like that. You need time to think, of course—'

'No, I don't, Tom.' She took a breath. 'I'm no longer in love with you.'

There was silence between them in which he seemed to shrink and she stared fixedly at a stain on the table-cloth. Raucous laughter, bursting from across the room, struck both of them as personal mockery.

After a long interval he asked, 'How long have you known?'

'About ten minutes.'

'Ten minutes!' He stared at her. 'For God's sake, Rachel, how can you be sure?'

'I'm quite sure. Don't ask me how.' She had met him this evening for the sole purpose of being reconquered. Any other of her intentions had been self-deception. 'I'm so sorry, Tom, it was completely unexpected. But you do see why it won't work?'

'Is that final?'

'I'm afraid so.'

'I don't understand,' he said, bewildered. 'Every-thing we had together, didn't that mean anything to you?'

She had only spent hour upon hour expunging it from her memory.

'Anything?' she said. 'It meant everything to me. When you took it away with you, I thought I'd die. You know what I did instead? I set to work to condition myself to life without you, to stop remembering, because you were driving me mad.'

He waited without moving.

'I didn't realize how entirely I had succeeded until this evening,' she added. 'I suppose it's like brainwashing. Can't you understand?'

'Frankly,' he said, taking refuge in anger and managing to sound petulant. 'I'm beginning to. This is revenge, isn't it? Getting back at me?'

She sighed. 'There is nothing to be revenged. Nobody was at fault. It was a question of survival. I'd lost you.'

'You could have waited before washing me out of your system like something easily disposable,' he said bitterly.

'Your parting was final,' she said, 'or so it seemed to me.'

'Because you wanted it that way,' he shot at her, and tossed back his drink in one violent gesture.

Slowly she collected her handbag, put away her cigarettes and lighter, sat up straight, preparing to rise.

'I've tried to explain,' she said quietly, not looking at him. 'There's no point in my staying.' She snapped the clasp shut. 'I'll tell you one thing, Tom, it wasn't easy, shutting you out. I'd hate to go through it again.' She got to her feet.

'Don't go.' His face crumpled. 'Please, Rachel.'

'I must.'

'I don't honestly know how I'm going to live without you,' he said in a low voice. 'I need you, you don't realize how much—'

She realized quite well; needing was not loving by a long way.

'I'll be around,' she said. 'You'll start again with someone new and thank God I didn't marry you.'

'Fucking hell,' he muttered.

She looked intently at him. 'You won't do anything stupid?'

'Like jump off Westminster Bridge? What is it to you?'

'What will you do right now?' she hesitated, anxious.

He eyed her, putting everything into his glare: hurt, anger, frustration, fear.

'How would I know, since you are not available? Get drunk and go and screw someone, I suppose.'

'Goodbye, Tom.'

She walked away rapidly, out of the semi-darkness into the glare of the marble hall without looking back. Outside it was already dusk, and tangy with autumn as she set off along Gloucester Road towards home. She had to fight an overwhelming desire to run back, fling her arms round him, put right the dreadful mistake she had made. But she kept walking blindly, clumsily, bumping into people coming out of the underground station. There was no mistake, merely a vast emptiness.

A bonfire was smouldering in the gardens of St Stephen's Church. She leant limply against the railings and watched the curls of blue smoke rising, remembering only the good things about him as if he had died;

his compassion when Christian was wounded, his affection for Emily. Emily would never forgive her if she knew what Rachel had done, would regard it as terrible treachery. She would judge from a child's perspective, seeing in black and white, unable to grasp the grey areas of adult entanglement.

In much the same way Rachel's brain chose solely white memories at this moment; a whole miscellany of them, ones that she had banished ruthlessly. The delight of skin against skin, the sight and scent of flowers, a seat in a country churchyard, the blue and white of a patterned cup and saucer, the smell of fresh coffee, ice-cold river water and his face laughing above her, stupid jokes that no-one else would understand, waking in the warm knowledge of being unalone. She did not try to stop them, allowed them the free run of her mind, because it no longer mattered.

She cried, all the same; not from regret or for what might have been, but for the sheer waste and the transitory nature of love.

Chapter Twelve

September slipped into October without Rachel noticing particularly. It was not that she hankered after Tom or longed to reverse her decision; but she missed those things he had provided for a brief and fatal spell, all of which amounted to a reason for living. There was a curious flatness about the days now, similar to watching a black-and-white film when accustomed to colour.

Sweeping up the first fall of leaves in the garden, she glanced up at the house, the unanswered question of selling always at the back of her mind. She saw the bulge in the mellow brickwork: the whole terrace had been thrown out of alignment from a land-mine exploding two streets away, fifty odd years ago. Before long the window frames would need repainting: facing south, they were the first to flake. The windows were like eyes to which she had grown used, full of benevolence, trustworthy and trusting. I can't sell, she said to herself, not yet, not for a while.

It was a day of clouds sliding stealthily across the sun. Gazing upwards, it seemed to her a face hovered, pale and disembodied behind the window panes of Tom's room. Then it was gone, a trick of reflection. His spirit come to haunt her? she thought with sour humour. Already there was a ghostlike quality in retrospect to the time they had spent together. But that was over and done with, finished; which was more than could be said for the ghosts who belonged. Why had they come? Why had they gone? Or was it not their way to leave, but merely to fade into the fabric of the house as woodlice and spiders retreated behind panelling? Perhaps because her mind was freed from obsessional love and looking for a replacement, these questions gently nagged at Rachel from time to time. They made her vaguely dissatisfied with the research she thought to have rounded off so neatly. Questions meant unfinished business, and she hated loose ends.

Louisa, who was to be married at the end of the month, wanted help in choosing a dress, much to Rachel's surprise. She had not been shopping with her daughter since she was thirteen. Little had altered. Louisa was as choosey and obdurate as in adolescence, marching from shop to shop in relentless pursuit of what she had in mind. At the end of a day spent in changing-rooms, watching her wriggling in and out of countless garments, Rachel queried the necessity of her own presence. She had made no contribution beyond remarking a dozen times, 'That looks lovely, darling.' No help, since Louisa would look stunning in a sack, a silken replica of which it now appeared she was trying on.

'I wouldn't have that,' remarked Rachel, craftily.

'Really?' Louisa turned, twisted, twirled in front of the mirror. 'Funny, it's the only one out of the whole lot I really like. Terribly Thirties. I'm mad about it.'

Twenty minutes later they were in the street and on their way home, carrying the dress, carefully wrapped in a large cardboard box.

'In return for the ruination of my feet on your behalf,' said Rachel, kicking off her shoes and slumping on the sofa, 'I want your opinion on something.'

'All right.' Louisa tore her thoughts away from hats and accessories reluctantly. 'Shall I get us drinks first?'

When they were settled, Rachel said slowly, 'The ghosts.'

'Don't tell me they've come back?'

'Not as far as I know. Do you have any views about their entrances and exits?' asked Rachel.

'I think they left because their aim was to get me out of harm's way,' said Louisa, 'but I've already told you that. The date of the fire was imminent and in some way they felt I was in danger, so they put the pressure on to make me leave.' She looked at Rachel. 'It all sounds so ridiculous now, doesn't it? But I was terrified at the time. I thought I'd suffocate.'

Rachel waited a second before saying, 'Do you suppose spirits retain the characters they had in life?'

'I've no idea, Ma. Why do you ask?'

'Because if they do,' said Rachel, 'only Lisa would have worried about your safety. Lilian didn't give a damn for anyone.'

'Perhaps she had a fit of remorse.'

'She didn't know the meaning of the word, by all accounts.' Rachel sipped her drink. 'Two separate influences, one good or at least harmless, the other evil, under the same roof. I think,' she said, 'they were here for different purposes, and probably at odds with each other.'

'So what was Lilian's purpose, apart from creating

a nasty atmosphere? To return to the scene of the crime?'

'Perhaps,' said Rachel uncertainly.

'And why this year in particular?'

'It might have been a reaction to you and Robin; a mother and baby, association of ideas. Or possibly, there is no reason. Fifty years may be like one to them. Who knows how time is measured in their existence?'

'Well, there you are,' Louisa said, 'you've answered all your questions yourself, satisfactorily. You're the one who claimed ghosts distracted you from the facts, remember? Why the sudden interest, since they've gone?'

'The facts are dealt with,' said Rachel, 'and somehow, it does not seem enough. Besides,' she added, 'I'm alone now with time to think.'

'I'm sorry about Tom,' Louisa said.

'Thank you, but it doesn't keep me awake any longer.'

'If you want to talk about it . . .'

'Not now. One day, perhaps.'

'I understand,' agreed Louisa, who did not understand anyone's reticence, but did her best. 'Will you find someone else to rent the room?'

'No,' said Rachel, rather too quickly. 'I've got a job,' she explained, 'and that will do for the moment. I told you about the toys, didn't I?'

Before Louisa left, she unpacked the dress and they hung it in the empty nursery cupboard, tissue paper protecting its shoulders from dust, to await her day of days. She wanted to be married from home, despite her usual disregard for convention.

'I still love this room,' she said, looking around her.

'Having been scared out of my wits hasn't made any difference.' She looked at Rachel dubiously. 'Are you all right in the house alone?'

'Don't,' said Rachel. 'You sound like Simon.'

'I didn't mean it like that. You would tell me if they came back, wouldn't you? I'd hate you to have the same experience as I did.'

'It's unlikely, but I'll let you know if I'm worried.'

On their way downstairs, Rachel added, 'I suppose Sim will be on at me before long to sell it. Another attack is due, I feel.'

'He's far too frightened to open his mouth,' said Louisa, grinning. 'Ever since you bawled him out over neglecting Emily.'

'It won't do him any harm,' said Rachel with satisfaction.

'You aren't going to sell, are you?' said Louisa, making the question into a statement.

'No, not for a while.'

'I'm glad, just as long as you're safe.'

Funny child, thought Rachel affectionately, waving her farewell.

Besides the usual archives, Rachel's toy research had taken her to parts of the country she had never seen; delving into small collections in both private houses and musty provincial museums: even a Shropshire cottage, home to one of the earliest rocking horses. Occasionally she drove to her destination, more frequently she went by rail. On one such journey she saw from the train window a lake banked by dense greenery, so similar to the one where she and Tom had watched the fish rising, her heart stopped beating: only to lurch

269

onwards a second later, ice-cold and demoralized.

One Saturday she took Emily to see Queen Mary's doll's house at Windsor Castle. As they stood in the queue, Rachel had the chance to study her granddaughter surreptitiously, and came to the relieved conclusion that her life had smoothed itself out. Her face was composed and tension-free, expressing only disapproval of the child in front of her demanding the lavatory. The expression changed to concentrated rapture, well worth the wait for the doll's house as she gazed at Victorian life in miniature. After lunch at the Old House Hotel, they gave the ducks on the river the remainder of their bread rolls, smuggled out of the dining-room.

'How's Alexander?' asked Rachel tentatively.

'All right,' replied Emily carelessly; silence for a time, while ducks dived and squabbled over chunks of bread. 'Actually, he doesn't look quite so creepy now,' she said eventually.

'They do improve with time,' said Rachel. 'Human babies are the ugliest form of new-born young, apart from birds.'

'He's quite good. He doesn't cry much, rather like Bins. Yukky Françoise has left, did you know? Mummy's got a nanny instead, until Alexander's a bit older.'

'Better than Françoise?'

'Much. She doesn't look like a nanny. She dyes her hair and wears jeans, and she knows how to play Monopoly and Racing Demon.'

'Sounds like a good choice.'

During the drive home, Emily asked, 'Why aren't I staying the night?'

'Because Daddy is taking you to the zoo tomorrow.'

'I hate the zoo, it's boring. And smelly.'

'Darling, he *is* trying,' Rachel pointed out.

'I know. I'm trying too. I wish we didn't have to bother. Things work out better when you don't try too hard; like painting at school. Is Tom at home?' she asked out of the blue.

'No. Tom has gone for good, I'm afraid.'

'I didn't have to try with him.' Emily looked at Rachel, who kept her eyes firmly on the road. 'Why has he gone? Did you stop liking him?'

This was too near the mark for comfort. After a pause, Rachel said, 'Sometimes, when you like some-one a great deal, you imagine them to be what they are not. That's roughly what happened.'

'You mean you can go off people,' Emily agreed. 'Like Lucinda. She was my friend. Then she stole my india rubber and swore she hadn't, but I found it in her pencil box, so I've gone off her.' She sighed. 'But Tom's different, of course.'

'Not all that much,' said Rachel gravely.

As they entered Datchet, she thought of Florence Codie, tucked away in her rest-home down a side turning.

'I know an old lady who lives here,' she said to Emily. 'Shall we stop off to see her?'

'Do we have to?'

'No, of course not. But I'll tell you who she is – the Rumbolds' housekeeper, Florence Codie. I thought you might like to meet her.'

'She must be awfully old.'

'A fair age, yes.'

'You've met two people now who used to live at

Consort Terrace, haven't you? Lisa's husband, what's-his-name—'

'Robert.'

'Robert, and this housekeeper.' Emily thought for a moment. 'Is Lisa's mother alive as well?'

'No. She died a long time ago.'

'Oh good,' said Emily cheerfully. 'You wouldn't want to meet her.' She settled back in her seat. 'I think I'd rather go home and not stop off, if that's all right. Shall we have tea when we get back?'

Rachel sat in bed that night, ostensibly writing up her research notes, in truth reflecting on Emily's words: 'You wouldn't want to meet her.' The unequivocal statement of a child, needing to deal in facts, to get her ideas sorted and stacked and labelled, so there could be no chance of misunderstanding. Numbers were important to her; two living people, one dead person. And one dead love affair, Rachel added to herself. Turning out the light, she lay with her eyes open to the darkness, suffering an unexpected wave of nostalgia, missing the concept of a lover rather than the man himself. Tom's absence was complete, the empty other side of the bed a certainty. She felt no such assurance in the case of the ghosts. She held her breath, listened: absolute silence, not a creak, not a groan from stretching timbers. Yet they were there; she was conscious of their mute breathing in the very structure of the walls, poised, forever ready and waiting on the borders of their time and the present. Monitoring the vibes in the air until the right one, a word, a gesture, an unremarkable happening, triggered them into action.

She was, for the moment, unafraid. But she had to

admit to a growing abhorrence of Lilian Rumbold. Lisa was welcome to come and go as she pleased. It was possible to live with the victim of an inhuman crime, difficult to accept the perpetrator. Should Lilian renew her presence, then that was the factor which might tempt Rachel to abandon the house, it occurred to her before she slept.

It was supposed to be a quiet wedding; so Louisa had assured her mother. Now Rachel found herself giving a drinks party for them in the evening, there was a lunch laid on for family only at a Chelsea restaurant and twenty of Louisa's friends had failed to reply to Rachel's invitations. Ten days before the wedding, her nerve was failing her.

'Do find out who's coming,' she pleaded over the telephone to Louisa. 'I must know. It's getting close.'

'They're bound to turn up. Just count them in.' Louisa's tone was snappish. 'Don't fuss, Ma. I'm beginning to feel exhausted just thinking about it.'

How like Louisa, Rachel complained to herself. They should have flown to the West Indies to get married if they did not want fuss. But she knew perfectly well how much she would have hated that. Phyllida came to lunch, full of home-brewed philosophy.

'All weddings are the same,' she announced. 'They bring the worst out in everyone, like driving. Mothers weep all through the service from sheer relief it's almost over.'

'This is a register office,' said Rachel. 'There's no time to weep. The whole thing is signed and sealed in two minutes.'

Beneath the veneer of panic about the arrangements

lay a far deeper fear that Louisa would slip away from her in married life. It was an unwarranted and ridiculous qualm, for how could the signing of a piece of paper make any difference?

'You won't be losing a daughter, but gaining a son,' chanted Phyllida, reading Rachel's thoughts with uncanny perception.

Rachel ignored this. 'Louisa does make things as complicated as possible,' she said. 'Take the arrangements regarding Robin. Camilla is going to have him while they're on honeymoon, since she's got a nanny and I've got Emily for the whole of half-term. But instead of leaving Robin there the day before the wedding, Louisa is bringing him here for the night because the nanny is away and won't be back before Saturday evening. Louisa doesn't trust Camilla to look after him on her own. The poor little boy will be passed around like a parcel.' She sighed. 'I know Louisa will be impossibly jumpy the night before; she'd better have a room to herself, and Emily can share the nursery with Robin.'

'Hearing you talk,' said Phyllida, 'makes me thank the Lord I only have one, and he's the other side of the world at present.'

At the thought of Phyllida's son, who was said to have some rather peculiar habits, Rachel thanked the Lord he did not belong to her. She poured two glasses of wine, cheered up and started to count her blessings. They stuck to non-controversial subjects during lunch, both making a conscious effort to be nice to each other. Rachel was aware of being welcomed back to the sisterhood of single women, but she owed Phyllida a favour and hid her irritation.

'Don't worry,' said Phyllida kindly as she left, scooping up the second mail from the doormat and handing it to Rachel. 'It'll be all right on the day, you see. Just a question of survival.'

Rachel carried the padded envelope to the drawing-room and opened it, prising off the liberal sellotaping with difficulty. Inside was another brown envelope with a letter attached, addressed to her in an unknown handwriting. Mystified, she drew out a single sheet of paper headed, THE BIRCHES RETIREMENT HOME, DATCHET, BERKS, and began to read.

Dear Mrs Playfair,
I regret to have to tell you that Mrs Florence Codie passed away peacefully in her sleep on 10 October. I found the enclosed envelope amongst her effects, addressed to you with instructions that it should be posted after her death.

I apologize for not informing you of her going at the time. Unfortunately, the envelope was only discovered quite recently, and since she had no living relatives, I did not think it necessary to place a notice in the newspapers. Please contact me if you require any details concerning Mrs Codie's place of burial. She had an indomitable spirit, and will be greatly missed within our little community.

Yours sincerely,
Susan Whitehead. (Matron.)

Letter in hand, Rachel remembered a wheelchair

parked on the lawn, resembling a small boat on a deserted ocean, and felt her eyes prick with tears. 'Indomitable spirit'; in all probability Codie had run the place. She opened Codie's package slowly, guessing correctly at the squashy contents before she pulled out the slim wad of used envelopes, held together by an elastic band into which was tucked a letter of explanation. The writing was spidery, and wildly erratic in its direction.

'Dear Madam', it began. (Rachel realized she was greatly favoured to be accorded the title.)

Seeing as how you took an interest in Lisa, I want you to have these letters. They'll let you see how things was, bring her to life for you, like. Three of them's what I wrote to me sister Gert, she passed away some years back and they come back to me with all her other things. Couldn't bring meself to chuck 'em away, don't know why. Other letter's from Lisa to Gladys what was a friend of hers, they was Land Girls together. Gladys send that one to me when she hear of Lisa being killed, said maybe Nat would like to have it one day. Well, he read it, but he leave it in my keeping because of the little boy getting hold of it when he weren't old enough to read about such things. There's a key I put in one of the envelopes. Ain't no point in sending it you, won't fit none of your locks, but it's to show you what I told you were Gospel truth, and there's the evidence. Chuck it out, I would, it's got a wicked history to it.

By the time you get this I'll be pushing the daisies up, I've had my innings. It were nice you coming down to see me, very kind I calls it.

Wishing you all the best,

Yours truly,
Florence M. Codie.

Rachel finished the letter with a sense of loss, and slid the elastic band off the envelopes, holding them in her hand for a moment without removing the letters. She had always known there must be letters, buried perhaps at the back of someone's drawer and long forgotten. But Codie, of course, would never forget her night of terror, her private holocaust. Rachel went downstairs to make a cup of tea before starting to read this personal account of Lisa.

The letters were dated. Curled on the sofa, she placed them in chronological order, guessing, since they spanned half a year, that most of the story was contained within them with the exception of the final episode. Codie's writing had been steadier in those days, the grammar and spelling no different; but she conjured up a graphic sense of time and mood which transported Rachel into her world, Codie's world, and kept her there, engrossed. Immune to the ring of the telephone, she read quickly through all four and then began again at the beginning.

She accompanied Lisa through each stage of her last year: into the air-raid shelter where the American fed her sips of Bourbon, and the air was full of dust and fear, and the start of something fatal. ('She come home two o' clock in the morning, her face a sight, all smears and grime . . . an expression on it I never see before. All lit up.') Where Lisa went, Rachel followed, in the

277

blacked-out streets of wartime London, into bed and the arms of Nat, to Norfolk in bleak loneliness, down these stairs to confront Lilian with her pregnancy. The lines spoke to her in the voices of Lisa and Codie and Lilian, branding themselves on her mind. ('They're prejudiced against Americans like Nat ... I never understood until now what people saw in making love ... With Nat I don't need practice, it's like dancing ...' 'The girl's pregnant, knew it the moment I seen her ...' 'I wouldn't have minded dying if I'd killed Nat's child ...' 'I can see her now, walking on them Cornish sands with the bairn ...')

When she had quite finished, Rachel was crying. She had imagined she already knew the story, that there was nothing more to be discovered. All she had known in fact were the bare bones. Codie had fleshed them out, breathed life into the dead so that they gestured and spoke and acted in Rachel's presence. The effect was emotionally exhausting; she dabbed at her face with a wet tissue. The last hours of Lisa's life were missing; understandably so if one considered Codie's anguish. Rachel was not sorry to be spared the finale; imagination was enough. She folded the letters and laid them on her desk, wondering what to do with them, exactly where to file them. She found it impossible to throw them away; they were part of the history of the house and, besides, Codie had entrusted her with their safe keeping.

The key was another matter. She tipped it out of its envelope on to the desk reluctantly. It lay there, an innocuous household object, slightly rusted. The rust seemed to her the colour of dried blood: a murder weapon, no less. She stared down at it in morbid curiosity, then shoved it back in the envelope and dropped it in the waste-paper basket. The letters stayed where they were, awaiting a resting-place. For all the insight into private lives that they provided, the ultimate questions remained unanswered. She was none the wiser about the dead.

The first signal of their return happened three days before the wedding. Rachel had spent an hour of the morning diffidently explaining her wishes to the caterers, a frighteningly professional couple recommended by Renton. Part of their job, it seemed, was to raise the final bill to astronomical proportions.

'Does it *have* to be vintage champagne?'

'For a wedding reception? Oh, I think so, madam.' (Thinly veiled glances of contempt.) 'Now the smoked salmon on brown-bread squares. This is always a favourite. One needs double the quantity you suggest, I'm afraid.'

She saw them out with relief and sank into a chair, querying whether any ritual celebration was worth the trouble and the overdraft. Then she thought of Louisa, and decided it was indeed worth it after all. Presently, her mind now on her daughter, she decided to transfer Louisa's dress from the nursery cupboard to the spare room next to her own, where shoes and hat were already laid out. Up in the nursery, the battered family cot stood against one wall, awaiting the occupation of Robin. Emily would be lost in that double bed, she reflected, glancing at the expanse of white bedcover; and then, her eyes caught and riveted by one object, moved slowly towards it.

Louisa's dress was carefully spread out across the

bed, off-white silk crêpe arranged in soft folds, waist nipped in, sleeves at right angles. Tissue paper lay beside it, neatly folded in four. Rachel's brain raced this way and that like a squirrel in a cage, hunting for a logical explanation, knowing quite well one did not exist. She opened the cupboard and found the yellow silk hanger over which she had seen the dress draped with her own eyes. Taking it down, she rehung the dress hurriedly and with fumbling fingers. There was a pervading smell as the material swung against her; a smell reminiscent of clothes stored in attics and fur coats belonging to elderly relatives. Mothballs: a commodity that had disappeared with the advent of air-fresheners and a host of high street dry cleaners.

Rachel gave the room one last searching look before leaving it, taking in only its serene innocence. She rigged up a line in the garden and looped the hanger over it so that the dress could air in the sharp east wind and the sun. A 'Thirties' style; Lisa might well have worn something similar as a young girl. There was no doubt in her mind that this was Lisa's doing. The dress had been arranged with a kind of loving care, as if she wished to please. Rachel tried to get on with her long list of things to be accomplished within forty-eight hours, without much success. Her concentration was weak, and there was a hollowness in the pit of her stomach which she refused to admit was panic. She did not mind in the least Lisa's re-emergence; Rachel realized she was expecting it, had never quite believed in the girl's absence. But it raised the possibility of Lilian's return. Her distaste for Lilian's spirit had grown into something a great deal stronger; she hated the woman, and the idea of her inhabiting the same house had suddenly become an unacceptable threat.

This would have to happen now, she thought; nothing must spoil Louisa's day, Louisa's peace of mind. For a brief moment Rachel longed for a solid human presence, a comforter, an ally; longed for Tom, even Henry, to walk through the front door. She needed advice, but from which source? The local vicar? This idea she discarded immediately; from what she had seen of him she judged him to be a muscular Christian, a believer in healthy bodies begetting healthy minds, the sort who would regard exorcism with suspicion. Her thoughts turned to mediums, seances and, finally, to psychical researchers. Seconds later, she was jotting down the address of the Society of Psychical Research and dialling the number. They were situated in a mews off Kensington High Street, a stone's throw away. She considered this to be a propitious omen, and an hour or so later she was seated at the kitchen table, eating a sandwich and flanked by pamphlets, tracts and a library book, all on the subject of psychic phenomena.

Emily telephoned in the evening, bursting with the news that she had won a school prize for history.

'That's wonderful,' Rachel told her, recalling a similar event in her own life, and the pride that went with it. 'What's the prize?'

'It's called *A History of England*,' said Emily, 'and that's not very wonderful. It's really babyish. Granny?'

'Yes?'

'I'm sleeping with Bins in the nursery on Friday night, aren't I?'

'That's right. You don't mind, do you? Louisa really needs a room to herself on this occasion.'

'I don't mind, I like Bins, but can I move into the room next to yours when they've gone?'

'Certainly you may, but you'll have to sleep in Louisa's sheets. I'm not making up another bed.'

'Oh, that's all right.' A pause. 'I don't see why Louisa needs a lot of room just because it's her wedding. Why isn't Vijay staying, too?'

'It's a tradition – I'll explain when I see you.'

'Oh, all right. Granny?'

'Yes?'

'I can't wait. 'Bye.'

Neither can I, thought Rachel, looking forward not only to the company, but the comfort of another human being.

She had absorbed all the relevant information in the pamphlets and continued with the library book, finishing at one o'clock in the morning. The subject was gripping enough in its own right, had she been reading for amusement instead of searching for some form of defence. The Society of Psychical Research had been helpful and enthusiastic, offering to send someone round to investigate. She felt slightly foolish as she explained this was not necessary for the time being, that there was only sad, harmless Lisa in evidence and that Rachel's enquiries were merely precautionary. Call on us, they told her, at any time, handing her their literature. She found the offer reassuring, just as she found the man and the girl surprisingly earthbound and not the cranks she half-expected.

But despite all the goodwill and the reading matter, she was left with little to go by. There were several passages in the book which interested her, however. The prose was chatty, as if the author expected a readership with a low intelligence quotient.

'Try to think of time as a video, by which lives are recorded on film for eternity; our lives, in the present, being recorded alongside those that have gone before us. There is a happening in your life which is remarkably similar to that of a person who once inhabited your home. The spirit reacts to this similarity and is drawn back, believing this to be a replay of its own life. In other words, it is tricked into returning . . .'

The theory supported Rachel's own beliefs, even if it told her nothing new. There was a chapter devoted to malignant versus benign spirits and their separate patterns of behaviour, some of which was pertinent.

'Where an act of violence has taken place, there is evidence to believe the spirit of the instigator may return to the scene of the crime, as may the victim . . .'

It went on to describe various sightings, summing up with a paragraph that caught her attention.

'Spirits as a whole have one thing in common. They are searching for someone or something, be it an object or a person, or a resting-place they have been denied . . .'

She skipped several passages given over to poltergeists since it did not seem to concern her, except for the last few sentences.

'It is practically unknown for a malignant spirit to cause physical harm to a living person, although the mental aggravation caused can be severe. In such cases help may be sought from the Church, and an exorcism carried out. The simpler measure of placing a cross, of any description, where the spirit is used to manifest itself, has proved successful in some cases . . .'

That suggestion smacks of witchcraft, Rachel said to herself sceptically. Nevertheless, just reading about the subject, besides the offer of assistance, had combined to calm her. She turned out the light without a hint of her former panic, and ashamed at her attack of the jitters. The unwelcome thought crossed her mind that she might be slipping back to the way she was before Tom liberated her; obsessional about the house for want of a human substitute. Then she reminded herself that she had merely exchanged one type of bondage for another, and liberation had been accomplished on her own initiative, by leaving him. She kicked irritably at the bedclothes, unable to sleep. Wedding arrangements took over her mind, the things she had failed to get done weighing on her conscience, nerves of a different kind attacking her. How stupid, she thought, to waste all that time on some fanciful whim when there were flower vases to be found, glasses to be counted, silver to be polished, the large damask tablecloth lying in a drawer, probably not quite clean . . .

She slept, and continued to look frantically for these objects in her dreams. After an hour the telephone shrilled hysterically beside her and she fumbled the receiver to her ear, only to hear a click and the dialling tone. Too exhausted to be annoyed, she drifted off again until the sound of Consuelo's emphatic shutting of the front door woke her a great deal later than she had intended.

'What time tomorrow would you like us to deliver?' asked Jenny in the florist's.

'Between nine-thirty and ten, if you would.'

'You must be ever so excited, Louisa being the only girl.'

'Terrified, mostly,' said Rachel. 'Dreading things going wrong, like the flowers flopping over and dying.'

'Like me to come round and give you a hand?'

'No, thank you, Jenny, bless you. I'll manage.' She had already alarmed herself by the amount she had spent, buying every white flower in the market. 'You won't forget Louisa's roses on Saturday morning?'

The day passed in relentless preparation, to the accompanying dirge of Consuelo's Hoover. Everything but the arrangement of the flowers must be accomplished before Louisa arrived tomorrow, bringing Robin and her nerves with her. Consuelo was at her best before a party; she viewed it as a challenge, throwing off her natural lethargy and giving Rachel an extra unsolicited hour of her time. Together they pushed the furniture to the walls and removed the smaller items to the basement.

'It looks like a church hall before a dance,' commented Rachel.

'Is good when you have the flowers,' said Consuelo comfortably. 'Very much different.'

At the end of a long morning they reviewed their work, and sagged on to kitchen chairs with a glass of wine each in front of them.

'*Salud.*' Consuelo raised her glass. 'Happy days to Louisa.'

After a second glass she burst into tears.

'Oh, Consuelo, don't.' Rachel fished in her bag for tissues. 'It's supposed to be a happy event, a wedding.'

'Little Louisa.' Consuelo dabbed at her eyes. 'Is so

little when I come here first,' she sniffed, measuring in the air somewhere below her upholstered bosom.

'Well, she's a big girl now,' said Rachel, 'and you must cheer up or you'll get *me* going. Don't you dare do this on Saturday night.'

She had explained to the caterers that Consuelo could not be left out, however much she got in the way.

'Is all right now,' said Consuelo, beaming. 'Is the wine.'

The telephone rang. 'I answer?' she asked, proud of her erratic English.

'Yes, please. Say I'll ring back, whoever it is.'

'Is no-one.' Consuelo held out the receiver so that Rachel could hear the dialling tone. 'Just click and – poof! Gone.'

'That's the third time today.'

'Burglars,' said Consuelo ominously. 'Is what they do. See if is an empty house.'

'Or a wrong number,' said Rachel. But she was beginning not to believe in either supposition.

'Is for Louisa,' Consuelo said before she left, handing Rachel a small wrapped box. 'For wearing at her wedding. In Spain, no girl get married without. Also, all girls is married in church, in Spain,' she added severely.

'Yes, I know. But Consuelo, you've already given Louisa a present.' It was standing on the piano, wrapped in paper printed with silver bells; a singularly hideous vase, as Rachel had been shown. 'You shouldn't have spent so much on her.'

'I want,' said Consuelo, showing signs of further emotion. 'Louisa is like my own little girl.'

Rachel guided her hurriedly to the front door and out into the crisp air.

'You see.' Consuelo gestured towards the pale sun. 'Wonderful weather. Is good omen.'

With affection, Rachel watched her broad backview walking away a touch unsteadily, but lightly as a dancer, like many heavy women.

It's bound to be a crucifix, Rachel thought, which Louisa will refuse to wear because Vijay is Hindu and she has no faith of her own. Too tired to worry about minor problems, she put the box on the dressing-table in Louisa's room, and checked the dress. It hung untouched on the cupboard door, and smelled only of freshly aired material.

On television that evening, the weather forecast warned of strong winds reaching gale force in the north. So long as they stay there, Rachel reflected, half-asleep in her chair, trying to raise the energy to get herself to bed. When the telephone rang at ten o'clock, she let it continue without answering. It stopped, and started again within seconds. Galvanized into action, she yanked off the receiver and hissed at it furiously: 'Look, will you bloody well leave me alone or I'll call the police.' There was silence, but no click. Then a voice said mildly, 'Well, that's a nice welcome, I must say.' Tom's voice.

Oh no. No, no, no, this was all she needed. 'Have you been persecuting me?' she asked coldly.

'Does that really sound like me? But someone has, obviously.'

'Ringing up and ringing off, driving me nuts. Sorry if I've maligned you. How can I help you, Tom?' she said as noncommittally as possible.

'I saw Louisa's engagement in the papers and wanted to wish her luck.'

He paused. 'Or am I too late? Is she already married?'

'Not until Saturday. You're just in time.'

'Well, if you'd give her my love and best wishes.'

'I certainly shall. Thank you.'

Another of those dreadful pauses. Did he imagine he would get an invitation?

'And how are you, Rachel?'

'Fine. And you?'

'Fine.'

'Not divorced yet?' she asked idiotically, mentally kicking herself for a fool.

'Not yet; merely lonely and celibate. And you?'

'You know me, devoted to my solitude.'

What a pathetic conversation: why not terminate it, she thought?

'And still at the same address, apparently?'

'Obviously. Here I am.'

'I'm not surprised. I know it's the love of your life, the house.'

'Perhaps. At least it's reliable.' She gritted her teeth, refusing to rise to the bait.

'Unlike others you could mention, I suppose? Anyway, it's good to hear your voice. I have to confess I had an ulterior motive in ringing you; just to hear you.'

'I see. Well, now you have—'

'I wondered if we could meet for a drink, or a meal. No strings, of course.' He laughed. 'I don't think either of us wants to go down that path again. But it seems ridiculous not to remain friends—'

'Sorry, Tom.'

'Sorry what?'

'Sorry, I'm going to bring this conversation to an end now. I'm planning on an early night. And I don't honestly want to meet you.'

'Ever?'

She sighed. 'I can't be specific about time.'

'All right if I try again in a month or two?'

'If you must. It was you who made all those calls, wasn't it?' she said suddenly.

'Me? Perish the thought. Good night, Rachel, sleep well.'

It depressed her, this juvenile example of small-mindedness. What had he hoped to achieve by irritating and even alarming her, or was that precisely his objective? She climbed into bed and darkness without bothering to read, and lay there feeling disillusioned. She had never wanted to think about their final parting; now his call had forced her to do so. Had she really hurt him so badly that he was driven to playing vindictive games? He still had the power to wound her, with his snide remarks about her love for the house. She put out a hand and touched the wall, imagining she could feel its friendly response, bonding them together against all adversaries. He was the only man she knew who regarded bricks and mortar as a dangerous rival. She recalled other critical eye-openers: his unforgivable remarks about Robert, his sarcasm and the sudden burst of angry sex which was so unlike him. And she realized all at once just how unlovable he had become and felt sad for him, and for the bitterness that was all that remained between them.

There was no time the next day for retrospection. The sun shone but the wind blew strongly, bending the tops of the trees. Her mind was full of little items such as did she possess a hatpin to secure Louisa's cartwheel of straw? The flowers arrived in armfuls of white paper; sprays of small chrysanthemum, lilies, old man's beard, Japanese poppies. She divided the bundles between the drawing-room and dining-room, where the vases stood waiting. Morecombe, woken from the indifference of old age by a sense of restlessness, followed her about, getting under her feet.

'You'd be better off in your basket,' she told him, struggling to insert a tall stem into its chicken-wire holder. He growled in reply, which was not his habit. She turned in surprise and the chrysanthemum lurched to one side. Morecombe was crouched flat on the carpet, hackles up, teeth bared, before giving a plaintive whine and scuttling from the room.

Rachel stayed quite still, waiting for the inevitable smell of scent and tobacco. Her hands were icy and the palms prickled. But the scent of the lilies overrode any other, and the sight of her desk changed her fear to incredulity. The top was a mess of torn-up paper, stray bits scattered on the carpet below; engrossed in the flowers, she had not so much as glanced in that direction. She knew they were the remains of Codie's letters before she started to pick them up, letting them fall from her fingers hopelessly. Besides the litter, the pigeon-holes had been emptied. Cheque-book stubs, packets of paper-clips, old letters and receipts lay in chaos but undamaged amongst the debris, as if a desperate and haphazard search had taken place. She found a carrier bag and collected every scrap of paper she could find, shivering as she did so, just as Morecombe was shivering downstairs in his basket. A mounting fury rose steadily inside her as she cleared up; outrage at this wanton act of destruction and invasion of her privacy. She glared across the deceptively peaceful room at Lilian Rumbold's favourite space and yelled at the top of her voice: 'You unutterable bitch!'

'The flowers are great, you've done them beautifully,' said Louisa, gazing appreciatively, glass in hand, surprisingly relaxed. From the hall could be heard Emily's admonitory tones as she prevented Robin crawling up the stairs.

'Do they really look all right?' Rachel eyed the large drawing-room arrangement critically. 'Nothing seemed to go smoothly this morning.' She sighed. 'I expect I was trying too hard, as Emily put it recently.'

Louisa bent to kiss Rachel's cheek. 'Thank you, Ma, for everything. I'll say it now because by tomorrow I'll probably be mildly hysterical.'

'Nonsense,' said Rachel distractedly.

Louisa glanced at her sharply, noticing her mother's face drained of colour.

'Are you feeling OK? You looked exhausted.'

'A bit tired, that's all. And hungry, actually. I haven't eaten much today.'

'I'll get supper. I'd like something to do.'

'What about Robin's bath?'

'I'll put him to bed first. You put your feet up with a drink and the paper.'

'Can I bath him?' asked Emily from the doorway.

'You can do everything if you like.'

'Put him in his sleeping-bag?'

Rachel lay on the sofa like an obedient child and

listened to them climbing the stairs, Emily's voice saying, '*Up* we go,' encouragingly. She hoped they would not be long. They were being kind and considerate, but more than anything, she needed their company. *The Times* lay in her lap unread, while she tried to keep her mind strictly on tomorrow's celebrations, to stop it veering off into dark corners. The necessity of hiding a nameless panic from Louisa, of remaining outwardly normal, gave her a feeling of dreadful isolation.

The wind had gained strength in the night, stripping a new carpet of leaves from the trees. Through the kitchen window, Rachel watched them being lifted and tossed, flurries of red and gold in the sunlight as she gave the children their breakfast.

'Where's Louisa?' asked Emily.

'She's having breakfast in bed this morning. Being spoilt.'

'It must be fun, getting married.' Emily finished the careful peeling of her boiled egg and pushed the shell neatly to one side. 'Everyone being specially nice to you. Shall I cut Bin's toast into soldiers?'

'Yes, please. And take the top off his egg, would you?'

'Mind you,' said Emily, pursuing her theme, 'they won't be living together now, will they? Which is a pity.'

'Why, for Heaven's sake?' asked Rachel, putting a spoonful of cereal into Robin's mouth.

'Being married isn't so interesting. That's what people at school thought when I told them, anyway.'

'Oh, Emily,' sighed Rachel. She mopped up Robin's face and took a longed-for drink of coffee. 'Did you and

Robin sleep well last night?' she asked, changing the subject.

'Sort of.' Emily dipped a toast soldier into yolk and guided it in Robin's direction. 'Actually, something really strange happened, but I slept all right after that.'

'What do you mean?'

'After someone tried to tuck me in. I thought it was you at first.' She selected another piece of toast. 'So I said, "Hallo, Granny," and then I saw it wasn't. Ow! Bins, that's my finger.'

Rachel lowered her coffee cup slowly to the table.

'You mean, you saw someone?'

'Oh yes. But it wasn't just anyone. It was Lisa, you know, Mrs Rumble's daughter.'

There was silence. Emily looked at her grandmother guardedly.

Pulling herself together with difficulty, Rachel asked, 'How do you know it was Lisa?'

'Because of her hair. It was very pale, almost white, just like you said. And she was young, and that was all I could see, really.'

'Em,' said Rachel, 'could you honestly be sure? It was dark—'

'There was Bin's nightlight, it wasn't quite dark. I'm absolutely sure.'

'Perhaps you were dreaming—'

'I knew you'd say that,' said Emily with composure. 'But I know I was awake because Bins was snoring, well, kind of snuffling, and I couldn't go to sleep.'

Robin, deprived of food for a moment, shrieked like a steam-whistle and knocked over his mug. Milk streamed from every corner of the high chair.

Emily slipped from the table. 'I'll get the cloth.'

293

Rachel cleaned up pensively, concentrating on the job in hand without speaking.

'You think I'm making it up, don't you?' Emily said.

Rachel straightened, looking at her injured expression.

'No, I don't,' she said seriously. 'You wouldn't do that, I believe you completely. But please don't say anything to Louisa just now. Not today.'

'I wasn't going to. Bin's bib is sopping. Shall we take it off?' Emily undid the tapes, unconsciously admiring the kissable nape of his neck. 'Lisa's dead, so she must be a ghost,' she said, 'and Daddy says there isn't such a thing. I'm glad I've seen one,' she added triumphantly.

'Seen what?' Louisa, pale and yawning in a white robe, stood in the doorway holding a tray.

'You haven't eaten a thing,' Rachel said reproachfully.

'I can't,' said Louisa, unloading the tray by the sink. 'It sticks halfway down.' She kissed the top of Robin's head and drew up a chair next to Emily. 'I'll have another cup of coffee, though.' She glanced at Emily feeding Robin the last of his egg with fierce concentration. 'I'll give you a job as nanny any time you like, Em. What's all this about ghosts?' she asked.

Emily turned pink with the effort of silence. Rachel put the coffee in front of Louisa and passed the sugar. Louisa looked from one to the other and laughed.

'Oh, come on,' she said. 'I need a diversion, my stomach's riddled with butterflies. Anyway, it's no use pretending, because I heard. Em's seen the nursery ghost and the ghost is Lisa.'

'You were eavesdropping,' Emily said accusingly.

'No, I wasn't. I merely overheard. Is that piece of

toast going begging?' Louisa took it from the rack and helped herself to butter, her appetite apparently restored. 'You don't realize, Em, but you've solved a mystery. The nursery spirit has been around for years, but none of us have ever seen her.' She looked at Rachel. 'Funny, it never crossed my mind it might be Lisa; did it yours?'

'Only very recently,' said Rachel.

'Emily must have psychic powers,' continued Louisa through a mouthful. 'Amazing. I wonder who else she'll—'

'Louisa,' Rachel warned.

Emily was again pink in the face, this time from anger. 'You knew! You knew all along there were ghosts and you didn't tell me.' She glared at Rachel. 'Why not?'

'Only,' Rachel said feebly, 'because you might have found it frightening. And Daddy and Mummy would have disapproved.'

'I wouldn't have said. You didn't trust me.' Tears swam behind Emily's glasses. 'Well, I shan't trust *you* ever again,' she said as she marched from the kitchen and fled upstairs.

'A great start to the day.' Rachel sighed. 'I knew something like this would happen.'

'Sorry,' said Louisa. 'Don't worry, I'll go and have a chat to her. She'll forget all about it in the hoo-ha of the wedding.'

'Emily never forgets,' said Rachel, 'but she might forgive, and that's up to me.'

Louisa lifted Robin from his high chair. 'All the same, it does make one wonder who else she's capable of seeing,' she remarked.

'It's late,' said Rachel. 'Time you started to get ready.'

They stood in bright sunlight, Vijay and Louisa, while Simon captured them for posterity with his video camera against a notice board that read: REGISTER OFFICE & DEPT. OF SANITATION & PUBLIC DRAINAGE. Arms entwined, Vijay smiling, Louisa laughing as her hat took off and her skirt billowed up her perfect thighs in the stiff breeze. Also caught on film was Emily's figure chasing down the Kings Road and retrieving the headgear from the legs of a bus queue. The ceremony was over. With varying degrees of relief they crossed the road by twos and threes in cheerful anticipation of lunch. Rachel felt as if she had lived a full day already.

The day had burgeoned into a rush, with all the usual last-minute hazards such as laddered tights, mislaid articles, and the unusual one of Emily's hurt feelings. Rachel, seeking to make amends, had found her on her bed, chewing her hair and reading.

'Would you like to come and get dressed in my room?'

'No, thank you,' replied Emily politely.

'I'd like to explain,' said Rachel to her unresponsive back, 'but I can't do that while your nose is in a book.'

Emily rolled over and stared at the ceiling.

'I meant what I said. You might well have found the thought of ghosts a frightening one.'

'I'm not a *baby*,' Emily said distantly.

'No,' Rachel agreed, 'but there are a great many grown-ups who would be scared by the idea. So try to understand how it was I didn't tell you.'

'Are you frightened?'

'No, I'm not. I don't believe they can harm one.'

'Then I'm not either.'

'All the same, I shall be very pleased to have you to keep me company for a week.'

Emily sat bolt upright. 'Why?' she asked. 'Don't you like being alone because of the Lisa ghost?'

'I don't mind Lisa in the least,' Rachel said truthfully. 'But I always love you being here, and ghosts are no company at all.' She added, a little unfairly, 'It won't be any fun if you no longer trust me, though. If you'd rather be at home—'

'I wouldn't.' Emily wriggled with the effort of giving in gracefully. 'I'm sorry I said that,' she said gruffly, and flung her arms round Rachel's neck.

'Perhaps I deserved it. Are we all right now?'

'Mmm. Granny?'

'Yes?'

'Will you tell me all about it from now on? You won't go on having secrets? Promise?'

'I promise.'

Emily released her hold, quick to consolidate a victory. 'You said "ghosts". There's another one, isn't there? Not just Lisa?'

'Look, I've promised, and I'm not sliding out of it. But in an hour and a half Louisa is getting married.' Rachel gave her granddaughter a kiss and got to her feet. 'We've got all week to talk. Find your dress and let's make you beautiful.'

Camilla had good taste in clothes, and Emily wore a black velvet pinafore dress printed with minute pink daisies. On her head was a hat of her own choosing, of crushed velvet shaped like an inverted flower-pot with a frilled brim, which looked ridiculously apposite. And as she returned now, clutching Louisa's hat and flushed from running, Rachel saw quite suddenly how she would be one day; never pretty, but very probably beautiful.

As for Rachel, there had been time to make herself presentable and that was all; she felt only half put-together. But it was Louisa's day, and no-one would notice the bride's mother. With Robin in his pushchair and Emily by her side, she waited to cross the Kings Road by the Sydney Street traffic lights. They changed to red, discharging a two-way stream of pedestrians from either pavement. Amongst the sea of passing faces, that of Tom appeared alongside, smiled and vanished like the Cheshire Cat. Emily tugged at her sleeve.

'That was Tom,' she said as they reached the pavement.

'Was it?' said Rachel vaguely. 'Well, it wasn't exactly the place for a chat.'

While they walked the hundred yards to the restaurant, she decided he had not been there by chance; it was too much of a coincidence. She wondered whether he was turning into a snooper; a nuisance. How typical that he should see her in the role he despised: her family's keeper. It no longer mattered, for she had come to despise him equally.

The weather broke the next day. Rain, driven by gusting winds, lashed furiously at the windows, and the sky was an implacable blanket of dark grey. Emily was delighted.

'It's an indoor day,' she said, and Rachel knew quite

well that she was expecting to be fed information without any interruption from outdoor activities.

It was not easy to keep her promise, Rachel realized. There were things at which she baulked when it came to telling Emily. The contents of Codie's letters, for instance, were not for her ears, with their descriptions of pregnancy and attempted abortion. Nor did Rachel consider it wise to divulge the destruction of the letters. She believed even now that it was possible for Emily to become scared: Rachel herself could no longer pretend immunity to fear. If Lilian had to be mentioned at all, then it must be a strictly censored account, vague enough to make her frankly uninteresting. It was best to concentrate on Lisa, who haunted the nursery solely for the harmless and pathetic purpose of finding her child.

Lilian had attended Louisa's reception. Rachel had come upon her at that daunting moment before the first guest arrives and one is faced with the barrack-like vista of a large and unpopulated room. It seemed impossible that the caterers, coming in and out with bowls of olives and clean ashtrays, should remain oblivious to the smell. And then Louisa had arrived, looking as fresh as at the start of the day, and her eyes widened.

'*She's* here.'

Rachel nodded and shrugged, attempting casualness. But she was shivering in the warmth, and Louisa had brought her a drink swiftly and without fuss, and scribbled the telephone number of a Mauritian hotel on a piece of paper.

'Promise to ring me if you need me,' she said.

'Darling, what can possibly happen?' said Rachel; all

the same, she put the number away with a sense of relief. Shortly afterwards, people started to arrive and the drawing-room to fill. For the next three hours all her concentration was taken up in remembering names and making introductions and refilling glasses. Whether Lilian's spirit had survived the din and crush of the party, or whether it had faded away, there was no way of telling. There was no sign of her when at last Rachel gazed round an empty and slightly dishevelled room. She supposed she was lucky in that flowers had not been wrenched out of vases, that no poltergeistic vandalism had occurred. Only the uneasy knowledge that Lilian was capable of such acts remained.

The caterers, however extortionate, were true professionals, and Rachel came downstairs the following morning to find everything cleaned and tidied away where possible, the rooms hoovered and the furniture replaced: in the wrong positions, certainly, but the intention was honourable. They had even locked up for her, and the key to the back door mortice lock was missing; but it was the only thing with which she could find fault. There were dishes of leftover food covered with cling-film residing in the larder.

'No smoked salmon,' said Emily, disappointed.

They stared down at the flaccid and unappetizing remains of last night's delicacies before shooting them into the bin. Smudges under Emily's eyes bore witness to the unaccustomed excitement. She had fallen asleep in an armchair halfway through the proceedings, and Simon had carried her to bed.

'She never woke up properly,' he told Rachel on his return. 'Couldn't even say Louisa's name properly: kept mumbling about Lisa.'

'Really?' she said vaguely. 'There are two people over there with nothing to drink. Could you . . . ?'

'It was a lovely party,' Emily said at lunch. 'I wish Christy and Kate had come, though.'

'So do I. But he's had a lot of leave; he couldn't ask for more.'

'Vijay let me drink some of his champagne.' Emily yawned. 'I can't remember going to bed. I expect I was a bit drunk.'

'We'll both take our hangovers to bed this afternoon and sleep them off.' Rachel looked at the ever-darkening sky. 'The best place in this weather.'

'Granny! You promised to tell me about the other ghost, remember?'

'Later.'

And later, dozy from her sleep, Emily said, 'I suppose it's Lisa's mother. She's the only other dead person.'

'Yes,' agreed Rachel. 'I believe it is. But I've never seen her.'

'How do you know she's there, then?'

Rachel gave her the watered-down version of Lilian.

'I can't smell anything,' said Emily through a mouthful of buttered toast. She stared at the place which, according to Rachel, was Lilian's favourite corner. 'Is she here now?'

'I don't think so.'

'I don't think so either. I'd probably see her if she was, like I saw Lisa.' There was a certain superiority in Emily's voice at being thus gifted. 'Where do ghosts *go* when they're not actually here?' she asked.

'Who knows? Back to where they belong, perhaps.' Rachel reached for her mug of tea. 'Although I have a feeling they don't quite belong anywhere, like displaced persons, which is sad.'

'What's a displaced person?'

'Someone without a country or a home.'

'Perhaps our ghosts think this is still their home and we shouldn't be here.'

'There is a theory,' said Rachel carefully, 'that spirits are searching for someone or something. In Lisa's case, I imagine it is her baby.'

'I wonder what her mother's searching for? Maybe it's the baby, too.'

'I think not.'

But Rachel wished fervently that she knew the answer. If it was the crown jewels themselves, she would have laid them gladly on her desk in order for Lilian to swipe them and be gone.

'I don't think she liked children,' she said, 'from what old Florence Codie told me.'

'She sounds perfectly horrible,' said Emily coldly.

'Not very likeable, I agree.'

'I knew she wasn't,' Emily remarked, 'otherwise she'd have saved Lisa. It's quite easy to rescue people from fires. You put a wet cloth over your head and crawl along on your hands and knees. We learnt that in fire drill at school . . .'

The fire drill lecture continued at some length and the spirits were forgotten for the time being.

'Is it winter now?' asked Emily as she went to bed.

'It certainly seems to be,' Rachel said, listening to the wind whining in the trees and rattling the windows.

'I'm glad I'm sleeping in this room, next to you.' Emily thought for a moment. 'Lisa won't find anyone to tuck in tonight.'

302

'Poor Lisa.'

'Yes, poor Lisa. I'm not frightened because you're not frightened, but I like this room best. You're not frightened, are you, Granny?'

'Absolutely not,' Rachel swore.

But she was, with a cold, illogical fear that prevented her entering the drawing-room unaffected. Why should the presence of a child engender security? She thanked God for it as she went round the downstairs rooms, locking the french windows, until she came to the back door, which was locked indefinitely. Having to go out the front way to the dustbins was a nuisance; tomorrow she would call the caterers and ask them what they had done with the key. She kept a bunch of them hanging from a ring in one of the cupboards: there was no earthly reason to separate one of them.

No *earthly* reason: the alternative solution came to her in a flash as she stared at the bunch in her hand; Lilian, key, nursery door, in that order. The caterers had left the keys on the kitchen table after locking up: if they were the object of Lilian's search, then there they were, laid out for her to find quite easily, omnipresent as she was. Rachel sat down abruptly, her knees trembling. She made one brief attempt to dismiss the idea as the product of a fevered imagination, with no success. She knew already that the caterers would deny any knowledge of the matter. All this could have been avoided had she left Codie's key on the desk with the letters. Anger rose in her from the sheer inconvenience caused by Lilian's spirit; but overriding that was the thought that this detestable woman, apparently capable of theft and destruction, might also cause harm. And for the first time, Rachel was forced to acknowledge a very real and helpless terror.

Emily came dancing down to breakfast, wearing Louisa's crucifix round her neck. It had been left behind on the chest of drawers by mistake.

'By-mistake-on-purpose, more likely,' said Rachel, who had not slept well. 'Louisa's extremely thoughtless. Consuelo gave it to her as a wedding present. If she knew it wasn't appreciated, she would be terribly hurt.'

'Is it real gold?' Emily held it under the light.

'Yes, it is. Consuelo is very generous.'

'Can I wear it? Just for now, I mean?'

'As long as you remember to take it off when she comes to clean.'

Amongst the mail was a letter from Robert, thanking her for letting him know of Codie's death, and going on to give an account of Montmiral in autumn. He wrote well, and his descriptions brought a sudden flood of longing to be away from London and the house. The black, difficult-to-decipher writing gave her a sense of balance, so that the day did not seem quite as ominous as before. It occurred to her how wonderful his immediate company would be: he would know what to do.

The rain had stopped. It was a sunny, blustery day with clouds scudding before the wind.

'What shall we do?' asked Emily.

'Let's go for a really blowy walk. I feel like some exercise.'

'Oh, Granny, must we?'

'As far as the Round Pond,' said Rachel firmly.

'There were gale warnings on the news this morning; this bit of sun won't last.'

'Can I take Christy's old boat? The one in the toy cupboard?'

'You may, so long as you're prepared for it to capsize or get stuck in the middle of the water.'

This was precisely what happened: the little yacht, no longer seaworthy, sailed bravely to the centre of the pond and keeled over. Sadly, they left it there, and walked onwards to the Palace, to gaze through the railings at its perfect façade. Rachel pointed out the windows of Queen Anne's nurseries, a new one built for each short-lived child.

'Her face is said to appear at one of the windows.'

Emily stared and stared, trying to conjure up this vision through the blank panes.

'I suppose she's a bit like Lisa, looking for her baby.'

'Or babies, plural, in poor Queen Anne's case. She had fourteen of them.'

Over the roof of the Palace, a giant black and purple cloud loomed like a bruise in the sky. Rachel called to Morecombe, who was nosing around in the grass. Progress homewards was necessarily slow because of his advanced age, and by the time they reached the house the first huge drops of rain were spattering the pavements. Indoors it had become as dark as night. The dog pattered to the drawing-room, stopped short, growled and fled downstairs. Rachel's heart sank as they followed, to find him shivering in his basket.

'What's the matter with him?' asked Emily, stroking his head and making soothing noises.

'Dogs don't like ghosts,' said Rachel flatly.

Emily's head shot up. 'Is she there, what's-it . . . Lilian?'

'I expect so, since Morecombe's upset.'

'I'll go and look, shall I?' said Emily, her eyes sparkling.

'No,' said Rachel with unusual vehemence. 'I'd rather you didn't.' She started to lay the table for lunch, clattering knives and forks into position.

'Why are you cross?' Emily asked primly.

Rachel glanced at her. 'I'm not – oh well, yes, I am, actually, but not with you. It's not being able to open the back door, and the missing key and so on.'

'You didn't mind yesterday,' Emily pointed out, unaware of how maddening she was being.

Halfway through a rather silent lunch she asked thoughtfully, 'Can you make ghosts go away? For ever and ever, I mean?'

'I believe so,' said Rachel. 'One can have them exorcized. It's a religious thing, a kind of ritual performed by a clergyman to lay restless spirits.'

'I think that's what we should have done, then,' said Emily.

'Really?' Rachel said cautiously. 'For what reason?'

'Because it's this Lilian ghost that's making you cross, isn't it, not the back door at all, really?' Emily spooned up the last mouthful of chocolate mousse and looked at her grandmother squarely. 'You're never cross, not as a rule,' she said.

Rachel smiled at her and sighed. 'It isn't that easy to find the right clergyman. Not all of them approve of exorcism or believe in wandering spirits, you see.'

Emily considered this for a minute or two. She was remembering how angry her mother had become when she ran into the road without looking. Camilla had been frightened, that was why. Anger and fright seemed to go together. She decided not to mention the fact to Rachel.

'Oh, well,' she said carelessly, 'we'll have to think of something else, then, because Morecombe's awfully scared and it isn't fair. Can I watch telly, Granny?'

This was an unusual request from Emily. 'Yes, if you want to. What's on?'

'*Ghostbusters Two*,' said Emily succinctly.

Rachel laughed, put to shame by this light-hearted approach.

While Emily watched the film, Rachel tried to settle down to bill-paying and letter-writing. Her mind wandered. She had a strong desire to write to Robert, but various inhibitions were getting in the way. 'For all its obvious beauty,' he had written, 'I don't appreciate this time of year any longer. I suppose it is all a part of growing old, and I dislike being the wrong side of winter ... The spring is worth waiting for here, though, the meadow flowers in bloom, carpets of wild cyclamen amongst them. I wish very much that you could see them for yourself in April or May.'

There was a note of yearning enclosed in the last sentence, which she guessed to be as near a definite invitation as he was prepared to make. She wondered whether he were unwell, or perhaps a little in love with her, and the idea made her uneasy. She did not wish to be fallen in love with, or have to deal with the complications that would ensue. Emotional involvement might well force her to give up a welcome line of retreat, and she did not want that either. She

307

did not, at present, know how to reply to him.

She thought of Henry, and then of Tom, and decided that she was not a good chooser of men. Both of them, in their own ways, had drained her self confidence, left her one notch down in her own estimation: less courageous, less capable of decisiveness. Small wonder she clung to the house like a lover. Allowing a mere touch of the supernatural to reduce her to nervous shreds was an example of her dwindling moral fibre. She pushed the paperwork to the back of her desk abruptly. Emily had the right attitude: if an eight year old managed to treat it as a joke, then so could Rachel. 'I refuse to be intimidated, you old bat,' she said over her shoulder to Lilian. The room was unoccupied, as it happened, but doubtless the woman hovered somewhere close enough to get the message. It was Emily's half-term; nothing should be allowed to spoil it. Music from the television denoted the end of the programme. The rain had stopped, and in the communal gardens of the square Rachel knew a Hallowe'en party was about to start: a measure taken by desperate parents to stop their children wandering the streets, ringing doorbells and demanding 'trick or treat'. Secretly Rachel had hoped to avoid this social event. Now, repenting of her churlishness, she called downstairs to Emily.

Half an hour later they crossed the road to the gardens, Emily transformed by hideous witch's make-up and carrying the yard-broom. The wind had strengthened, striking them a great sideways buffet so that they stumbled and clung to each other, laughing. A bonfire was alight on the lawn, and a crowd of adults and children were gathered round it, their faces pink from the glow. One of Rachel's neighbours, the sort of woman who was born to organize, came forward to greet them.

'Hallo, Rache. I say, you've grown, Emily. Hardly recognized you. Is that a contribution to our refreshments? Great! Dump them on the table over there. We're going to bob for apples in a moment. You'll have a go, won't you, Emily?'

'What do I have to do?' Emily asked cautiously, as she was led away, a reluctant participant.

An hour later, the party was in full swing. Children in the guise of witches and warlocks screamed around the gardens, chasing each other manically in and out of the shadows. Anoraked parents, their voices loud from the intake of red wine, made almost as much noise. Emily flashed past in hot pursuit of a warlock, pelting him with apples and giving blood-curdling yells. Rachel, watching in amazement, burst out laughing. She felt suddenly and illogically happy. Overhead, the trees bent and moaned before wild gusts of westerly wind. A child slipped, fell and started to howl. The organizer dashed from group to group, saying, 'Time to call it a day. I've heard from the Park police: there's been a warning of force-nine gales. Will some of you help to douse the fire?'

In twos and threes they straggled through the gates, 'Good night' ringing in the air as they parted company. Rachel closed the front door breathlessly against the weather, and stared at an unrecognizable Emily. Her hair hung in damp strands, her witch's make-up had smudged down cheeks and forehead, and her eyes glowed.

'That was great!' she said, airing her blacked-out front tooth in an awful grin.

'It was rather, wasn't it?' agreed Rachel. 'You seemed to be giving that poor boy a hard time.'

'He wasn't "poor" at all,' Emily replied. 'He said I was the ugliest girl he had ever seen.'

'Well, of course you were. Witches are meant to be ugly.' Rachel tossed her anorak over a chair. 'You certainly got your own back, anyway.'

'He cried when I threw the pail of water over him,' Emily said with satisfaction. 'Pretty pathetic, really. None of the apples hit him, though. It's difficult to aim when you're running.'

Rachel sighed in mock despair. 'I only hope I never meet his parents.'

Where was her prim, Victorian grandchild now? But in truth she was quite intrigued to see Emily letting her hair down for once. Perhaps this unpromising interlude, standing frozen in a gale drinking indifferent wine while a gang of children ran riot, had been a success for both of them. Or perhaps it was the bliss of getting warm again. Something had relieved her nervous tension, and they spent a relaxed evening playing beginner's chess, which was Emily's current favourite.

Absorbed in their game, they were scarcely aware of the howling wind. There was a certain smugness about being comfortably battened indoors, while outside other poor wretches struggled with the elements. A muffled crash in the garden broke Rachel's complacency. She went to the french windows and peered into total darkness.

'What was it?' asked Emily beside her.

'I don't know,' Rachel said, 'but I have a nasty feeling it was a tile.'

She switched on the television to hear the weather forecast: 'Strong winds reaching gale force, with gusts of seventy to eighty miles an hour, are expected to hit South-East England during the night . . . car journeys should be avoided unless strictly necessary . . . people weighing under eight stone are advised to stay indoors.'

'That's you and me,' Rachel said. 'We'd be blown flat on our faces.' Emily giggled. 'Or sail over the roof-tops like Mary Poppins.'

'In answer to many worried callers,' said the announcer, 'this is definitely not a hurricane.'

'That's what they said before the last one.' Rachel switched off.

Upstairs, the sound of the wind was greater.

'It roars,' said Emily, 'like the sea.'

Rachel wedged the windows to stop the rattle. 'Don't worry if you hear a few crashes and bangs,' she said. 'There are bound to be some dustbins bowled over tonight, and bits of broken tree and so on.' She kissed Emily's forehead, the only part of her visible above the duvet. 'You're not frightened, are you?'

'Of course not.' Emily gave a wriggle. 'It's quite exciting.'

Rachel understood what she meant. How lovely to be eight years old and not bound to worry about how many tiles were loose. The roof had not been inspected since the nineteen-eighty-seven gales. The acacia tree also worried her. As she watched it sway wildly, black against paler black, a sudden blast bowed its head towards the ground. She drew the curtains hurriedly: it had stood up to worse than this, one could but hope. The draught whistled under the door, chilling her ankles. In bed, she read for an hour until her eyes felt heavy and, looking in on Emily, she found her asleep and the duvet slipping sideways. Rachel covered her carefully: the crucifix was round her neck, nestling in her pyjamas. She did not stir; but Rachel's sleep was light and restless, the noise of the wind never leaving her subconscious.

There were footsteps, and the crying of a baby, and an intermittent banging. Emily listened, completely awake on the instant. The banging was obvious; a door or window swinging loose in the gale. The footsteps could be Rachel's, going to investigate. It was the baby that interested her: she had not heard it cry since that very first time when Rachel refused to discuss it. Lisa's baby: or was it, Emily wondered? Only dead people became ghosts, and the baby was alive and living in America; so Rachel said. She lay there, turning the matter over in her mind, while the banging and the fitful wail persisted.

Her ability to see Lisa made her feel important: no-one else seemed to have the gift. She would like to find out if it could happen again, to prove it wasn't a fluke. Curiosity was strong enough to draw her from the warmth of the bed to the door of her room. It was ajar, and the landing light was on as a concession to her fear of the dark. She held her breath: the night was full of noises, creaks and groans and rattles as the house stood its ground against the wind's battering. There was no sound from Rachel. Emily put her foot on the first stair to the top floor with a quite pleasant frisson of nervous excitement, and climbed softly upwards. She stepped bravely into the pool of darkness on the upper landing and switched on the light.

The nursery door was shut: the banging came from behind it and the wind whistled beneath it. There was a key in the lock which fell to the floor as Emily turned the handle and peered in. The crying was fainter now, and seemed to come from a long way off. She could make out the shadowy lumps of furniture, and two more fluid shapes that leapt suddenly, wildly towards her from across the room. Her heart in her throat, she fumbled for the switch and flooded the nursery with light: one of the casement windows was swinging back and forth on its hinges, and the curtains were billowing in the blast of cold air. She let her breath go in a great sigh of relief, and the thudding in her chest slowly subsided: of course they were curtains, anyone could see that. There would be no Lisa now, bending over a cot as she had imagined her. Lisa was as much a creature of darkness as Emily was of light: Emily knew so, and she had made a nonsense of it. She stood, shivering in the freezing draught, feeling stupid and rather cross.

Three things happened in rapid succession. In a sudden and violent gust the window crashed inwards with a noise of breaking glass, the nursery door slammed shut and the light went out. Emily stood rooted to the ground before flinging herself at the door and struggling with the handle. Outside, the landing and the stairs and the lower landing were one enormous black void: the whole house was in darkness. At the first tentative step, her bare toes caught in the worn patch of carpet. She landed on her knees, feeling the crucifix dig painfully into the palm of her hand and the chain snap from her neck. The darkness closed round her like a tangible thing: crouching back against the wall, she screamed at the top of her voice.

The crash of the window woke Rachel. She realized there was a power failure by the time she heard the screams. Nightmare visions of attack from intruders gripped her as she stumbled across her room in the dark and out on to the landing.

'Emily! Where are you?' Her shout cracked in the middle with fear. The screams stopped. Emily's voice came from above, caught on a sob.

'I'm up here. Please come and get me, Granny. I can't move.'

'Are you hurt?'

'No, but everything's dark, I'm scared.'

Why on earth had the child gone up there? 'Stay there. I'm getting a torch. I shan't be long.'

Rachel groped her way to the clothes cupboard and felt around for the large upstanding torch kept for such emergencies. She located it amongst the shoes and dragged it out. The battery was failing, and gave a dim glow instead of its normal powerful beam, but it was better than nothing.

'Can you see the light?' Rachel called at the foot of the stairs.

'Only just,' Emily said waveringly.

'All right. I'm coming up now.'

Rachel was halfway there when the pressure began: it blocked her path like a soft, implacable wall. For a moment she thought all the upstairs windows must be open, that the force that held her pinned against the banister was part of the unprecedented gale. She used all her strength to move upwards, but a weight more

314

powerful than herself was not only preventing her but pushing her inexorably backwards. The air was being pressed from her lungs: the blood rushed to her head and throbbed in her ears. For a terrifying second she felt herself falling and grabbed at the banister rails, clinging on desperately. She remembered Louisa.

'Granny! What are you doing?' Emily's voice was hoarse with panic. Sprawled on the stairs, Rachel could think only of survival.

'Emily,' she said, 'you have the crucifix. Just throw it towards me, please.'

She tried to make her voice matter-of-fact: but the weight was intense, suffocating her, so that the words came out in a strangled whisper.

'I can't! I daren't move, Granny, I'm frightened—'

'Do it!' whispered Rachel in despair.

She waited. She thought, I mustn't faint: then there came the barely audible sound of the crucifix as it landed on carpet, two steps above her. The gold glimmered in the feeble light from the torch.

A rush of air swept past, fanning her cheek, and was gone on the instant. The pressure lifted as suddenly and completely as it had begun, leaving her oddly light and disembodied. She lay where she was, limp with relief, taking great breaths and trying to gather the strength to move. A waft of scent lingered in her nostrils: for the last time, please God, let it be for the last time, she prayed.

'Granny!' Emily's tone was peevish.

'I'm coming.'

She pulled herself upright weakly and, grasping the banister, clambered the remaining steps to the top landing. Emily was crouched by the nursery door;

Rachel knelt, and gathered the shivering bundle of granddaughter in her arms.

'What took you so long?' Emily asked accusingly, clinging to her with icy arms and legs.

'A touch of cramp. For a minute, I couldn't move.'

Was it merely a minute? It had seemed like eternity.

'You're shaking,' Emily said.

'I was worried about you. Whatever made you come up here in the middle of the night?'

'I wanted to see Lisa again, but I didn't. Then the window broke, and the lights went out, and—'

'No more for now. We've got to get you warmed up. Hold tight.'

As they crept slowly downstairs by the hazy glow of the torch, Emily said through chattering teeth, 'I didn't see Lisa, but I saw her mother. I'm getting quite good at it, aren't I?'

The morning was bright and still, as if the storm had never been. It left behind a trail of destruction, however. Rachel's garden was strewn with twigs and minor branches, and some of the taller plants had been flattened. In the park, a dozen or more trees lay prone, their giant roots wrenched up and sadly exposed. The damage was not on the catastrophic scale of the nineteen-eighty-seven hurricane, but it was bad enough for people to exchange their experiences in the shops; someone's glass-house had disappeared, to be found in another garden a hundred yards away; somebody else's front door had been blown in; a bicycle had been sighted, bowling along the street of its own volition. There were dark mutterings of ecological disaster, the ozone layer and the greenhouse

316

effect; and once again, tree surgeons were at a premium.

Rachel's story remained her own. No-one would have believed it; in the clear light of day, she herself had difficulty in believing its authenticity. She might have written it off as a waking nightmare brought on by over-tiredness: if it had not been for the evidence of Emily.

The two of them had spent the rest of the night in Rachel's bed, sharing bodily warmth and the hot-water bottle. They slept late, waking to find the electricity restored and lights burning everywhere. Neither spoke of the night's happenings; Emily was unusually quiet, and Rachel was busy on the telephone, trying to find someone to repair the window and replace the tiles. Not until they were in the garden, making a start on clearing the debris, did the subject arise.

'Are you cross with me?' asked Emily.

Rachel stopped raking. 'Of course not. Should I be?'

'Mummy would be. She's always cross if I make her frightened.'

'It's understandable,' Rachel said. 'Perhaps I was *too* frightened to get angry. In any case,' she added, 'you had a reason for your night-prowling.'

Emily scraped up a handful of twigs and dropped them.

'Eek! There are creepy-crawlies under all this.'

'Use the rake, then you won't see them.'

Emily sighed and looked around her. 'We haven't done much, have we?' She eyed Rachel. 'There are things I want to ask. You won't get cross about that, will you?'

317

'Stop making me sound like an ogre.' Rachel pulled off her gloves and tossed them into the wheelbarrow. 'We've done enough for now. Come on, let's go and find something to drink.'

They sat by the fire in the drawing-room, Morecombe stretched out in front of the flames like a small, fat doormat.

'What was the crucifix for?' asked Emily.

'It is supposed to lay spirits to rest; particularly the bad ones.'

'I thought so.' Emily drained her glass of Coke. 'Because that's when Lisa's mother flew past you. She went so fast she really did seem to fly,' she said. 'And then she disappeared.'

'Down the stairs?'

Emily frowned. 'I don't know. She just – vanished.' She looked at Rachel. 'If you couldn't see her, how did you know she was there?'

'I have always known; partly from her scent,' Rachel said. And, as from last night, her killing instinct, she added silently.

'It's funny,' Emily said. 'I always thought Mrs Rumble was fat, but the one I saw was tall and thin, and her hair must have been black because it didn't show in the dark.' She considered a moment. 'We never liked her, did we? Was she *really* bad?'

'She was not a good egg,' said Rachel lightly, 'from what I have learnt.'

'Has the crucifix got rid of her for ever, d'you think?'

'I very much hope so. It's a symbol of goodness, whether you believe in Christ or not.' Rachel rubbed Morecombe's back with her foot. 'He's a good barometer; he wouldn't be lying here if she was still

318

around. By the way,' she added, 'I've found the key to the back door.'

Emily's eyes grew round. 'Was it upstairs, by the nursery?'

'Yes. How did you know?'

'I guessed. It fell on the floor when I opened the door, and the nursery doesn't have a key. Did *she* put it there?'

'I believe so.'

'Why?'

'I think she was probably one of those maddening people who insist on a place for everything and everything in its place,' Rachel said, prepared to go no further.

'But it wasn't the right place.'

'All keys look much the same. She got it wrong.'

'It's lucky,' Emily said cheerfully, 'that we're not afraid of ghosts, isn't it?'

Rachel did not answer at once, the naked terror of the previous night fresh in her memory.

'Very lucky,' she agreed eventually, picking up the empty tumblers. 'Any more questions, or shall we have lunch?'

'Only one,' Emily said. 'You won't ever live anywhere but this house, will you?'

Rachel looked round the room, the late autumn sunlight reviving the faded colours of carpet and curtains; its tranquillity restored.

'I'll stay,' she said, 'for a long while yet.'

Emily sighed with satisfaction, her queries dealt with and tidied away neatly in her mind.

'That doesn't mean I shan't leave it occasionally,' Rachel added, 'for a week or two. A change of scene is a good idea from time to time, however contented you are within your own four walls.'

'Holidays, you mean?' Emily made a face. 'Our holidays will be really boring now there's Alexander. Boring old Isle of Wight, boring old sandcastles. I suppose,' she said enviously, 'you'll go somewhere exciting, like France.'

'Exactly,' Rachel agreed. 'To a place called Montmiral. I thought you might like to come with me,' she said carelessly.

Emily stared at her, turning slowly pink. 'When?' was all she could utter.

'How about the end of May, for the summer half-term? The late spring is worth waiting for, so I'm told, with all the meadow flowers out, and carpets of wild cyclamen.'

Emily, quite overcome, buried her head in a cushion.

THE END